BOURBON STREET

Digger knows what it's like to be on the bottom. He's been there most of his life. But he's got a plan to put him on top. And nothing is going to get in his way. Sure he has to betray a friend, but Johnny would have betrayed him first if he could. Of course, now Ma Vivaldi and Leon are looking for him, looking to bust his head, or worse. But they can be avoided if he can just stay away from Bourbon Street. All he has to do now is get past Mr. Trigg and arrange a meeting with the real boss, Vitolo Giannini, and he's in. He's got a smuggling set-up that is so perfect, Giannini will *have* to deal with him. What could go wrong….?

HOT CARGO

Ed Brody needs the work or he wouldn't have joined the crew of the old oil freighter in the first place. The captain, a fat man named Croup, introduces himself with a gun in his hand. And then there's Sheba, a young, red-haired temptress that has no business on the boat, even if she *is* married to the guy in charge, a crippled old man named Ringer. Brody figures they're smuggling Ringer and his wife down to South America. Then he watches as the crew loads crates filled with jet engines aboard. When he realizes that they're headed out of the Gulf toward the Atlantic, he knows that there is something a lot more at stake here than smuggling. Now he just needs to live long enough to do something about it.

G. H. OTIS BIBLIOGRAPHY
(1924-1992)

Bourbon Street (1953)
Hot Cargo (1953)

As Otis H. Gaylord
The Rise and Fall of Legs Diamond (1960)

As Peter Dawson (ghosted after author's death)
The Savages (1959)
Yancey (1960)
The Texas Slicks (1961)
The Half Breed (1962)
Bloody Gold (1963)
Showdown (1964)
A Pride of Men (1966)
The Blizzard (1968)

BOURBON STREET
HOT CARGO

G. H. OTIS

INTRODUCTION BY GARY LOVISI

Stark House Press • Eureka California

BOURBON STREET / HOT CARGO

Published by Stark House Press
1315 H Street
Eureka, CA 95501, USA
griffinskye3@sbcglobal.net
www.starkhousepress.com

ISBN: 978-1-951473-16-7

Cover design by Jeff Vorzimmer, ¡caliente!design, Austin, Texas
Cover art by James Avati, 1955
Book design by Mark Shepard, shepgraphics.com

First Stark House Press Edition: November 2020

THE SEARCH FOR OTIS
BY GARY LOVISI

Every once in a while you come across a writer whose work you really enjoy. Sometimes it's a new author, but often the discovery of a neglected writer from the past can offer just as much pleasure, if not more. The thrill of discovery always brings wonderful dividends when you come upon such an author. In this case it is a relatively unknown 1950s paperback author — G. H. Otis.

Back in 1996, I began a search for information on G. H. Otis. As far as I could tell he wrote only two excellent hard-boiled crime noir novels: *Bourbon Street* and *Hot Cargo*. Both novels appeared as paperback originals in 1953 from a long-defunct, often-forgotten, certainly obscure, lower-end, small paperback publisher of the era: Lion Books. Lion was influential in its day though, specializing in hard-boiled crime and noir fiction, publishing fine original works by Jim Thompson, David Goodis, Robert Bloch, David Karp, Richard Matheson and others. G. H. Otis sits comfortably with these masters.

The two books by Otis are good solid work, well ahead of their time and in many respects, hard, crisp, lean, clear and fascinating. Two fine, classic books. Then that was it! As far as I knew, he wrote those two books and nothing else! Why? There was not a peep from him afterwards, not another word, no more books at all. What happened? Did he write any other books? I began to wonder about G. H. Otis, and the more I thought about him, the more I was sure that the name had to be a pseudonym. If that was so, then who was G. H. Otis? So I extended my search.

Walking Down Bourbon Street

Bourbon Street (Lion Book #131) is the better of the two books, in my opinion. The cover blurb — that on many paperbacks of the era often exaggerated, if not outright lied about what the book was about — this time it tells it right and true:

"A loot-mad thug takes New Orleans apart! Savagery prowls the back alleys of New Orleans while a gunpunk tries to pull the deal of his life. A novel of America's crime rulers — and of the people they own and crush."

For once, the blurbs got it right.

The inside teaser page goes a bit further and proclaims the hero as a noir villain who finds himself:

Trapped by a gutter…he looked at the street. Dark and dirty and twisted. Bums in the alleys, sleeping off the no-food days and rotgut nights. Cockroaches crawling over their faces. Yellow-skinned girls waiting under the yellow lights, waiting for the New Orleans spenders to come down to the Quarter for a night of slumming. This was what he had run from. He had broken in a man's face, made a blood-deal with the syndicate, sold out a woman who loved him and ruined another he loved. All this, just to get off the street. And now he was back. And the shadows were waiting for him. And there was no place to run.

And let me tell you, the blurbs do not exaggerate. *Bourbon Street* lives up to everything they say and more! The 'hero' (actually an early anti-hero), is a tough guy, a former alky bum named Digger Mulcahy. His hard-boiled narration offers a fascinating insight into his life, world, and thoughts.

Handling Hot Cargo

A few months later, Lion Books published the second Otis novel, *Hot Cargo* (Lion #171, with cover art by Robert Maguire). The blurbs tell it best:

"They carried 129,000 tons of explosive oil — and a TNT woman."

And on the teaser page, the blurbs add:

A shipload of hungry men — and one man-starved woman. The tropic nights were still and sticky. The engine room was a steam bath, airless and smelly. The drums of oil were tinderboxes, ready to blow star-high.

But, nothing was as hot as the bare-legged woman named Sheba who strutted the decks and turned 19 love starved men into a shipload of fevered animals.

But still — Brody thought — he could get the ship through, get it to its port, even though one engine was gone and the crew was drunk.

He'd get her to port.

Except there was no port… The only place they were going was to a midnight rendezvous in the middle of the ocean — where a five-inch gun was set to smash Brody and his ship straight to hell!

Once again, as with *Bourbon Street*, the blurbs for *Hot Cargo* do not lie. They don't even exaggerate! The cover art by Robert Maguire shows Sheba dancing provocatively for the horny male crew on a hot tropic night, enticing them to fight over her, to spill each other's blood for her, as Brody looks on — wanting her more than all the others but knowing she's deadly poison.

The hero here is Ed Brody, a character similar to Digger, but not the twisted and vicious anti-hero that Digger is. Brody is a more cynical loner, tough and sharp, more decent. Brody is on the run, Otis never tells us from what.

Hot Cargo, like *Bourbon Street*, is an incredible tour-de-force, a hard-boiled, realistic, often brutal story about a brutal world and the people who make it that way. It is quintessential noir at its best.

Reading Otis

So what about my search for Otis? Who was G. H. Otis? Thanks to the kind assistance of veteran scholars Victor Berch and Bob Briney, and an assist from Jeff Vorzimmer, I was able to piece together the following story. Even today with the publication of this new edition by Stark House Press in 2020 — and even though the internet makes it possible to find a lot of data on authors that was not available in 1996 when I first wrote the original article — the irony is that it is still near impossible to find much on this author today. My search for Otis has led me to this incomplete conclusion — but I present what I know here in the hope that some day someone will be able to fill in those unknown areas. So here is what I have discovered about the author known as G. H. Otis.

G. H. Otis was Otis Hemmingway Gaylord, Jr. He was born September 8, 1924 in Boulder, Colorado, and died February 26, 1992 at 67 years of age, in Boulder, Colorado. Upon graduating from high school in 1942, he joined the Navy where he served for the duration of World War II. He attended the University of Colorado and worked his whole life as an ad rep for newspapers. He was married, with one child, and he never made a living as an author.

It is also asserted by some that in the 1960s Gaylord wrote some soft-core adult paperbacks (commonly known these days as "sleaze"), however I could find no evidence of his having written any of these type of books; nothing has ever shown up.

Through the Copyright Office in Washington D.C., I received reports that offer the following additional information on this author who has become an enigma to me.

The copyright application for *Bourbon Street* (actual publication date by Lion Books was March 27, 1953) was received by the Copyright Office July, 1953. At that time Gaylord gave his home as Aspen, Colorado, but it is shown in one of the other forms that in June of 1953 that he was actually living in Mexico City, Mexico. Gaylord's agent at the time was Marguerite Harper, located at 50 East 42nd Street, New York, New York.

Five months later, the application for *Hot Cargo* (Lion Books publication date was November 13, 1953), received on December 28, 1953, shows things a bit different. Gaylord's address in December, 1953 was 703 11th Street, Boulder, Colorado and his agent had been changed to DA Magazine Management Inc.

However, Gaylord did write one book under his real name — only one — *The Rise and Fall of Legs Diamond* (Bantam Book #A2079, paperback original, 1960). This movie tie-in novel is based on a screenplay by Joseph Landon and has cover art by Stanley Zuckerberg. The film featured dapper Ray Danton in the title role of the crack shot gangster, and was directed by Budd Boetticher, famous for his Randolph Scott westerns.

Gaylord turns up next in, of all places, Walt Disney Studios in California. Their Employee Records Department gave me what little info they had on file for him after so many years: a short note that Gaylord was an advertising manager for nine months, from July 4, 1965 to April 30, 1966. I have not discovered any more data about his life from this time, to his death in 1992.

My search took me online, and I also asked knowledgeable scholars and collectors I know for any further information, but there is nothing more on Otis, or Gaylord. One almost wonders, did he want to be found? He did write with some authority about New Orleans of the era, and about working on an oil tanker, so he may have had some of this experience in his life that he put into his two books for Lion. Perhaps.

Otis Hemingway Gaylord, writing as G. H. Otis, wrote two damn fine hard-boiled crime noir novels that should not be forgotten. He was a hell of a fine writer. That is why I am so elated that Greg Shepard of Stark House Press has decided to publish this new edition that collects these two terrific Lion Books by Otis, books that have now become noir cult classics. Once you read the novels that make up this book you will take a deep dive into the grim wild world of hard crime noir.

I envy you reading these books for the first time, or re-reading them in this new quality format. I know you will enjoy them. You will never forget them! Although I haven't ended my search for Otis, at least with is new Stark House Press edition, you can find these two spectacular reads, and maybe you will even begin your own search? Enjoy!

—Brooklyn, N.Y.
June 2020

Gary Lovisi is a crime author who sells, collects and writes about rare and vintage paperbacks. Under his Gryphon Books imprint, he publishes *Paperback Parade*, the world's leading magazine on collectible paperbacks of all kinds. You can find out more about him or his work at his website: www.gryphonbooks.com or on Facebook.

BOURBON STREET

G. H. OTIS

PART I

The room wasn't much, a come-down from my apartment—an airless room in a crummy hotel. It was furnished with the usual soiled overstuffed chair, chipped dresser and creaky bed. The cockroaches were free. But I could wait. Things were going to get better very, very soon.

I was lying on the bed near the street window trying for a breeze. Sometimes there's a breeze that dries the sweat and cools the body. Most of the time there isn't.

It was dark now, not that it lowered the temperature any. It's always humid-hot in New Orleans. An occasional interior light began to give the outside buildings shape.

Up and down this street lights have a habit of blinking on and off. Cocktails … Lounge … Oysters … French Cuisine … The Absinthe House … The Olde Absinthe House … The New Absinthe House (take your pick) … The Music Box … Louis Prima's. But only a few signs had been turned on and the narrow street looked deserted. Anyone who wanted to get planted at a bar rail now knew the doors were open—knew the doors were wide open twenty-four hours a day.

Below me the buses rolled by, empty now and dimly lit. The city was taking five.

But in the French Quarter, this breather is more like a gasp. Waiters would only have time to clean ash trays and sweep cigarette butts into corners before the suckers rushed back for a fling at the club bars with their naughty and untalented strippers, watered-down drinks and Dixieland. No cover, no minimum. Two beers, two bucks, mister. Like it or leave it.

I could leave it!

I had lain here all afternoon trying for that breeze and watching the suckers, and now pretty soon I would get up and climb into a cool shower. Cool, that is, if it was one of my lucky nights. Even the water rarely gets cold. After the shower, I would take my time about getting dressed. I could have a good dinner—at least I could still do that. A lot of the boys in my business wouldn't get a good drink tonight. Some of the boys I knew had gone south to Mexico, or further. Or maybe they were working on the docks, or maybe like most they were in jail. They wouldn't have a cool suit and, especially, they wouldn't have a good meal.

But first I had to think it over.

So I fired up another butt and relaxed. I had it figured right, but still I had to go over it. That's the only way to be. That's why I'm still clean while some have gone south and others are doing the book in a federal brake.

New Orleans had been my luck. I had landed here broke and low-down—so low that I slept in the streets without caring anymore at all. I could have gone on being a wine bum without half trying.

I fell in and came out smelling like money instead.

I found a guy in an alley one night while I was looking for something easy to steal. He had been sapped and rolled. I had gone over him fast, but whoever had got to him hadn't left me a thin dime. He was an old guy, pink-cheeked, fat and manicured and his clothes were good. His suit and shoes would hock for a couple of bucks at any used clothes store on N. Rampart Street, or I could ease him onto his feet and get him home. That's usually good for a few dollars to a grateful citizen.

To strip him was risky, a sucker play. The second choice just took time. Hell, I had no place to go. I took him home.

He turned out to be a smalltime bookie who made his own contacts and collections and always carried a roll. That's why he was sapped. But he hadn't given me dough. He looked me over, my 200 pound, six foot two inch frame, and gave me a job—a job I could like. I became his runner.

I made the rounds of bars, barber shops and beaneries, picking up the bets that had been left with porters and waiters, and Fatso stayed healthy in his room.

He was just one of hundreds of small operators in the city, but he was on the inside and he opened the door as wide as he could for me. It wasn't long before I had a couple of clean shirts of my own and could start letting bourbon burn out my guts instead of rot gut.

Nobody rolled me, although it was tried. We did pretty well and when the old boy unfortunately fell down a long flight of stairs and brained himself, I was left sole heir to a going and growing business.

It was too easy. I didn't know how much I had to learn.

When the reform platform man got elected mayor in 1946, it was just a laugh to the boys and I laughed right along with them. The reformers didn't change anything.

On a local scale, the authorities couldn't muster the power to control the parish officials, and the parish officials had their hands in deep, with the help of a little legislation.

The law read that gambling constituted a misdemeanor and that state officials could not be indicted for compounding a misdemeanor … a neat bit of legislation.

Gamblers need cooperation to exist and with the threat of prosecution removed, parish authorities had always been more than ready to cooperate. The long green was not incidental.

But the reform movement should have been a warning. Everything from bingo to barbuit stopped dead when a man in a coonskin hat made a big hit on television in New York a few years later. The Kefauver Committee gave the locals impetus.

I still had dough in the bank, but there wasn't going to be anymore from where that came. Not for a long, long time. It was going to have to be something new from now on and there weren't many choices. Too many Federal, State and even County Grand Juries had seen to that. Too much reform had put the rackets out of business for the first time in history.

But I had already picked my spot. Only a few things were still going, run by the biggest operators in and out of the country. They played games too big and complicated for anyone to call a recess on, but you didn't send them your card and go into business just like that. You had to have something they could use, something they wanted; not a gun or guts. Unemployed thugs were a dime a dozen. What the big men always needed was an angle, a gimmick, a money maker that would pay better than prohibition.

I had an angle.

All I had to do was get to the man and I was almost there. Anytime now, tonight, tomorrow, any day now I would be in. I would be in or dead.

I had looked for a wedge and found it—a wedge of spring steel that could snap back and cut my head off. You don't have a casual what-the-hell working agreement with the man I'm trying to do business with. He takes a hold on you that breaks only when you break and rots only when you are rotting at the bottom of a bayou. This is more than I've ever done; farther than I've ever gone. They say that to be part of the syndicate is to live in hell.

I don't have to go all the way. I can still drop it whole, but when I think of the sleazy rat holes I have put up in, the dirty, sweaty, tiring, unpaying jobs I've had on the boats and docks of the Gulf, and of the punk bum I was, I know I don't want to chuck it.

I got up and shuffled into the bathroom for a shave and shower. One thing you learn here—never move fast unless, of course, there's action. The heat will dehydrate you until you feel like the day after

New Year's Eve.

I turned on the shower and let it run while I shaved. When I finished, the shower water was just a shade cooler than tepid.

Back in the bedroom, I opened the closet and pulled out my navy blue silk shantung suit and laid it on the bed. I chose a white sheer batiste shirt and plain silk shantung tie. With my narrow brimmed Milan hat and dark perforated calfskin shoes I was all set to be seen.

The head doctors say that everybody compensates. When you're six feet two and tough with a face that's just a little out of whack and a voice full of gravel, you're going to try to look good someway. So with me it's clothes. I'm not saying the girls object. They like my nose slightly flattened and the little scars in my eyebrows and they especially like someone who looks strong enough to break backs.

I snagged my breast pocket wallet from under the junk on the dresser. I opened the top drawer of the bureau dresser and eased out my bottle of high test sour mash bourbon. After three inches of this a man can glow in the dark. Only from now on I had to be bright in the right ways ... so I just took two inches, flicked off the light, locked the door and headed for the street.

Bourbon Street—fourteen blocks of bistros. Not many years ago, it had been fourteen blocks of bordellos with more history than Basin Street.

The Court of the Two Sisters, Lafitte's Blacksmith Shop, The Absinthe House, all more than a hundred and fifty years old, now quaint little bars. Jean Lafitte, General Beauregard, Andrew Jackson and a host of other famous men had lived here.

Lafitte had been an honest blacksmith, a pirate in hiding and a planner of the defense of New Orleans and patriot all on this same street. You'd never know it now. Every bar employs a sidewalk barker to tell you all about how the little ladies are going to move all, shake all, show all, step right in, a new show in five minutes—a spiel as phony as a panhandler's plea.

I shouldered my way up the sidewalk toward Arnaud's and a bowl of crawfish bisque.

The dinner had been all that Arnaud's brags it is. I was standing outside letting things grumble into place in my stomach and feeling good about it, when I noticed little Bennie, the junker, standing on the other side of the street trying not to look like Bennie, the junker.

Maybe I'd been too preoccupied. That's a nice way of saying I may have been careless.

He was standing sideways to me watching something up the street.

Bennie is an errand boy, tramp, sneak thief, a habitué of the street with Banjo Annie. Where he sleeps nobody knows. But mostly Bennie is a junker, a full-time addict.

To my right was Bourbon Street with its crowds and lights. To my left was Royal Street, deserted by the tourists at night. I walked toward Royal while he was still stargazing, turned the corner leisurely and flattened into the shadows against the building.

I didn't have long to wait. He came around the corner like a commuter after the five-fifteen.

I grabbed him by the front of his soiled coat and spun him into a doorway. He tried to bring his foot up, so I let him have it easy but solid once in the sweetbreads and on the back of the head with the heel of my hand as he went down. He wasn't out, just gentled.

I stepped out of the doorway and had a look. We were alone.

I picked him up, propped him in the corner and took a handful of his coat in my fist. He wouldn't look at me; just gasped a little.

"You're pretty busy these days, Bennie."

He kept his head down.

"I've seen you around a lot lately, Bennie Boy." I tightened his collar for him with my grip. "You must have been by my place half a dozen times today."

He squirmed, just to test me, so I slammed him with my free hand. It hurt and I could see he was beginning to get scared.

"I ain't done nothing to you, Digger, honest. Lemme go."

"Look, Bennie, you're not even sweating. No cough, no yawning, no sneezing. If I shook you down, I'd find a little heroin or opium. Since when did you give up the weed for the expensive stuff? You're loaded with dope."

"I don't know what you're talking about."

"Okay, maybe I'll case you and take away your candy."

He was going to be stubborn, so I spun him around and pinioned him with my left arm and started to frisk him. That did it.

"Digger, you wouldn't … okay, okay."

He would have screamed it, but he was panicked.

I straightened him up and stepped back. At least I knew he wasn't packing a rod. If he ever owned one, he had hocked it for his snow a long time ago.

"Whatta ya wanta know?" he asked.

"Who hired you to watch me?"

"A guy uptown."

"What guy?"

"This guy comes up to me in front of Pat O'Brien's and asks me can I tail someone."

"Why do you say an uptown guy if he tagged you in front of O'Brien's? Tell it."

"Okay, I know he's uptown 'cause I've seen him at Walter's, that big cafeteria on St. Charles Street. He's the manager or night man or something."

I placed it all right. The big man wanted to know what I was doing with my time. If I was seeing any strangers. If my habits were good.

"Okay, Bennie, I'm not sore. I'm sorry I roughed you up."

He couldn't believe his ears.

"I was just worried about a tail, that's all," I said.

"Gee, Digger."

"This guy probably thought I was grabbing one of his very own babes—just a jealous guy."

"Yeah!" Bennie said.

"Well now, Bennie, I don't want to have a jealous husband taking shots at me, do I?"

"Gee, no."

"So you just go on tailing me and calling in. You call in, don't you?"

"Yeah, Bayaud 6-6023, every ..."

Then he stopped. That's the trouble with a hophead. They wake up too late to shut up.

"Thanks, Bennie. You can follow me around. I don't mind that, only don't get too close. You stink. You smell like death," and I hit him hard just behind the ear and left him there with one more reason to hate the little world he lived in.

Back on the street, I picked a club bar without as much neon as the rest and found a place empty at the bar.

A bored cigarette girl, in long black hose and high heels, with hardly anything else barely covering plenty of everything, was circulating among the customers.

When she saw me, she brightened and headed my way.

I had headaches enough.

"Hello, Digger," she said.

Very original.

"Hi, Baby."

"You haven't been around."

"It's Lent," I said.

"It is?"

She took a deep breath and her chest swelled. She didn't have to.

"You never came back," she said.

"That's what I told you at the time."

"Okay, Digger, but if you change your mind, I haven't moved."

"And the key is in the mailbox," I reminded myself.

She laughed, sold me a pack of butts and pushed the tip back at me. She moved off swinging her hips.

It was wasted ammunition.

I gave the bartender an order for a double Walker's Deluxe on the rocks and let my muscles relax.

Bennie wasn't going to tell anyone I was wise. He liked his snow too well. He could pick me up later at any one of the places I hang out at in the Quarter. I hadn't gone any place different, or seen anyone new for months, except when I had gone out of my territory to plant the seed for my big try. That's the way I was playing it, very cool. No dames. I wanted the man to know I meant business.

Now I had a phone number. I didn't need it. I knew who it would lead to in the end, but it would be helpful to know who this particular bird was and where he fitted. You never can tell. It would be something to do tomorrow. Better than watching the tourists from my bedroom window.

I left two bucks on the bar and shouldered my way to the door.

Outside again, I headed toward Vivaldi's.

Ma and Johnny would be there waiting to start our nightly game.

Ma Vivaldi, or the Mrs., or Ma, whatever you chose to call her, was an enigma to the wealthy people in the Quarter. She didn't make a splash with her dough and she had plenty. She owns a string of thoroughbreds that aren't dogs. She also has a bunch of real estate scattered around town and three little bars in the Quarter. The bars are all dumps off of Bourbon on the side streets. Only the oldtimers, the winos and occasional drunken sailors who have lost their way ever patronize them. It's an open secret that she loses her money on them.

No one is ever literally thrown out of her places. They are "escorted out." If you get too drunk to stand, you are welcome to sleep on the floor. No extra charge. Nothing fancy, just dime beers and wine and rot gut for fifteen cents. If you are broke, you can even put one on the cuff.

She is maybe fifty years old. She always wears a tailored jacket like a man's, expensive cut, and skirt to match. She wears low-heeled shoes that the ladies' ads like to call "sensible" and silk hose. She is always neat, manicured and just from the hairdresser, and she is small. Ma isn't five feet tall, but she can look and talk like a very big woman, and I guess she is.

Ma makes her headquarters in the joint on Toulouse Street. There isn't even a name on it, just an electric sign that says "Beer" in small letters above the paint-cracked door. A few old tin beer advertising signs hang lopsided on the outside walls. I pushed open the door and went in.

Leon, the regular bartender, was reading a mystery down at the end of the bar while another bartender took care of the few customers.

I straddled a stool in front of Leon. He didn't even look up.

"How they hangin', Digger?" he said.

I didn't have to answer. He always asked it. He finished the page and turned a corner over to mark the place, slammed down the book and gave me his smile. I smiled back.

He dived under the counter and came up with the bottle of good stuff and a clean glass all in one terrifyingly swift movement. I'm always fascinated to see how fast he can still move. Leon had been a pug too. We had even fought some of the same boys. Only I had quit young, almost before I got started good. Leon hadn't quit until the commission's doctors had retired him—not for scrambled brains altogether; it had been his eyes.

He poured one carefully and gave me his smile again like he was proud or something.

"Anybody home?" I asked.

"Yeah, the Mrs. and Johnny," and he nodded toward the back.

I tossed down the drink and got up.

"Saloon," he said.

"Hot dog," said I.

It's a game that he plays, so I play it with him. He laughed and I headed for the back room. I didn't pay, we understood each other.

The back room was a barren, box-like place. A large poker table, a shaded light hanging above it and an odd assortment of wooden rung chairs were the only furnishings. A small opening high up with an electric fan in it gave ventilation.

Ma and Johnny were seated at the poker table. Ma with the news section of the *Times Picayune* and Johnny poring over his inevitable racing form.

I knew they wouldn't return to normalcy until they had digested what they were reading from cover to cover, so I picked out a chair that had four legs that were reasonably the same length and sat down.

I snagged the sports section out of the mess of papers on the table and sat about whiling away my time. Once this had been a hot poker room. Now it was a library.

I had gotten to know Ma in this room when I was getting started with my own book. She was hard to be close to and it had taken time. But it was a boost to be known as a friend of Ma's and I had been glad to spend the time. I had thought that she held something against me, but if she did, it was forgotten now and I was as close to her as anyone, except Leon. There was something nobody could touch between Ma and Leon. I never could find out what. Nobody could.

Johnny was a different matter. I had respected Johnny. I had met him here too. He had been established and when I was getting started he had looked big. He steered me plenty in those days and eventually we had made it a partnership. With our combined rolls we could book bigger bets and before the lid came off, we had just about all of the downtown traffic we could handle. Johnny had been a rock in those days—Know-how and steel nerves to back it. Thirty dollar shirts and a hotel suite to match. But he was slipping. It wasn't that he didn't live in a hotel suite now. Hell, neither did I. He just didn't look so sharp anymore. His clothes didn't have that well-pressed edge and when he looked at you his eyes didn't bore right in like they used to. Maybe he knew he was a has-been.

Ma put her papers aside. "How about a little game?" she said.

Johnny carefully folded the form and put it into his breast pocket. "I don't mind."

"You're on," I said.

"I'll get Leon out of the bar while you clear the table," said the Mrs. and she looked at Johnny. "And a fresh deck."

Leon always made up the fourth these days: the real reason she hired an extra bartender. We played our game tight and we played not so much for stakes but for blood.

Johnny sat looking down at his hands as I gathered the newspaper and tossed it onto an extra chair. He hadn't looked me in the eye since I had come in.

I had seen it coming; tonight was the night. It was to be for more than blood; we would play for the flesh too.

The game of hearts is played by octogenarians, invalids and kids under twelve. It doesn't demand the uncanny cooperation between partners of whist or employ the multiple combinations of bridge.

About the only four-handed game it beats is two-deck canasta.

But when experts play hearts, things happen. Hearts is a direct attack or defense game. The guy that hedges gets clubbed.

As in bridge, the high card takes the trick, you can slough when you're void. You have to follow suit and the man that wins the trick leads. The idea is not to get any hearts; they count one point apiece against you. Low man wins. The only complication is the Queen of spades. It counts thirteen points against the person who gets it in a trick. A score is kept and the payoff comes at the end of the game. No money is in sight and the vice squad stays home. A nice friendly game is hearts.

A good player can tell just about what his opponents have in their hands after the second trick has been played. If you know your players, you can tell to the card what they hold.

Sunlight was beginning to show behind the whirring blades of the fan in the wall before we were ready to quit.

My mouth tasted dry from too many cigarettes and shots, and stale air hung over the table in a cloud despite the fan.

Leon was still playing his close-to-the-vest, deliberate game.

Ma was as shrewd as ever. She changed her tactics to suit her hand and she never got careless.

Johnny was the goat. He had played erratically, taking chances. There just aren't any chances in a game as cut and dried as this and the more he lost the higher he had pushed the stakes.

I had glanced at Ma and she had nodded, so up went the stakes. With Leon it was okay. I knew Ma would back him.

We had been playing at a hundred per for the last hour.

Leon was down a few. Ma was about even, so it was Johnny that would owe the kitty a couple of grand.

He ran his hand over his face now and tried to shake the fuzz out of his brain.

He had been lapping it up. At top form, he never would have dipped his beak when he was doing business, and tonight he had meant business.

The hand was almost over. Leon had taken a heart and Johnny had taken four on a fool try at shooting the moon.

If you can take all the hearts *and* the Queen of spades, you get twenty-six points taken off your score.

We each had three cards now with Leon leading on my left.

He had nothing but good cards left. Low ones.

The lead was the deuce of hearts.

Across from me, Ma played the ace of spades and on my right, Johnny flicked out the three of hearts carelessly.

I held the four and ten of hearts and the six of clubs.

Eleven diamonds, twelve clubs and ten spades had been played.

With the two hearts in my hand, I could account for eleven hearts. Two still out.

The Queen hadn't fallen. I could duck this trick with my four but those other hearts were the five and six. Hearts would be led right back to me and I would be stuck with the lead in clubs. And the Queen.

I took the trick with the ten, a four hundred dollar gesture, and led back the four.

The five or six would top me and no one could lead back to me in clubs. I held the last and only one. I could relax and watch someone get hit with that thirteen hundred dollar pasteboard, the Queen of spades.

The Mrs. was out of hearts. Leon's play safe technique wouldn't allow him to lead a low card away from a high one and lose his protection. Was Johnny caught again? I would find out now.

Leon covered my four with the five. But he could have *both* the five and the six.

Ma played the two of spades. Her last card I knew was the Queen. She had been waiting for a chance to give it to me. In this game everybody gangs up on the winner so that the point spread won't get too big.

It was Johnny that played the six of hearts. He automatically gathered in the cards and laid down his last card. The three of diamonds. He looked white.

Everybody knew that the only other diamond out was the deuce.

We didn't even bother throwing our cards into the center of the table. Especially Ma. She didn't seem to have the heart to give him the Queen.

Johnny reached for the bottle, but it was a dead soldier.

Leon got up quick to get him a fresh one from the bar. Nobody said anything. Ma pretended she was busy adding the score.

Personally, I didn't care. Money—it's nice to have it to lose.

And that was it of course. Johnny didn't have it. That's why the funeral. Four grand maybe, and he had been baling it to take to the bank a year ago.

He had sunk pretty low. Getting into the game on credit like a cheap speculator. This was a strange twist. It had been Johnny that had taught me how to handle speculators.

Only it wouldn't be Johnny's way. He was right where I wanted him. For him I had something special.

Leon came back with the bottle and poured one around.

The Mrs. broke the silence. "There's forty-eight hundred bucks in the kitty and Digger wins the jackpot."

"Gee, Digger, you're the champ," Leon said admiringly.

"Yeah, he's come a long way," said Johnny. His bitterness showed.

"You were a good teacher," I told him. "I'll pop for the ribs." The winner had always paid for the breakfast which Leon would pick up from an all-night barbecue next door.

Johnny finished his drink and got up unsteadily. "Not for me," and he walked to the door. He turned and looked me in the eye for the first time like he used to. "I'll see you tonight with the dough."

All eyes were on me. I hated him.

"Okay, Johnny. No rush."

He looked relieved. He waved a limp hand and went out with a little of his old swagger.

Later, the Mrs. and I sat eating barbecue and gulping coffee. Leon was out checking the bar receipts.

I looked her over, as neat and chipper as when we had started. I wondered if she ever got tired.

She dropped the bare rib, wiped her face fastidiously with an oversize napkin and took up her coffee. "You were rugged last night. I can see why you've kept the nickname Digger."

I had run a ditch digging machine in a swamp crew once. We were laying a pipeline through the roughest country I'd ever seen. I had been the digger ever since.

"You were pretty hard on Johnny," she continued.

"He asked for it," I said.

"He was trying to get a stake."

"I'm not his meal ticket."

"He was yours when you were getting started."

"I had plenty to match his roll."

"Yes," she said, "that's right you did. Youth, good looks," (I laughed at that) "and a fast brain," she went on. "Maybe you were too big for him from the start."

I offered her fresh coffee from the carton and she held out her cup. I poured us each one.

"If he wanted a handout, why couldn't he ask," I said. "We've never eased the breaks toward anyone in a game before."

"I've tried to loan it to him. He's still too proud."

"I'm surprised you would let him speculate in your game."

"I know. Maybe I'm sentimental. I hoped he would get lucky."

"You never get lucky when you press. What did he do with it all? He should have had twenty-five to fifty grand laid back."

"Some dame."

I could hardly believe it. Johnny, the iron man, had been had by a dame. It was the one thing about him I didn't know.

"She went through everything and when he was clean she left him," said Ma. "It ruined him. He wanted to marry her. Now he's a flat tire with no place to go."

"Why don't you fix him a place? He's good with horses," I asked.

"I don't really need him and he knows it. He thinks it's charity." She toyed with her cup. "Are you going after the dough he lost last night?"

It was a curve. She wanted to know how mean I was.

"I'll sleep on it."

"What are you going to do now?"

"Sleep."

"That's not what I mean, Digger. What about that oil deal you told me about. Is that rich Dunbar going to put up the dough?"

This was part of my big plan. This was the angle that would make me appear legit. I wanted it talked about. I'm glad she had remembered it.

"I don't know yet. It takes time to work out the details."

"I hear you have been hanging around Antonio's."

That shook me. I wasn't prepared for it.

"I like to play dominoes," I said.

"Let me tell you something, Digger. They play more than dominoes at Antonio's. You know as well as I do that Giannini's old crowd has taken over that place. At least the outer fringes of his crowd. If you think you can get protection from someone there to open up again, you're mistaken. Gambling is dead in this town. Even Giannini can't fix gambling. I know."

Inwardly I sighed with relief. She thought I wanted to open my old book. I smiled. "You hear a lot, Ma. Who told on me?"

"Stick to this oil deal. It sounds good."

I got up to go.

"Thanks for the advice."

"And by the way, you've had a tail on you."

"Yeah. Little Bennie."

"Bennie? I didn't know about him. It was another guy. An out-of-town boy."

A double check! "Who was it, Ma?" I tried to make it sound unimportant.

"I don't know. Loud dresser, pink shirt and hand-painted tie. I heard he checked on you at the docks, with the pilots and skippers you used to work with."

"You do hear a lot, don't you Ma?"

She tried to pass it off with a shrug.

"Someday I'm going to find out who you really are," I said.

Her smile faded.

"Is that a riddle?"

"Maybe."

"I hope the day doesn't come when I have to find out who you really are." It sounded deadly.

I said, "So long."

I walked over to Bourbon Street. A bum was lying in a doorway on the corner. A cockroach was perched on his lips investigating his putrid breath. It scurried down his shirt front as he stirred in a drunken dream.

I stepped off down the street fast. I couldn't forget that I had been a lush once too. I never would be again. The big man was taking the bait. The guy who had been checking on me at the docks belonged to the big man. I had expected that. He was making sure I knew my business, that I could do what I said I could do.

I was going to make a pile of money. Enough money so that I'd never feel the bugs and cockroaches crawling on me everytime I saw a lush passed out in a doorway.

I pushed on down Bourbon Street toward my hotel.

Tomorrow was going to be a busy day.

The house phone woke me at noon and I stood under the shower until I was awake, then shaved.

I put out my new rayon gabardine, single breasted suit and a basket-weave shirt and picked out a pair of nylon mesh slip-on shoes.

I stopped before the mirror. I looked sharp. If my nose weren't flat, I could pass for a cotton broker uptown, but my nose and the scar tissue over my eyes always gave me away. Somehow they always knew. But why think of that. What do I care about people.

To hell with it. I had places to go.

When I reached the street, I lit up. It was an excuse to check for a guy in loud clothes wearing a hand-painted silk tie. He wasn't around so I hailed a cab and gave the driver an uptown address.

Nobody tailed us and I sat back and relaxed.

A year ago it was hard to get a cab on Bourbon Street, unless you wanted to go to a cat house. Cabs lined the curb bumper to bumper, but each driver was a worker for a particular house or lady.

You couldn't hire one for an honest fare. They made more waiting for the sailors, salesmen and hayseeds that could stand to buy it. A hell of a lot more. They used to call Louisiana the land of Huey, harlots and Hadacol. Huey Long was dead. Nobody knew where the harlots were. Only the Hadacol was left. What a place!

The cabbie let me out on a corner near the telephone building and I took a look around. Nobody I knew.

I ducked into a little French cafe half-way down the block and headed for the phone booth. I was connected with my party and after a little wheedling got what I wanted.

I stepped out of the booth and over to the bar to wait.

I was half-way through a two pound T-bone when she came in.

She was tall, five-eight in heels, dark hair and big brown eyes. She was lush as tropical fruit. But I had seen all that before.

She plunked herself down on the stool next to me. She didn't have to say anything to let me know she was sore.

"Breakfast?" I asked.

"That's just like you. Breakfast at one o'clock. Calling me at work and asking me to do something that is very much against the rules. Really!"

She was wearing one of those dresses sliced down the middle from throat to waist and her chest was working hard.

"Digger, you rat. Why don't you come around anymore? The only time you see me is when you want something."

"What did you find out?" I asked her.

She handed me a piece of paper. I folded it and put it in my pocket. We were alone at the bar, but you can't tell.

"It's an unlisted number," she said. "We have instructions to change it every month and we send the bill to 'Bartholomew and Henri.'"

"You mean it's listed under one name and billed to someone else."

"Yes, that's often done. Bartholomew and Henri is an accounting firm that takes care of the business of absentee owners or people on long vacations."

"Very neat."

"Does this help?"

"I'll let you know." I had finished my steak. I had my info and I was in a hurry. I got up, dropped a ten spot on the bar and headed for the door.

"Where are you going?" she shouted.

"I have a date," I told her, "with a very beautiful girl."

Another cab toted me back toward the French Quarter. On the way,

I took a look at the name on the piece of folded paper. It was familiar. James Twigg.

Mr. Twigg had appeared before the Grand Jury. His script had been dull reading. "I refuse to testify on the grounds that it may tend to incriminate me." And since the poor man didn't appear to know anything, he had been dismissed. But he was big potatoes. Big enough to stay out of jail while men that had worked for him took the rap. Mr. Twigg was the man all us bookies had paid our protection money to. Not directly, of course. I was going to take an interest in Mr. Twigg. He had a lot of my personal money.

I told the cabbie to let me out at Toulouse and Royal. We went four blocks out of our way working the one-way streets getting to my corner, but the breeze blowing over me in the back seat made it worthwhile. The job I had to do was going to be a hot one.

I paid the driver, scaled him a buck and walked into the entrance of the W.P.A. Art Project Exhibition Gallery. Only high domes visited here and they were too engrossed in the exhibits to watch each other. That made it perfect for my purpose. I went up to the second floor and made like a high dome.

I worked my way around the walls looking at the paintings until I came to a row of double windows overlooking the street. Nobody had come in after me, so I knew if I had a tail, he would be down there waiting for me.

I took a look.

It was a busy sight.

A steady stream of people plodded along. Tourists gawked into shop windows. Street hawkers and peddlers were shouting. Cars honked loudly as they whizzed by.

There were a couple of hundred people on the street. If my boy was there, the odds were that I'd miss him.

I watched tourists ask perfect strangers to snap their picture against bastard colonial French façades, ten-year-old kids sell pralines, Italians sell fresh vegetables, and Creoles from the coast peddle shrimp, but I didn't spot my boy.

From my window, I could look directly across the street into a row of three not-so-fancy second floor apartments. I fastened my attention on them. All three apartments had doors that opened onto a communal balcony.

The doors were shut but the window of the middle apartment was open. I couldn't see inside.

Nobody stirred into sight. I divided my attention between the street and the apartments.

This wasn't a popular room of the gallery. Not many people came in. When someone did, I moved around looking at the pictures until they left, then came back to my window. I was bored. There weren't any pictures I liked and nothing doing outside.

I was about ready to give it up, when the door of the middle apartment opened and a man walked out on the balcony, blinking in the hot bright sunlight. He wore pants with the suspenders hanging and a soiled undershirt. He was barefooted. It was my old pal Johnny.

He held a cup of coffee in his right hand and with his left he scratched his rear. I could see behind him into the apartment now. I had half of what I wanted to know. Johnny was alone. I didn't know if I had a tail, but I would have to chance it. Time was running out. If I was going to set it up, today was the day.

I went downstairs and across the street fast, dodging traffic. If I was being watched, this play might be missed.

I took the steps two at a time and could feel the sweat rolling down my back by the time I reached the doors at the head of the stairs.

I took a deep breath and tried the middle door. It was unlocked. Johnny was getting absent-minded in his old age. There were people in the Quarter who would steal the carpet off your floor.

I walked on in.

From the doorway, I could see Johnny sitting on the wrought iron railing of the balcony sipping his coffee and yawning.

The apartment was a one-room efficiency unit. Murphy bed, hot plate, small ice box, a couple of chairs and a small table. It was a mess. Empty bottles, clothes thrown around.

I slammed the door behind me and Johnny almost fell off the railing into the street. He recovered and rushed in to defend his castle. He stopped fast enough, when he saw who it was.

"A little jumpy, Johnny?"

He looked behind me, as if he would discover a hole in the wall.

"The door was unlocked," I explained.

He still didn't say anything; just looked at me suspiciously. So I looked back at him with his suspenders hanging and his dirty bare feet.

"Nice place you have here," I said.

"I told you I'd see you tonight."

"Aren't you going to ask me to sit down?"

"What do you want, Digger?"

He hadn't lost all his marbles. He knew this wasn't a social call. I shoved an assortment of clothing from a chair onto the floor and sat down.

"I know you said you would see me tonight. With the money," I said.

He looked bad.

"But I know you haven't got the money," I continued. "Maybe I'm not worried about it." I was being very friendly.

I nodded toward the cup in his hand.

"Finish your breakfast and we'll talk."

He remembered that he was still holding the cup, looked at it and smiled.

"Yeah," he said. "Join me?" and he walked over to the hot plate.

This was better. More like I wanted it.

"No thanks, but you go ahead."

He filled the cup from a grease-stained coffee pot on the hot plate. He was warming to our little visit now, so I gave him the pitch.

He sat and sipped while I talked and was blinking hard before I was half done.

"You mean you will forget the four grand I owe you," he stammered, "but we couldn't do it. We would be closed down in an hour. It's too hot to run a crap game."

"I didn't say we, Johnny. *You* would run the game. I bank it."

He swallowed. "But then I would be going the risk."

Now he was getting the idea.

"That's right," I said.

"No thanks. I won't run a crap game for you no matter how bad I need a stake."

Now was the time. I got up and moved over to him, talking easy as I walked. I didn't need to be that careful, he was stunned by the idea.

"It can be done, Johnny," I said. "It's a delicate operation, but it can be done."

When I was directly above him, I brought my hand up fast and smashed the scalding coffee into his face, cup and all. He tried to roll away, but I was faster. As he rolled, I hit him in the side, right above the kidneys.

There wasn't any fight left in him, but I pulled him sitting with a grip on his hair and slapped him around.

"You welcher, you cheap speculator," I told him. "Who do you think you're dealing with, some punk off a banana boat?" I was mad. I slapped him again to let him know it. "This is Digger you're talking to. The Digger you taught to handle speculators. Are you saying 'I won't' to me?" and I hit him in the guts. I let go his hair and he fell back clutching his belly and moaning for air.

I let him gasp a few times and then took it up again. I couldn't afford to let him get set.

I pulled him to me by the neck of his sweat shirt and told him again.

"Run the game, Johnny."

He shook his head no.

So I used persuasion. I told him about how it is to have your legs broken and be left down by the bayou for the mosquitos and chiggers to chew up on a hot summer night.

And he said no.

So I worked on his kidneys. I didn't mark him any place it would show.

Pretty soon he stopped saying no and started saying yes. When I was convinced that he was convinced, I eased up.

He lay there sobbing for air. His eyes looked glazed.

I found a bottle with a slug left in it and poured it down him and he started to come around.

"Listen to me and listen hard, Johnny. You'll work Westwego one night, Gretna the next, then Algiers, then Westwego. Never the same parish two nights running. Then start over again. We can work for weeks that way. Don't admit any locals. The play will be strictly for out-of-towners. Don't use the same hotel or tourist court twice. Don't use any of the old hangouts and use honest dice. A squawk will stop us faster than the police. Have you got it?"

He had it, but I went over it and over it.

He was weak and scared, but I knew he would get up and go to work for me. He was afraid for his life. He didn't have to be. Murder is for psychos. There's no percentage in murder, ever. Only right now he didn't know how well I knew that.

When I was satisfied, I helped him to his feet.

"Go to a Turkish bath and get yourself fixed up. I'll send a guy around with the bank roll tonight. The two of you will work the big hotels and bars to drum up trade. Be careful who you approach. The first local you talk to will spill, then you'll get your head broken." I gave him a final warning. "You foul this up and if the cops don't kill you, I will. The man I'm sending around is my man. He has two jobs: to protect you and watch you, so don't try a fade out. Be here at eight sharp to meet my boy, but don't come back here again. He has a new stake out for you."

I walked to the door. "Remember, Johnny, this is your last chance for a bank roll. Louse it up and you will have more than the rent to meet."

I left him standing in the center of the room, a sick old man. My man. How I hate a has-been.

At the bottom of the stairs, I held up in the areaway. My watch read four p.m. It had taken longer with Johnny than I had planned. I scanned the street, but couldn't spot anyone that might be on me. This was getting a little wearing. When I saw the number one, I would put a stop to this fast.

I ducked out of the doorway and headed for Exchange Alley.

The Alley is three blocks long and is the only so-called alley in the Quarter, a lane so narrow that cars can't negotiate it.

Baptiste John's All Nite Eatery advertised Creole cooking. I knew better.

I pushed open the screen door and walked in with a couple of hundred flies flying fighter escort with me.

My man was in a booth at the rear stuffing his face with red beans and rice. I walked back and sat down.

Baptiste got a big smile on his face and was starting to tell me, "My, how nice to see you and pull up a steak and sit down," but I cut him off.

"Shut up and listen to me. It's all set for tonight. Have you got the dough I gave you?"

"Sure, Digger." He sounded hurt.

Baptiste was a Creole. He was sentimental, loyal and dumb. And he was ugly. I have never seen such an ugly man.

But he knew his engines. There wasn't a better diesel man on the Gulf.

"You had better have it all. Pick him up at eight sharp. Take him to the Roosevelt and Monteleone hotels. Make him do all the work. Stay out of it all you can, but watch him. Don't let him talk to any locals."

"I got it." He was all business now.

"I don't care if the game gets big or not. I don't even care if you lose the roll I gave you, only keep it going for a few days. Bring him here after each session and don't let him out of your sight. If this works, you can sell this crummy joint and you'll be back on the Gulf with all the boat under your pants that you've ever wanted."

"That's why I'm doing it, Digger."

"Use the place that we picked out across the river in Westwego tonight and keep in touch with me the way we planned." I got up. "Keep a cool stool, Baptiste, I'm counting on you."

I started to leave, but he called me back.

"Digger, are you sure this is necessary at all?"

"I know what I'm doing."

"Yeah, you know, but I don't. What's the big plan? What the hell is it?"

"You want me to get someone else?"

"No, Digger, but …"

I headed for my hotel room. I needed a shower and a change of clothes, and I needed a drink. I needed a drink bad.

The shower helped and a double shot was starting to untie the knot in my belly. I was too nervous. Everything was set. Things were working for me. I still had my luck. A couple more shots would set me straight, so I sat down on the bed.

I was already dressed in a dark blue suit and light blue loose weave shirt with a black knit tie. I was wearing my best pair of cordovan shoes. Now I could start thinking about dinner—pompano, maybe bouillabaisse and baked alaska. I could wash that down with Creole coffee, coffee so strong that it leaves an ink-like stain in the cup. I could finish with a pony of brandy, Grande Armanaque, thirty years old.

I could sit and sip brandy and let Johnny and Baptiste take my chances, and wait for the big man to make his move. The big man!

I was ready for him. I put down another slug of bourbon, got up and put Mr. Sour Mash back in his drawer. My .38 detective's special was his roommate. I took the .38 out and checked it. A two inch barrel and short round wooden handle. A lot of strings had been pulled to get me this gun. It was stolen from the factory and wasn't registered. I slid it back in the spring hip holster and put it in the drawer. I wouldn't need Mr. .38 when I saw Mr. Big. Mr. Big wouldn't be favorably impressed by a gun. If by chance I was wrong all the way, a gun wouldn't help. I would be dead before I could use it. The only weapon I would carry into that meeting would be my brain, so I was ready.

I hit the street in a good mood. Maybe too good. I shouldn't have taken that last shot of sour mash. Before I knew what was happening, there was a man flanking me on either side. They didn't say anything; they didn't have to. The guns slung under their armpits did all the talking.

They steered me to the curb staying close, but out of reach. In perfect time, they patted me down as we walked. One for each side. They didn't seem surprised that I was clean. A black Lincoln sedan shot up to the curb and one of the boys opened the rear door and climbed in, sat on the far side of the seat facing me and motioned for me to get in. His buddy shut the door, got in front and half turned so that he could keep his eye on me. Check and double check. They were hard boys and I admired their technique. I like to see a job well done.

The driver didn't have to be told to get rolling. He eased away from the curb and merged with the traffic on Bourbon Street.

Wish for and ye shall receive. There wouldn't be any pompano and baked alaska tonight. I was invited to give a command performance. My act had better be good. No half-baked Digger.

It had happened fast and I felt a little shaken.

The hood on my left in the back seat was a swarthy little guy. I recognized him.

His name was Louis Pappas, a Creole with a Greek name and a torpedo by profession. He would have had plenty of notches on his gun, if you could cut notches in a forty-five. Why do the little ones always carry the biggest guns? I had heard he sheathed a switch blade in his garter and was very good at in-fighting. That's why he was in back.

The boy in front was new. He watched me out of little pig eyes set close in a tremendous head. He was big and looked moronic.

The driver kept his eyes front. He wore a cap and from the height of him appeared to be a midget. Nice companions.

I wasn't scared. I knew my role backwards, but I was lonesome for my .38 special.

We took a left on Bourbon and another left onto a one-way street leading uptown.

Nobody talked. Pig Eyes and I tried to stare each other down. I started to go cross-eyed and gave it up. I didn't look at Pappas. The little Creole gave me the creeps.

The midget tooled the Lincoln across Canal Street and headed up St. Charles. He dodged in and out of traffic smoothly and not too fast. He was good.

We turned into Felicity Street fast and the car whipped down a ramp into a basement parking garage.

The midget took the Lincoln down a lane between rows of parked cars to the back.

The big guy in front jumped out, opened my door and stepped back, out of reach. I stepped down and Louis Pappas got out his own door. He came around the car and motioned toward an iron circular stair in the corner.

We went up, Pig Eyes ahead this time with Pappas behind me.

Below us, I heard the Lincoln take off.

The hood ahead of me opened the steel fire door at the top and we were in the stairwell on street level. We climbed two flights and went out into a corridor of what appeared to be an office building. All the frosted glass doors were dark except for one down the hall.

Abreast now, we marched down to it and Louis knocked. There wasn't any lettering on the panel.

It didn't matter. I knew who I would find inside.

But I was wrong.

The gent who opened the door was a big fat slob of a man. He was dressed in the best that money can buy, but it didn't hide the fact that he was a schnook.

He had the coloring of a man that spends his time in Swedish massage parlors and out of the sun. He was too pink to be true.

He had light red hair and eyelashes, and if he were stretched out on a serving platter, he would look like a boiled pig.

"Good evening, Mr. Twigg," I said.

He led the way through the reception room into an inner office. We followed. He walked behind the desk and sat down.

Pappas and the moron stayed near the door.

Nobody asked me to sit down so I sat. I lit up.

Pig Eyes walked over to me and slapped the cigarette out of my mouth. For the first time his face changed. He grinned so I kicked him in the shins.

His expression changed again and his right hand snaked for his gun.

Twigg yelled, but it was Pappas who saved my skin. He moved up behind the blimp and cracked him smartly on the neck with a rabbit punch before I could have moved.

The blow sent the big boy to his knees.

Louis was earning my respect. He helped the thing to his feet and deposited him in a chrome chair that looked too small to hold his weight. I relaxed and fixed another butt.

It was that easy. Already I had found out I wasn't to be hurt. Not yet anyway.

"All right, Digger, no more funny business," said Twigg.

I blew a smoke ring and waited.

Twigg waited, Louis waited and Pig Eyes held his head.

"You've been trying to see me," Twigg said. "You came along without any trouble. If you didn't have a story to tell, why did you come with the boys?"

"My life insurance lapsed," I answered. Let him blow. I wasn't talking. I had to be right. I had to be. Twigg couldn't be the big man.

He was upset. He came around the desk like a rainbow colored cyclone. He stood over me shaking.

"Maybe you would talk to Max?" The big tough looked up hopefully. "You talked plenty at Antonio's and around the docks."

I stared at him in disbelief. He must trust his henchmen plenty to hint at something in front of them.

"I've talked to very few people, Twigg. Sometimes *talk* gets around."

He blanched, then turned to the hoods. "Wait outside." They went.

"Now tell it, Digger."

"Go to hell."

He turned livid. The trouble with these pink-skinned guys is that you always know how they are taking it. They color too easily.

"Get smart with me and I'll let Max work on you," he snarled. "Or maybe you have heard of Louis' specialty with a knife?"

"You frighten me."

"I'll do more than that."

He was shaking and he looked like he meant it.

"Twigg, I wouldn't spit on you if you caught on fire. Get that straight. I won't tell you a thing, not a goddam thing."

He blew his cork. He ranted and threatened and I let him. When he ran out of dirty words, I suggested a few.

He was licked. He hadn't had a chance to start with.

"Get on the phone or send a telegram or whatever you have to do and tell the man," I said, "I'm nobody's boy but my own. I'll do business with him. Either that or I'm walking out of here."

I was bluffing.

He walked to the window and looked out at the night.

Twigg wasn't a tough guy. In the organization, his job was to be a committeeman, hail fellow well met, backslapper and front. Maybe he could do his own job, but as a tough he wouldn't scare a four-year-old.

He walked to the door and opened it.

"Watch him."

Louis and Max filed in and he closed the door tight as he went out.

Louis stood cleaning his nails with a gold pocket knife. Max watched me like a hungry bear.

Twigg would be using the reception room telephone calling an unlisted number.

The hook must be set deep. I hoped my luck wouldn't play out before I landed my catch. I was going to throw all the little ones back until I caught the prize.

We waited a long time. Finally, Twigg opened the door and called Pappas. They huddled in the reception room.

Louis was arguing, but Twigg was adamant. He could muster some authority when he was backed up by the boss.

Louis came in and motioned to me.

Pappas and I went out alone. Max looked sorry to see me go before he had a chance to break both my arms.

At the door Twigg stopped me. He was sweating. "You had better have something good. Personally, I hope you don't." He was having his fun now. "I want to read about it in the papers a month from now after they find your body. And I want you to know what else I told him. I told him about you and I said 'don't buy.' I told him he would be sorry. He listens to me, Digger."

The bleater.

And we went on out, down the cold marble hallway past the dark doors and down the empty echoing stairs and down that iron spiral stair, and I felt as cold as the hallway and empty as the stairwell.

This was it and I was scared.

Louis led off down the row of parked cars. The big Lincoln was nowhere in sight. He picked out an old black Plymouth coupe, fished a set of keys out of his pocket and climbed in behind the wheel. I got in the other side.

We ran out of Canal Street, switched over to Ponchartrain Boulevard, past the New Orleans Country Club and cruised along.

I could almost smell that rarified air of the rich.

This was Metairie, a Jefferson Parish suburb of New Orleans, known for its estate homes and beautiful gardens. Metairie is on a ridge, a few feet higher than the surrounding landscape. That's important when the main confines of the countryside are situated at a lower level than the Mississippi. Levees keep the river out and when it rains, as it often does, the rain has to be pumped uphill into the river. If the pumps are started late or break down, people in New Orleans proper go sloshing around in a couple of feet of water.

Louis suddenly turned off the highway and pulled up before the iron gates of a walled estate. A spotlight speared us. Louis blinked his lights in a signal and the gates swung open.

The car shot through and came to a stop at the gatehouse. Behind us the gates closed as ghostly as they had opened.

"Get out, Digger."

Louis had his gun in his hand.

I got out.

Inside the gatehouse I was frisked again. This time it was thorough. No gun, no knife, no razorblades in my hatband. When he was satisfied, he led me back to the car and we drove up a lane graveled with crushed oyster shells that glowed white in the moonlight. The lane was bordered with bougainvilleas in full bloom and as red as blood. It would be a pretty place to be buried.

We came upon the house suddenly. It loomed above us white, three-storied and ablaze with light like something out of a southern novel.

Louis parked in the circle drive and we went up the broad flight of stairs past columns bigger around than two men and across the wide veranda.

Louis stopped me at the door.

"A word of advice."

He was looking up at me and I could see the dislike on his face.

"Try to sell a bill of goods here and you won't last five minutes. He can't be fooled; he has brains he hasn't used yet. Back out now and you'll live; go through this door and he will have you fed to the crabs. I'll be the one that does the feeding. I'd like that."

"Ring that bell, punk," I said.

He almost choked on it, but he rang the bell. He would never be for me, but then nobody ever is in the rackets.

A butler opened the door, took our hats and ushered us into a library.

The rooms were tremendous. Old-fashioned high ceilings exaggerated and magnified the size.

The decor was as good as Twigg's was bad. Philippine mahogany paneling and deep Persian rugs. The furniture was solid stuff, built for real comfort and on the walls hung expensive paintings.

Louis stood at the door, tense, as if at attention. I wandered. An autographed picture of a famous movie actress stood on a Steinway grand. I was just about close enough to read the inscription when the big double doors at the end of the room opened and he walked in. Vitolo Giannini, King of Crime, Emperor of Evil.

He looked me over slowly, then let his glance slide past me to the grand piano. His expression didn't change.

He was small physically, but I knew he was big every other way. He looked like he could strut sitting down.

He came on into the room.

He dismissed Louis with a flick of his hand and we were alone. We studied each other in silence. When he was satisfied, he went to his desk, opened a folder lying there and read aloud.

"Hector Patrick Mulcahy."

I winced. It had been a long time since I had heard my own full name.

"Thirty-six years old. Born in Paterson, New Jersey of Irish, Polish extraction. Left home at age fifteen. Seasonal worker, picked fruit in California, cotton in Texas. Construction worker, road gang. Prize fighter, won fifteen, lost none. Killed man in street brawl, lost license, suspended sentence for manslaughter to enlist Navy, 1941, wounded, mustered out on medical discharge, 1944, as Chief Boatswain's Mate. Purple Heart, Silver Star.

"Worked on Gulf freighters, banana boats as seaman. Received second officer ticket. Lost ticket for drunkenness. Deckhand, seaman on oil exploration crews."

He hesitated.

"Lush! Gambler, bookie …" His voice trailed off.

He flipped the folder closed, but not before I caught a glimpse. There were a lot more pages.

He leaned with his back against the desk and folded his arms across his chest. His eyes held a cold look.

"What's this all about, Mulcahy? Why all the fuss about wanting to see me?"

He turned and tapped the folder as if it were already wastepaper, then pointed a stubby finger at me.

"Why, why? What leads you to me?"

I didn't answer.

"They told me you had nerve," he said. "I think it's only colossal gall."

"Mr. Giannini," I kept my voice calm, "if you didn't think I had something, I wouldn't be here."

He dropped his arm.

"They said you might be smart too," he smiled. "Let's hear it."

I picked out a comfortable looking easy chair and sat down.

"When I was in the Navy, they taught me to pilot landing craft," I started. "It was a soft racket except for the Japs and I liked the sea, so when I got out I went back to it. I worked my way up and got my civilian ticket. I rode freights, tankers and banana boats between the States and South America. Am I boring you?"

"I know all this."

I lit up.

"After I lost my ticket I bummed the docks. Things were rough. That was the second time I'd lost a chance for a good living. First the fights, now this. I finally landed a job with an oil exploration outfit. The tidelands oil had been discovered and there was a rush to get it. These exploration outfits worked right off the coastline mapping the ocean floor just like the geologists do on land." I stopped. My throat felt dry.

I was coming to the hard part.

"We used boats about a hundred feet long, any old tub we could get. The Navy had snapped up just about everything afloat.

"Our geologist would map off a ten mile square of water and we would go over it a half mile at a time. We took a sounding of the depth and a sample of the mud and moved a half mile and did the same thing until we had covered the whole ten miles."

"Mulcahy, I am not in the oil game and I am a very busy man."

The hell he wasn't in the oil game. He didn't know it, but he had just bought in. I continued as if I hadn't heard him.

"The authorities got used to seeing us out there because we stayed out ten days to two weeks at a time, almost in the same spot. We only came in to fuel and stock up and went right out again."

His eyes lowered to slits as I went on.

"We used to wave at the patrol boats and planes because it was a lonely job, but they never paid any attention to us.

"I thought at the time what a perfect rendezvous those boats would be for smugglers. Of course, I never mentioned it to anyone because it was so preposterous."

I gave him a grin but he was preoccupied and didn't notice.

He strolled around the desk, sat down and picked up pen and paper.

"Mulcahy, you interest me. I would like to hear some more of this, ah, preposterous idea."

"You can call me Digger, Mr. Giannini."

He grinned. "All right, Digger, tell me why you think this would work and how you would do it."

I had known he would listen. The Feds had knocked off one big smuggling ring after another. Whoever controlled the import of opium from Arabia and Red China, cocaine and the other opiates for the junkers, controlled a great portion of the underworld.

There were other angles too. Jewels, gold and securities were worth double their value in countries behind the iron curtain.

Everything had a price someplace. The problem was to move it. Now I had to give him the full picture, so he could see it.

"Tideland operations are going full blast again. Private operators quit when the government threatened to take them over. Congress has passed a bill stating the government doesn't own the oil. The Supreme Court wrecked the bill, but the government's not sure of its rights. Besides the geologists' reports are top secret and are given only to the oil company that hires the survey. You can turn right around and survey the same section time and time again for other companies. This will be good indefinitely.

"The tidelands extend from the tip of Mexico clear around the Gulf to the tip of Florida so that you have thousands of miles in which to base your receiving boats. Deliveries can be made there from the West Indies, Cuba, Haiti, Jamaica.

"There are tidelands off the coast of California. With a boat there you can bypass Mexico and Canada and the Border Patrol. The Far East can send the stuff direct.

"These boats can be serviced by plane. Just wrap the junk in a cork container and drop it near a boat for a quick pickup.

"Back at the docks the delivery is transferred to a company truck with the trash or in empty food crates. There are never any inspections. These boats don't need a sailing clearance. Just like your own private customs station." I stopped. I had told him all I should. Now I wanted him to ask me questions. And he did.

"How close could we work to Tampico, Mexico?"

"An hour's speed run by motorboat, less by plane."

"And Cuba?"

"A few hours."

"What about a Federal license for these boats?"

"A regular marine license in the company or owner's name is all that's needed."

"How much do they cost?"

"Plenty, but not as much as the equipment. They have to be fitted to do the legitimate job. If they are working legit as well, they will more than pay for themselves."

He sat back, made a house of his fingertips and stared at the ceiling.

"You come to me, yet no one else can pin me down to a Federal rap for this type of operation. Why, Digger?"

"I once knew a guy in Tampa. I saw you with him one time. He was shot six months ago trying to escape the Feds. I don't have to mention names, but he was the biggest operator in business, but now his company is kaput."

"You guessed right on that, Digger," his smile faded, "but it isn't healthy to know too much. What makes you think that I need you in this caper. It's true you brought it to me and maybe I can use it. But what will keep me from taking you for a cruise on my yacht in Ponchartrain Lake and coming back without you?"

I would swim or sink with my answer. I took my time about it. I wasn't in a hurry for a swim in a concrete bathing suit.

"Mr. Giannini, you can't possibly do it without me. I'm the only man you can find who knows the Gulf men well enough. Those boats need a crew of eight. Where would you get them? The first ex-thug, bootlegger or guy with a record that appeared on the dock would throw suspicion your way. You need a pilot, engineer and geologist who all have to have licenses. Yet they have to be willing to look the other way when someone drops a boat hook and picks up that cork-lined package. Can you get them?"

I waited. He didn't answer.

"I can," I said. "Then there are the dock men, the storekeepers, suppliers, ship's chandlers and government inspectors. They know me. I know them. You put one of your old cronies on that job and the G-Men will be buzzing like flies. You can't make a move anymore."

I waited.

He sat.

"My record is old. I haven't been picked up for a Grand Jury appearance. Everyone you know has been. There's no one else you can trust. It's got to be with me."

He got up. "I like your story, Digger. Only don't be sure you are indispensable. Nobody is. Let's have a drink."

I could use one. I was wound as tight as a fishing reel with a 500-pound marlin on the other end.

He brought a bottle out of the liquor cabinet.

"This is my favorite, but maybe you would like something better."

It was sour mash.

"Mr. Giannini, I admire your taste."

He poured about four fingers. I did admire his taste.

I washed that tight taste out of my mouth and had another.

"Digger, I'm going to think about what you have told me. For your sake, I hope there aren't any bugs in it. I like you. If I can use it, we will have a lot to talk about. In the meantime, don't talk to anybody and play it cool."

We finished our drinks and he walked me to the door.

"If you want me to play it cool, take those stumblebum tails off me and have people stop asking for my pedigree. Somebody will get curious to know why I've become so popular."

"You're right. You have a good head." He gave me a level look. "Keep it tight on your shoulders. I'll have you driven home."

And he did, except that's not where I was going.

I sat in the back in the limousine that carried me toward town. It was a plush ride.

When we reached Canal Street, I picked up the car phone and made a long distance call to the chauffeur.

"Stop the car, James."

I felt like crooking my little finger in the approved style. Maybe his name wasn't James. He didn't stop.

"Pull over to the curb."

These servants weren't milk toast old family retainers. Mother Giannini had been a scrub-lady in Gretna and Vitolo had never known the loving care that mammies and servants can lavish.

This hired hand was an ex-con that was being looked after in his old age.

You had to speak his language to be understood. He pulled over.

He was upset.

"Mr. Giannini gave me instructions to take you home, sir."

"I have decided to take the air. Ring off, old man."

I slammed the receiver down and jumped out.

"Ta, ta, Mac."

His name must have been Mac. He ground the gears getting away.

I was pleased with myself. I felt like celebrating.

I hoofed it back to Ponchartrain Boulevard, but instead of going that way I kept straight ahead on Metairie Road.

It was a nice night for breaking and entering. The moon was hidden now by scudding clouds.

I came to the Golf Club and turned down Palm Avenue.

When I found the right estate I grasped a hand hold on the brick wall, got a leg up and jumped over and made a perfect three pointer in an azalea bed.

The grounds were a four acre miniature of the formal gardens at Luxembourg. I made my way toward the lighted library windows.

I crossed the flagstone terrace on my tiptoes and got to the edge of the French doors. The room was a study in brazen opulence. In the faint light of a single lamp, silk and satin shimmered, velvet glowed and polished wood was reflected like flames.

Low, soft hassocks and wide, long couches exuded comfort.

She sat in a chair reading, holding the book in one hand while the other swung at her side rattling the ice in a tall cool one.

Her legs were stretched out in front of her, encased in sheer hose. They were long, fully turned, willowy legs. Her hips flared excitingly then tapered to a slim waist.

Her hair was the color of fresh honey, bleached by the sun and it hung to her shoulders in graceful lines.

Her face was tanned golden to match her fine arms and her delicate features spelled breeding with a capital B.

She took a long pull on the drink, sat it carefully on the floor and put her head back on the chair as she fanned herself. The top of her blouse was undone.

It truly was a hot night.

One of the French doors down the line had been left open for ventilation. I walked over to it and entered the room.

"Fancy meeting you here," I said.

She came out of the chair like a guided missile, her hand at her mouth, choking on a scream.

I sailed my hat toward a couch and fished for a butt.

"Oh, God," she moaned.

"Don't faint, Eldeese. I've seen you before."

She folded her arms over her chest. Her eyes were still wide and frightened.

"How did you get in?" she breathed.

"By registered mail. I'm waiting for a receipt." I made myself comfortable.

"You can't stay here."

I got that hard feeling in my gut. Why did she have to bring that up? I was as good as the next guy.

"It was different then." She was ready to cry and saw the look on my face. "I don't mean …" Her eyes appealed to me, but I let her struggle.

"But … I was alone then." She wasn't helping herself any. "Oh, damn."

It was the same old story. Rich man's daughter, guy from the wrong side of town. It was always being thrown at me. I used to get sore and blow my top. Now I got sore, but in a different way. I could hurt this gal plenty, break her down, make her crawl.

She shrugged her shoulders, strode to the French windows and pulled the drapes.

"That's better," I said.

"Why do you make me feel this way? It's you *I* should be mad at. I know you are cruel, selfish and a warped person."

I got up and moved in close.

"So." I put an arm around her and she stiffened.

"Go away, Digger. I'm happy now. You don't bother me."

"Sure. It's easy to forget."

She relaxed a little.

"Let me go, Digger." It didn't sound final.

I put my other arm around her and pulled her to me gently.

"Don't make me start all over again," she pleaded. "I had forgotten."

I gathered her in till she was pressed tight against me.

Her arms stole slowly around my waist and she began to melt.

Her head came up and she looked at me, pleading with tears like pearls on her cheeks.

But her arms tightened, her fingers dug into my back and she kissed me—a hungry kiss.

I picked her up and carried her to the couch.

She lay there looking up at me, her smile was soft and her eyes looked far away.

"I haven't forgotten. I've only been waiting," she said.

As I lay down beside her she whispered, "Turn out the light."

"Build me a drink," I said as I lay back and let my muscles stretch and fall back exhausted.

She was a very happy girl. When the skirt was in place, she knelt by the couch.

"Like me?"

"Love ya."

She threw her arms around me.

"Do you really love me, Digger?"

"Let's not talk about love. Talk about liquor."

A fleeting expression of hurt crossed her face but she brightened, gave me a peck of a kiss and stood up.

Eldeese was a prize. Young, fresh and desirable. That her old man owned more oil than Standard of New Jersey didn't hurt. But she was no debutramp.

She was just at loose ends.

That had been our trouble. We had met at the Club Forest over a high stakes crap table. She was too young to be in the joint so I took her away from it all. That night we parked in a lonely spot on the levee.

She wasn't a wild kid or a fool. I had just been the guy that looked like the real thing.

We saw each other on the quiet—lake front bingo parlors or at a secluded bar.

Her old man found out and had me investigated. Nothing he heard was good. He sent me a warning and I sent the warning back to him beaten to a pulp.

He told Eldeese, of course, and she didn't care at first, but with the pressure of her family and friends growing stronger all the time, she began to change.

I liked it that way. I was growing tired of her as a steady diet and I had finally let her have it. I had told her to take her dough and society and shove it. I had laid it on pretty thick and she was hurt.

What the hell. It had been a long time ago. But you never forget.

She came back in while I was thinking.

"See, I remember." She held up a bottle of sour mash.

"I'm surprised Papa would allow common stuff on the premises," I said.

"It's not Father's, it's mine."

She plopped down on the floor next to me, slit the stamp on the neck with her fingernail and uncorked it like an expert. Her eyes stared levelly into mine.

"I have my common streak too," she said and winked.

I took the bottle and gave myself a drink. This was the third bottle I had sampled tonight. The third time's the charm. The bourbon went down like a submarine. It was as hot as a blast furnace, then cooled and became charming.

She accepted the jug and swallowed a large one.

"Very neat. You used to be a Pink Lady lapper."

I took back the bottle and helped myself.

"By the way, where is your old man?" I asked.

"Upstairs."

I sat bolt upright.

She uncorked the bottle from her lips and added, "Asleep, I hope."

"You mean all the time ..."

"Yes," and she giggled.

"I need a drink."

It was a tall one.

She crawled up beside me and took her turn.

"I hope he is a poor shot," I said.

"So do I."

We agreed.

I awoke to cries of street hawkers. "Blackberries, getcha-blaaaberries. Oysters and shrimp, not limp, jumpin' fresh oysters and shrimp."

The day was in full swing in the street below my window.

"Blaaaberries ... Shrimp, shrimp, not limp."

The street noise was out of tempo with the bells in my head. I made it to the house phone and got connected with room service. My tongue tasted like the inner sole of an old tennis shoe.

I ordered a tank car of tomato juice and black coffee to match.

The waiter must have started out by way of Nome, Alaska. It was taking him too long to reach me with the serum. I wasn't impatient, just dying, so I used the oldest remedy known to man—the hair of the dog.

There was just enough sour mash left in my own bottle to make the noises in my head fade to a tiny tinkle, and by the time the waiter appeared, I was only strong enough to get up and let him in.

He carried the breakfast tray in and I glanced out into the hallway, but I didn't see his dogsled. Management must have made him leave it in the lobby.

I didn't have a piece of whale blubber on me to tip him with, so I gave him the usual buck.

"Mush," I said.

He got out fast, looking scared. Didn't understand his own language, I guess.

I alternated shots of tomato juice and coffee until the walls stopped hurtling around, waited until the bathroom door came by again and jumped through.

I must have shared two quarts with Eldeese and when she had poured me into a cab, she had been sober.

I stood under the shower until my head rejoined my body.

I called the valet and told him where to find the body and chose fresh duds from the closet.

I was going to need a new wardrobe. Winter was coming. I played with the idea.

Winter, new friends, the race track opening, Mardi Gras. I would be meeting people. High class. I could join the club at the track, no more standing at the fence to watch the bangtails run. For all this I would want a new wardrobe. A trip, maybe Bermuda or Mexico City.

I clamped the lid on my dreams. If I wasn't careful, I would be wearing a pine box overcoat and very little else.

I was dressed by the time the valet knocked. This crummy hotel couldn't afford their own, so they subscribed to an outside cleaners.

I waited while the valet gathered up the dearly departed and I went out right behind him, locked the door and headed for the street.

As I waited for a cab, I scanned the block. Mr. Giannini had kept his word. No tail.

A taxi swung into the curb at my signal. I climbed in and gave him the address. He gave me a short fast ride and I gave him the change from a five. I felt charitable, like an oil man.

I had breakfast in a one-armed joint next to my building. Over coffee I gave a couple of the angles a go-around just for practice.

I had fifteen thousand tucked away and I was just about to spend it. The next few days would tell the story. If things didn't break for me, I should have a getaway poke. There wasn't enough for both. What the hell, I'm a gambler.

I cashed a check for pocket money in the New Iberia Bank, then took an elevator to the sixth floor of the office building next door. Down the corridor I stopped at a door bearing the legend, "Martin Epstein, Attorney at Law."

I opened the door and walked in. A very pretty girl receptionist gave me a bright hello, told me to be seated, that Mr. Epstein would see me in a minute.

The girl was Mrs. Epstein. She was tall, dark and well-made. Lucky Mr. Epstein.

A slim, well-stacked lady came out of the private office crying. The receptionist announced me on the intercom and I went in. Martin Epstein, attorney at law, sat behind a tremendous walnut desk. He was short, frail and bald. Unlucky Mrs. Epstein.

As I shut the door I could still hear the departing lady crying out in the hall.

"What did you do, pinch her?"

He swung his feet up on the desk and smiled.

"The case of the outraged wife. Her husband is a yentzer."

"A what?"

"In English, a cheater. Sit down, Mr. Mulcahy."

I sat. Martin had been my lawyer now for six years. He had a lot of my money and I had a clean police card. I always listened to what he said.

When I started to make book, I had looked around for my own lawyer. I heard about Mr. Epstein inadvertently. Some of the boys were laughing about a little lawyer who was defending a two-bit stickup. The thug signed two confessions before Martin got the case and had bragged that the five witnesses the prosecution had called up couldn't possibly identify him because, in his own words, "I was wearing a hat pulled down over my eyes and dark glasses at the time."

How he did it, I don't know, but Martin had won an acquittal on a technicality. That convinced me.

In court he wasn't impressive. He was half deaf and he looked like a ferret with his bald head cocked to hear what was going on. But he was the best legal brain in town and won his cases with monotonous regularity, and the D.A. hated his guts.

Myself, I loved him.

"I'm ready to roll, Martin."

"Fine."

"Have you got the contracts ready?" I asked him.

"Have you got the money?"

I smiled. He smiled back.

"Martin, why don't you go into this with me, on a retainer basis?"

"A retainer is always paid in advance."

"You'll get it in advance."

"No, Digger. The D.A. is waiting for a chance to get me. I'll take my fee for drawing up the contracts."

I didn't like that.

"You told me it could be handled, Martin." My voice was hard.

"What do you mean?"

"If you have me protected in the corporation setup, you wouldn't be afraid to be retained by the corporation."

He gave me a sharp look.

I had to be positive about this and there was only one way to feel safe.

"Am I liable under the setup you figured out or not?" I asked.

"No."

"I'd better not be because I'm going to make you a partner."

"Now see here, Digger."

"Do you want fifty thousand dollars or not?"

His eyes grew shrewd.

I got up and pushed his feet off the desk and sat down.

"I'm prepared to give you fifteen thousand now, for a retainer, and the rest monthly. Forget the fee for drawing up the contracts and corporation papers. That's chicken feed. If you have me protected, you won't be afraid to be my partner and be retained by the company. Fifty thousand a year buys a lot of chili."

"I see what you mean."

He opened the bottom drawer of his desk and produced a bottle and glasses. I gave him room to pour a couple. He shouldn't have to think on this long.

We sat and sipped. It was a brandy and good too.

Martin sat back and looked at me.

"The DA. would sniff this out as soon as I filed the papers for record." He flipped the intercom switch.

"Bring in Mr. Mulcahy's papers. All of them."

I froze. What was the little gink up to.

His wife came in with a folder and put it in front of him. He opened it and took out a legal document encased in blue paper.

"This is your corporation document." He tore it through the middle and tossed it in the waste basket.

I stood up. "What the hell."

He smiled. "We'll need a new one, if I'm going to be a partner."

He poured three drinks this time.

"A toast to a partnership, a very silent partnership," he said.

I drank mine in silent gratitude to the fates that be.

After his wife had left the room, he picked two more blue bound documents out of the file.

"Here are the contracts authorizing the leasing of *our* boats. Are you still in touch with the fall guy?"

"He's anxious to get started. I've been stalling him for months," I said as I took the contracts.

"Martin, I'm glad you decided to go in with me. But a word of caution. I'm the King Bee in this caper. The law would treat you like a mother if you stepped out of line compared to how I would handle it. Take your fifty thousand a year and give me legal advice. Nothing but."

"I know your reputation first hand, Digger. I think we will get on famously."

The little toad wasn't scared, he was smart. As my silent partner, he would make a mummy look talkative.

I put the contracts in my inside coat pocket and said goodby.

"Aren't you forgetting something?" he asked.

"What?"

"A little matter of fifteen thousand."

"Call me when you get the new papers drawn up."

He frowned. "You will have to trust me in this."

"That's the way I like it. We have to trust each other."

I closed the door.

Outside again, I went into a Walgreen Drugstore. The first telephone call got results.

"Baptiste?"

"Speaking."

"How are the pigeons today?"

"Off their feed, Digger. I have one in particular that wants to fly the coop."

"Did you clip its wings?"

"Man, I'll say, but it's still restless."

"Are you alone?"

"Yeah."

"How did it go last night?"

"Slow. We got a couple salesmen and a tourist. One guy wanted to bring his girl along, but we ditched him."

"Get a rumble?"

"No, but Johnny is no good at this. He was so nervous he fumbled all night. What the hell did you do to him?"

"Forget that. Take him out again tonight. I don't care if you kind of let it be known around now. We're set and the sooner I go into action the better."

"This is crazy, man. How do I know I'm safe?"

"Because I'm telling you. Relax, you're just about to earn a big pair of twin diesels to nurse."

"Okay, okay, I'll take him to Westwego tonight and Algiers tomorrow night. Is that it?"

"You remember fine."

I hung up and called another number.

A high voice answered with "The Dunbar residence."

"Is Mr. Dunbar in?"

"Who is calling, please?"

"Mr. Mulcahy."

"Oh yes, Mr. Mulcahy, Mr. Dunbar left a message for you. He is in New York and will return this weekend, on Saturday. He tried to get you before he left and failed. He seemed to be very anxious to talk to you."

"I'll call back on Saturday."

The phone booth was stifling so I got out.

Dunbar was with his rich friends in New York. I didn't need him yet anyway. I didn't have the boats nor the money to buy them. I hadn't hired the crews or bought the equipment. I was going to have to move fast and here I stood with my finger up it waiting. I couldn't rumble until I had Giannini convinced.

PART II

There was a bar without business just off Canal Street so I gave them mine.

There was only one angle that bothered me. The no-name angle. That quirk in my plans that I couldn't foresee; couldn't cope with. Why? Because I wasn't even there.

In every deal there is the chance of getting caught by accident.

You can't ever be positive in the rackets. All you can do is plan the best you know how.

Then I got it. I was beginning to walk the tightrope. Live from day to day, eyes constantly open, alert. Waiting for the unexpected.

It's a price you have to pay.

I dropped into the hotel for a shower and change. There weren't any messages so I figured everything was going smooth.

I was supposed to meet Eldeese at six.

It was an early hour for dinner but we would welcome the privacy of an empty dining room. I phoned the bell captain to send a fresh quart and the bellboy and I shared a couple when it was delivered. He didn't have any information for me. A combined force of bellboys can pool more information than the F.B.I. Nobody had been nosing around.

I got to the Vieux Carré Restaurant by six thirty. Eldeese outguessed me. She got there at a quarter of seven.

We became cozy over Martinis at a corner table.

The Vieux Carré is maybe the best French restaurant in the quarter. The place is run by an Irishman and in this town that's as it should be.

We dined fine on crawfish bisque and lingered over brandy. Eldeese was wearing a taffeta strapless gown.

As the restaurant filled up, she drew more and more admiring glances. Her old man would get the bad news before he was out of bed in the morning.

"Don't frown, Digger, it makes you look mean."

"So?"

"I like you for other reasons too," she laughed.

"Let's get out of here," I said.

"As you wish, sire."

She tossed down her brandy in a most unladylike fashion. Maybe that's why we got along. Sometimes she *was* a broad.

I signaled the waiter and paid the fare while she went to powder her nose.

When she came out of the powder room, she gave me a look.

"Let's get drunk."

"We don't have to."

"Can't take it, eh?"

"I'm beginning to wonder."

"Take me places, Digger."

"What about your old man?"

"To hell with him. By now everyone in town knows I'm out with you."

"Where to?"

"Every place. It's been a long time since I've been in the Quarter."

"We're on our way."

We started in the biggest, noisiest club on the street. The music stank and the drinks were terrible.

We skipped from joint to joint and by midnight we were drinking our shots straight to avoid water poisoning.

Even without the gambling and girls, New Orleans is a wicked city. The Quarter jumped at night to the tune of bacchanalia. Fourteen square blocks on a perpetual carnival binge.

That mousy third clerk from back home acted like a combination Casanova and Diamond Jim Brady when he hit Bourbon Street. Perfect strangers became your dearest lifelong friends. I don't know what it is but the street affects people that way.

We had drunk our way through just about everything there was by the time we hit Lafitte's Blacksmith Shop.

It was comparatively quiet here. I looked at Eldeese.

Her eyes were shining with suppressed excitement.

I waved the cabbie away. We weren't far from that lonely spot on the levee and that's where we were going.

The sun was blinding hot on my face. I threw an arm over my eyes and lay still.

I had kicked the sheet off in my sleep and I lay naked, letting the sun bake my body.

Holy Toledo, another one of those mornings. What was I doing getting frazzled every night when I would need all my strength and wits about me soon.

I came to enough to order coffee on the house phone.

A shower helped revive me and the coffee supplied the final crutch.

I dressed in a rush and got out of there.

In the street the bright morning light hurt my eyes. I squinted as I crossed to the shadows on the other side. My feet took me aimlessly toward Esplanade Avenue. Where was I going? I didn't know. It was going to be a long, long day.

I found a cafe.

The joint was empty. Too late for breakfast, too early for ten o'clock coffee. My rules were my own so I had coffee. The thought of breakfast made my stomach slide toward Cuba.

Nobody else came in, the waitress was too ugly to play games with, and even the buzzing flies seemed bored.

It was too early to call Baptiste. I was going to let Epstein call me. To hell with Eldeese.

I watched the second hand go around on the electric clock over the counter.

Time dragged by like a sluggish tortoise. A watched kettle never boils.

I left some change on the counter and hiked myself out.

I found a record shop up the street, but sitting in a booth listening wouldn't help. Cigarettes tasted like rope in my mouth. I'd had too much music last night. Too much of everything.

Why was I so nervous? I looked behind me. No shadow. Must be the salt air.

By noon I was on pins and needles. I found a pay station in a department store and dialed Baptiste. The bell rang on the other end a long time.

"Hello," a voice answered.

"Baptiste?"

"Yeh."

"Are you clean?"

"Huh? Oh, sure," he yawned.

"Get the cotton out of your head. What's the story?"

"Gees, Digger, you woke me up."

"Tell it."

"Tell what? There ain't nothin' to tell."

"Do you want me to come choke it out of you?"

"Don't get sore. We did fine last night. Big game, we won a bundle."

"How big a game?"

"Like you planned. We let in some of the hep boys. Everybody is starved for action."

"Good. Any beefs?"

"Like you said, I let Johnny do the approach. Only a few wouldn't buy."

"Anyone we know?"

"Yeah. They maybe worked for a certain somebody once."

"Good. Algiers tonight."

"One thing." He stopped me from hanging up.

"What?"

"About Johnny. Remember I told you how nervous he was the first night?"

"Yeah?"

"Well, last night he was cool as ice. You know what I think?"

"He's going for a stake so he can try a runout," I told him.

"How d'you know?"

"I expected it. Watch him like he was your unfaithful wife."

"How long, Digger?"

"Tonight. It will be tonight." I was guessing.

I hung up.

On the street a guy in a hurry bumped me. I almost hung one on him before I caught myself.

This hustle and bustle could drive a man nuts.

I found a car rental agency and bought a twenty-four hour ticket. I needed wheels under me, someplace to go. The car might be handy to have for other reasons later on.

I sped out Elysian Fields Avenue breaking the speed laws on open stretches.

I felt better. I pulled into a roadside park on the lake front and got out.

I watched old men fish and young girls sunbathe and babies trying to launch play boats.

At dusk, these same people would come back with bushel baskets and nets to trap the shrimp that fed on the sandwich crusts and refuse of the day.

I spent a nice afternoon. I motored over to the yacht basin and looked at the boats and had a cool lunch on the veranda of a cafe facing into the lake breeze.

I was relaxed by the time the sun set. I jockeyed the car into town in the gathering darkness.

I was relaxed and set and I wanted to be where they could find me when my time came.

I found a parking place on Toulouse and walked around to the Hotel.

I had messages. Epstein had called, Eldeese had called three times, but the kicker was a note that two men had paid me a visit. They had declined to leave names. I got up to my room and had the desk send me a bottle.

I was in the shower when the knock came on the door. I shut off the water, wrapped a towel around my middle and went to answer it.

I stood to the right of the door jamb.

"Who is it?"

"Jimmy."

I unlatched the night catch and stepped back.

It was the bellboy with my bottle.

I shut the door after him and latched it.

"Uncork it and have one, Jimmy."

"I can't stay long. We're busy tonight."

He poured two in water glasses on the bureau. I watched him.

"I had visitors this afternoon," I said.

He laughed. "I thought you would be calling for me."

"Who were they, Jimmy?"

"New to me. Not the vice squad or regular cops. They looked like private dicks and they were loaded for bear."

"How do you know that?" I asked.

"I brushed up against one of them. He had a blackjack in his pocket that was as big as a baseball bat. The other guy had the same kind of bulge in his coat."

I peeled a ten and a five off my roll.

"The ten is for you. Give the fiver to your relief and tell him to tip me if they're here when I come in or go out."

"Thanks."

He saluted me with a finger and went out.

I started to dress. The two strangers didn't bother me. That would be Eldeese's father sending his warnings in pairs now.

I picked out my navy blue suit. It was designed to disguise the .38 detective's special. I wore the special belt with a clip for the holster.

From the bottom drawer I drew out a pair of calf skin gloves and tried them on. They fitted tight, as good as the bandages a prize fighter wears under his boxing gloves. People don't know how easy it is to break a hand.

I stripped the gloves off and stowed them in a side pocket and opened the top drawer. The .38 special was bedded down next to my sour mash. I passed up the bourbon and lifted out the gun and checked it. A handful of extra cartridges went into my pocket and the holster and gun on my hip.

I buttoned my coat, turned off the light and went out.

Back at the car I sat in the front seat behind the wheel and looked around for a place to stow the gun and cartridges.

With my pen knife I made a slit on the left hand side of the seat down near the door. I put the gun in it, handle up, and practiced a draw. It would work fine. I put the cartridges in the slit and the gun on top of them.

There was little chance I would get to use the gun. The odds were a hundred to one that I wouldn't even be in this car later on, but I couldn't afford to have it found on me. My play was based on the idea that I had nothing to hide. I felt better with the gun this close. It wasn't good but it was the best I could do.

I had dinner at Arnaud's as usual. It was getting late. By this time Johnny and Baptiste would be rounding up the customers.

I ate slowly, dragging out the hours.

After coffee, I ordered brandy and looked at my watch; eleven p.m.

No action. I watched the door and waited. The minutes ticked by. Still no action.

I paid and left. Outside the sky was overcast and there was the smell of rain in the air. It would cool things off.

I walked down Bourbon looking into faces. Nobody.

I turned down a sidestreet and stopped before a dirty-colored building with a lonely beer sign over the door.

The door was open so I went in, crossed to the deserted bar and sat on the end stool.

Leon looked up.

"Hi, Digger, how they hanging?"

"Ma in?"

"Nope, too early."

He dived under the bar for the good bottle and a clean glass. His reflexes were still conditioned for the ring and he would never quit moving fast until he died.

I kept my seat on the end stool so that I could watch the street through the open door.

Leon left the bottle on the bar and I sat and sipped.

Cars rolled by outside occasionally, but few people. A Ford, a Buick, a Cadillac, a Lincoln.

That was it. I waited about four minutes and the Lincoln went by again, slower this time.

I gave it two more minutes and stood up.

"Tell Ma I was by."

I started for the door.

"Saloon," he said.

"Hot dog," said I.

I turned left on the sidewalk and started back toward Bourbon. I almost got there. A guy jumped out of a door way and jammed a gun in my ribs, hard.

"Easy now," he breathed. Another hood came from behind the cars parked at the curb. They patted me down good.

The Lincoln pulled up and we walked over to it.

The back door opened and I saw the smiling moronic face of Max, Twigg's boy.

"Get in, you son of a bitch."

"Okay, Pig Eyes." I started to step in, then lunged, throwing a straight right as I went. I bounced his head off the heavy bullet proof glass of the window and he slumped down, cold. The back of my head exploded as I reached for the door handle on the opposite side and I fell on top of him when they hit me again with the sap.

When I woke up, I thought it was still dark. But it wasn't, I just had my eyes closed. I was tied with my arms behind me in a straight backed, wooden chair. I tried to move my feet but my ankles were shackled tight to the legs.

I looked around me.

"Good evening, Mr. Twigg," I said.

He didn't answer. Neither did Max or the other thug. I didn't know him socially anyway.

I was in a narrow concrete room. Where? A storeroom in the subterranean parking garage under Twigg's office. That was my guess. Nobody would hear me holler down here.

Nobody talked. They sat and smoked and Pappas cleaned his fingernails. Nobody even looked at me. I tried my ropes. I could move my body an inch either way. That would help me stand what was going to happen.

Twigg looked at his watch.

"To hell with waiting," he said. He came over and stood in front of me.

"Where's Johnny?"

I looked up at him innocently. "Johnny who?"

"Save yourself some grief. You and Johnny are running a floating crap game."

I looked amazed. "I am! Then what am I doing here?"

"You're in no position to get smart." His voice was steely. "This town is cold and that's the way the chief wants it. He's mad, Digger, awfully mad."

"So am I, you fat apple-knocker."

His face turned brick red. He held his half-smoked cigarette in front of my face.

"What did you call me?"

"Fat, you gink," and I spat on the cigarette.

He lost his head and slammed the butt into my face but it had gone out and I only felt the sting of his hand.

"Take him, Max."

Max stepped up and with a smile on his face looped a right at my nose. His aim was a little high and I turned my head and rolled as much as I could as he landed.

He hit me high and my ears rang but he almost cracked his hand.

He stopped and glared. I smiled. He whipped out his handkerchief and wrapped it around his fist.

"Don't mark him," said Twigg.

Max started in on me with intentions of breaking my ribs.

He got set and whistled one at my breadbasket. I rolled in the chair and blew out through my nose, a pro trick of making the gut as tense and tough as possible.

He tried it a couple more times, harder, and I rolled and snorted.

I laughed at him. He was getting to me but I wouldn't let him know it.

"Somebody hold him still," Max said.

The strange pug came around behind me and clamped an arm around my neck and shoulders.

That hampered my movement and cut off my wind.

I felt myself weakening as Max drove his big fists in like pile drivers.

I gulped air, got set, and threw my body weight in a last violent rolling motion. The chair went over sideways pulling the thug behind me off balance. He fell on top of me and Max almost turned around twice swinging at empty air.

I was lying there waiting for the kicks that were bound to come when I felt a cool breeze blowing on my face. I opened my eyes. Twigg was frozen against the wall, Max wasn't moving. Pappas was looking toward the door.

I craned my neck that way.

Mr. Giannini was standing in the doorway surveying us all with a very cool eye.

The guy on top of me scrambled to his feet. "What is this, Twigg?" said Giannini.

"He got tough."

"I told you to wait. What happened, Louis?"

"Digger got smart with Mr. Twigg. Max was softening him up."

"He doesn't look softened to me." He walked into the room. "What did he say?"

"Nothing," Twigg said sullenly.

"Pick him up," said Giannini.

Max and the pug lifted the chair and me to our feet.

"When are you going to learn, Twigg?" said the King. "You don't try to beat information out of a fighter. He won't talk when you hit him. He used to do that for money. Isn't that right, Digger?"

I was silent.

"With a fighter you use another method. Come here, Louis."

"Oh, Christ," I thought.

"Take off his shoes," said Mr. G.

Max unlaced my right shoe and yanked it off, almost taking my foot with it.

I was thinking fast.

Mr. Giannini poked a stubby finger into my chest.

"I put the lid on this town—no games, no dames. The Grand Jury has no squawk for six months. I like that. This is a bad time for me. A very bad time. You and your two bit partner start a floating crap game and I get calls from the cops in two parishes. I thought you were smart. When I saw you I didn't believe you had been a tramp. Now you louse up your deal for peanuts. You're still a tramp."

"That's just it," I said.

"What is, tramp?"

"The deal. I haven't seen Johnny for days. I don't know what he's doing. Whatever it is, it's not with me."

Giannini curled his lip. "Louis!" he called.

Pappas walked up. The switch blade was in his hand and I hadn't seen him reach for it. His arm no more than twitched and the blade was hurtling toward me.

The blade winged into the chair seat and stuck in the inch of wood showing between my legs. A drop of sweat ran down my face and dropped off my chin as I sat watching the knife quivering there.

"Talk, Digger. You haven't said anything yet," said Mr. G.

"Think about it," I told him, "you said it. Would I put a wrench in our deal for peanuts?"

"I don't know what to think about you yet."

"You looked me up. You know all about me. I bet you even know how much I have in the bank."

I waited a second to let that sink in. "Would I ruin myself for one, two hundred a night?"

He thought about it.

"Cut off my toes and we'll never do business, or do you want me to talk about that, here and now?"

He turned to the others. "Get out," he said.

When we were alone, he untied me. I got up and stretched. My stomach and ribs had already started to ache.

"My boys followed you to Johnny's house two days ago."

"He owes me four grand. If he's running a game it's probably my fault," I said sadly.

"Why?"

"I asked him for my dough. He was scared. This is probably the only way he can raise it."

"I want you to find him and stop him."

"Me?"

"I want you to stop him so he can't start again."

"I was his partner."

"Was, is right. I want you to teach him a lesson that the others in this town can learn from. Then maybe we can talk. When somebody comes in with me they got to prove their sincerity."

"Have you decided on our deal?"

"We'll talk about that later."

I thought it over. I had known he would set a price on my allegiance. It had worked my way. I had set up my own pigeon and now all I had to do was go knock it down.

"I'll do it," I said.

"Can you find him?"

"I can if anyone can."

"Louis will go with you to see that you do a thorough job. When you are finished, come back to my place and we'll talk."

I didn't like that. Pappas could foul up the job. There was Baptiste to think of.

"I'll do it alone."

"You'll do it with Louis."

"I may not be able to get in if he tags along."

"That will be your hard luck."

He went to the door and let the others in.

I tried to straighten my clothes while Giannini talked to Pappas.

"Ready?" said Pappas.

"Just about," I answered.

I walked toward the doorway. When I got abreast of Max I wheeled to him, feinted a left and crossed my right. He was out before he started to fall, but I nailed him two more times before he hit the floor and bounced.

"Ready," I said.

The next time Giannini wanted to see me, he wouldn't send Max. That boy wasn't welcome. I felt better.

Louis and I were cruising. He headed no place in particular, waiting for me to give out with a lead.

I was stalling. I couldn't shake Louis. That would look suspicious. If I went through with the job Johnny might blabber before I could get to him and Baptiste had to be protected. They could have *him* spotted too.

I needed Baptiste and he wouldn't stand still for a beating, but I had a safety valve. Now was the time to use it.

"Head for the Quarter," I said.

We drove in silence.

We turned into Bourbon Street.

"Slow," I said.

I pretended to watch the crowded sidewalk, looking for someone.

We rolled past the light, blazing, garish clubs and the chanting doormen, past Conti Street, then St. Louis.

Toulouse was the next street.

"Pull up."

He slid into the curb and I got out.

"Find a parking place and meet me back here."

"Why?" He was suspicious.

"We're scaring the chickens. Nobody is going to squawk to me if they see you in this car. You belong to the opposition, remember?"

He turned it over, nodded and pulled away.

As soon as he was out of sight I hot-footed it around the corner of Toulouse, got out my keys and unlocked the rented Ford. I was waiting for him, motor idling, when he showed.

I peeped the horn. He squinted at the car and came over.

"What is this, Digger?"

"Driving around in your car is worse than riding a police cruiser. I borrowed it."

"Fast work. You wouldn't be throwing a curve?"

"This could be my neck. I'm doing the best I know how."

"That's sensible." He got in.

I drove to Johnny's old haunts, double parked, went in and asked for the time of day, anything for an excuse. I went to every place except Ma Vivaldi's. At the last place on my list I rejoined Louis in the car with what I hoped was a gleam in my eye.

"I got an idea. Where did you say he was the first night?"

"Westwego."

"Then where?"

"Gretna."

"I think I see what he's doing. Westwego then Gretna. Two nights, two different locations. Westwego is as far west as he can go from Gretna. In between we have Harvey and Marrero. Tonight it could be any of those four, but it's not. It will be Algiers. That's as far east as he can get from Westwego and still be near the city."

"Did you get a tip back there?" He was watching me narrowly.

"Not exactly."

"Belch it up, Digger. There are six parishes bordering on New Orleans. We can't take all night."

"This is my caper." I let my left hand drop to my lap. "I call the plays." I was ready to go for the .38.

"Roll. We haven't got time to argue."

I let my breath out and shifted into gear.

We boarded the ferry at the foot of Canal and rode slowly across the Mississippi. I didn't enjoy the trip.

In Algiers I drove down Pelican and stole a look at a clock over a bank. I wanted to hit the game at its peak. If we walked in when everybody was intent on the game I had a chance.

In Algiers I found a parking place outside a dilapidated booze foundry.

"Is this it?"

"Not if I know Johnny. I know a lush who pays his rent here. He knows this side of the river."

"I'll go with you."

"Nix."

He looked at me again, probing with those sharp little eyes.

"Relax, Louis. I want Johnny more than you ever will."

I got out and walked into the honky-tonk.

Inside the air was as stale as a washroom without plumbing. I spotted a rum-dum at the end of the bar that would serve my purpose. I moved in next to him and signaled the bartender.

"A double and one for my friend," I said.

He turned his watery red eyes toward me. He needed a shave, a bath and new buttons on his fly. He was going to tell me to go to hell but the crisp ten dollar bill I slid across the bar stopped him.

I hoisted a couple with him. I needed the reinforcements. We hardly exchanged a word but it would look good to anyone watching from outside.

I left the change from the ten and blew before I got sick on the smell of him.

"Nice friends you have," said Louis as I got in the car.

"Yeah."

It was after two a.m. We left the main street and headed down a black top spotted with chuck holes. The road ended at a barrier over the river.

A run-down two story building loomed out of the dark. I made a U turn so that we would be headed away from the place and cut the lights.

"Stay here and keep the motor running. We may have to scramble," I said.

Louis reached over and flipped off the ignition and pocketed the keys.

"When we leave, there ain't going to be anybody left in shape to move."

He had one hand on the lapel of his coat.

"Let's go," he said.

I got out leaving my .38 behind.

The sign over the gallery read "Seaman's Haven." I followed him inside.

We entered a two-by-four lobby. A fat, bald, cigar-chewing night man was reading a paper behind the desk.

He eyed us narrowly as we approached.

"Do somethin' for you gents?"

"We want a room with hot and cold running dice," I said.

He studied it.

"You sure you got the right place?" he asked.

"Johnny told us to drop in," said Pappas.

"Second floor, gents. Room 200."

"Thanks," I said.

"Join us," said Louis. His voice was flat and a .45 was in his hand.

The fat man went white.

"I can't stand the ringing of bells," said Louis. "Don't play Santa

Claus."

Fatty came around the desk with his hands up.

"Put the dukes down and walk ahead of us."

We went up the stairs. From the end of the hall came faint sounds of clicking dice and mumbled exhortations to the gods of chance.

In front of the only door with light showing underneath we stopped.

"Knock the knock," said Louis.

The fat man hesitated.

"Don't risk it," said Louis.

Fatty gave three short raps and then one more.

The door swung open immediately.

Louis pushed the night man ahead. He tumbled into the room and fell and we rushed in after him.

"Freeze," said Pappas and he covered the room with his .45.

They froze.

There was a long wooden table pushed against the wall. Boards had been nailed to the sides to make a crap table. Around this stood about ten guys in a state of petrification. They gawked at us.

"What is this, a heist?" said one.

Louis leveled the gun on him.

"Clam up and move out."

They were frozen.

"Hit the bricks," said Louis.

They started to move toward the door slowly.

Johnny was staring at us stupidly.

The rest started to file out. Baptiste was near the end of the line and Louis was giving him the eye.

The last guy stopped and diverted attention.

Baptiste got to the door and I could hear him clumping away fast.

"What are *you* waiting for, an engraved invitation?" Louis was doing all the talking.

The guy who was hanging back was big, very big. He was dressed like a sport.

"What the hell is this? That's my dough on the table. I was covering more than two grand."

"You just crapped out," Louis told him.

The big guy smiled. I had to give him credit. He wasn't scared.

"The hell I did. This ain't a stickup or you would have taken the dough in their pockets."

"Smart boy!"

"I don't know from nothin' about your local war. I just flew in from

Miami."

"Your arms must be very tired."

He laughed. "Let me take my dough and scram."

"Take a kite, Mister."

The big boy got a determined look on his face.

"I'm takin' my dough."

Louis looked from me to him, comparing us. He got a twisted smile on his face.

"Take him, Digger."

Miami looked at me and I looked at him. He smiled a big toothed crooked sneer.

"Try it, sucker, and I'll tear off your leg and beat you to death with it," he said.

I pulled the skin tight gloves out of my pocket and pulled them on. It had to be. I would have to get into action to keep Johnny quiet, and maybe get my head torn off in the process.

I moved in and the sport's hands came up. I feinted, chopped and stepped back. He caught me hard going away. A counter puncher. He knew the rules.

I feinted again, hooked one high and stepped inside where his greater size would hamper him.

I got to his sweetbreads with both hands and he tried to bear hug me. I brought my arms up and cracked his Adam's apple to break the hold and stepped sideways before he could bring his knee up. I took a long step with my right foot that carried me in again but to his side and he whistled a left over my head. Just what I wanted. I caught him in the kidneys and he doubled over and hit on his head. It was the old-fashioned Dempsey roll.

"That's enough warmup, Digger," said Louis.

I looked at Johnny. His mouth was working but no sound came out.

"Get it over with before somebody tips the cops."

I got to Johnny before he could scream and drove him into the corner with short rights and lefts. I kept him propped there. Left, right, gut and face. His nose went flat like it had been hit with a brick.

Each time I landed, it made me sick.

My fists tore his left cheek open and the blood spattered my clothes and the wall each time I smashed him.

He didn't know it. He was out cold, hanging in air.

I gave him a final glancing right that sent his body skidding along the wall to collapse in a heap by the crap table face up.

I caught a glimpse and turned away. He didn't have any face left.

"Finish him," said Pappas.

I looked at him. His eyes burned with the excitement of a sadist.

"Go to hell."

I walked to the door and as I went out Louis walked over to Johnny's fallen form and stepped on his face. I could hear bones crack and give as I hurried down the hall. I wondered which one of us had killed him.

"Let's eat," said Louis.

"We're due back."

"There's time. We did a fast job." He felt expansive. "The boss will be up, he never sleeps, never rests."

I concentrated on driving. I didn't want to see that bloody, smashed face in my mind.

"I'm not stopping," I said.

Louis didn't argue.

The ride back on the ferry was hard. I sat behind the wheel trying to block off part of my mind. This wouldn't be the last job Giannini would ask me to do. It was his way of keeping a man ground down. Half killing a guy in a fair fight was different. Was it worth this? I had been a chump to think I could do it my way. There would always be a check on me now.

We didn't stop for Pappas' car but drove straight to the chief's estate. I was told to wait in the library while the butler led Louis off to another part of the house.

I lit up and made myself at home in the high-toned surroundings. It was a funny thing, I didn't feel uneasy here. I was made for this kind of living. The best or nothing. The only difference between me and any other guy with ambition was that I had to get it my way or maybe die trying. No salary, savings account and slow death security for me. I'd rather take a chance, my life against the jackpot.

Giannini came in and went to his desk. He looked neither happy nor displeased. He was Vitolo Giannini, the King.

He sat in the big chair behind the desk, his chin resting on his chest, eyes closed.

I waited. There was thinking I had to do too. If this was his way of getting me rattled, he was failing.

We waited a long time.

"I have given your proposition a lot of thought," he said.

Not a word about tonight. I had been slugged and beaten and had been ordered to chop down my own partner and not a word.

"I have been given to understand it can be done if handled correctly. I want to hear more."

I studied the ash on my cigarette. "The details will have to be left in my hands."

"What?" he breathed.

"If you have investigated, you know that I am the one."

"How can you know that, Digger?"

"Simply because I'm the one you're talking to." I was still bluffing, but he smiled.

"Nice guessing."

"Not guessing, Mr. Giannini, facts."

"Let's hear them."

"I handle the boats, the corporation, the oil exploration, the details … everything."

"I never do that. I would lose control. Control, that's the secret, Digger."

"You won't. Your men will make the pickup at the docks. I don't want to know what happens to the stuff after it passes through my hands."

"Uh, uh. That way I could get short changed. What do you take me for, a chump?" He laughed.

"Just the opposite. That will be my insurance against you having a kick. If it's gold or dope, my boys will weigh it to see that we are passing on the proper amount. I'll trust my boys, but I won't and don't want to know the people who deliver to us or who we deliver to. They are the ones I won't trust."

"Very good. I like that idea but I can't give you so much leeway."

"That's my price."

"It's too high."

We were bargaining, but I held the trumps.

"Who would be my partner, Twigg?" I laughed. "How would that look on the corporation papers?"

"There is no hurry about this. I can look around."

That was his bluff.

"What have you got going now? Slots?" I asked. "A gambling house?" I looked around the big room. "This is expensive. The upkeep here must run plenty. You have a million expenses. I couldn't begin to estimate your payoff around the country. What have you got coming in? You may have time. I doubt it."

I was getting to him. He studied me trying to make up his mind whether to read me off or not.

"Look, Giannini," I said, "gambling has been a ten billion dollar industry employing three hundred thousand workers. Those are facts. That makes it as big as the steel industry. Punchboards, slots, handbooks, wire services, and casinos handled it. They're all kaput. How do you make up the grift on that big an operation?"

He was listening now, so I went on. "The Miami crowd has gone to Cuba and Puerto Rico to set up new casinos but there is room for only a few. The Chicago mob tried horsemeat for hamburgers and pushed it with toughs just like in prohibition days. That fell flat. Next they tried stealing four state cigarette tax stamp printing machines and cornered the wholesale cigarette market. They got caught. Even if that had worked, it wouldn't fill a ten billion dollar hole. And last but not least, the Feds have slapped tax assessments and penalties against the rackets totaling over twenty million dollars just for the last half of the year." I gave that time to register. "What's your share, Giannini?"

"Let's hear your plan," he said impatiently. "I can't make a decision until I know the works."

That was better.

I went on, "I will have a corporation set up to own, but not operate small boats. A dummy corporation will lease the boats. The second outfit will assume all legal responsibility for their operation. I will see to it that the men I need will be hired to operate the boats and that the corporation will accept contracts to work in the areas where we need them." I stopped.

"Go on."

"That's all."

He got up and came around the desk.

"I can figure that much. Digger, I have to know."

"Okay, talk to my lawyer."

"Your lawyer!"

"Yeah, Martin Epstein. I just retained him for fifty thousand a year to protect the parent company."

Giannini was sore. "What does he know? What have you told him?"

"Nothing. He knows less than you do. You know his name and what the boats are really going to be used for. He doesn't. He gets a salary as a director and as the corporation lawyer. He's satisfied with the legal aspects and you know his reputation."

He thought it over. "Why did you have to bring him into it at all?"

"For our protection. If he will become party to it, I'm satisfied it's foolproof."

"That's smart but it could backfire."

"How?"

"He could wise up and raise his price."

"Would he?"

"No, you're right. He's too smart for extortion."

He went back to his desk and fiddled around with some papers. It was his turn to talk now.

"When could you begin operations?"

So it was that bad with him. Things were really tight.

"As soon as I get a hundred thousand bucks."

"What?" He came out of his chair again.

"We need three boats to start with. Equipment, salaries, a drydock layout and the renovation of the boats will take it all."

"Not from me, you won't take it."

"Not directly, no."

"What does that mean?"

"You'll arrange a loan for me. Regular interest, payments and the rest. I'm going to become a legitimate businessman."

"How do you get your cut out of that?"

"Eventually I'll own the boats. More immediately I'm going to charge you according to the traffic."

His eyes narrowed. "A holdup?"

"Not at all. I'll charge a nominal fee for whatever we deliver. A percentage. That way I'll be anxious to protect your shipments. The more we handle, the better I'll do and the better you do."

"How much, Digger?"

"You name it. I'm not greedy. My plan is for quantity so the charge can be kept low."

"Do you know how much stuff finds its way into the States in a year?"

"No."

"You can become a millionaire fast on one percent."

"Then that's what I want." I could always change my mind. I wanted him happy.

"The loan will be a problem."

"Then it's a deal?"

"I think yes."

He *was* happy.

He came over to me and I stood up.

"*Sciacchenze?*" and he held out his hand.

Our contract was this handshake.

I wasn't fooled. The sub-clauses would be brains and bullets and more binding than the law, as long as he wanted it that way. He could call it the other way too. I would have to be careful. Very careful.

I drove the rented car back to town. Dawn was showing red in the east but it wasn't a color I was fond of right now. There was still blood on my cuffs and shirt front.

On Bourbon Street I drove on past my own hotel and found an even cheaper place further down. The joint was only one jump ahead of a flop house but that was what I wanted.

I retrieved the gun and shells from the slit in the seat, locked the car and went into the hotel. The lobby was a two by four room, dark and deserted. I spotted a pay phone in the corner and climbed in.

My first call was to the car rental agency. The night man took my message about where they could pick up the car in the morning.

The next call took longer. I finally got Jimmy, the bellboy at my hotel. When he got on the line he sounded a little breathless.

"Yes sir," he said.

"What the devil took you so long? That old zook keeping you busy?"

"I don't know what you mean, sir. We don't have no girls here."

"Come off it, boy. This is Digger."

"Oh, it's you. You had me scared for a minute."

"You better leave that angle alone, Jimmy. This town is hot."

"This is a one nighter. We got a convention. What do you want, Digger?"

"I've got a job for you. Listen close. Have my trunks sent up to the room. Pack everything except one suit and a change. Have the trunks checked to my name at the Union Station. Bring the change of clothes to me at the Regal Hotel two blocks down the street from you. Can you do that?"

"I got it. It will take time."

"Bring me the clothes first. You can keep that bottle of sour mash for yourself and hustle it up."

"I'm on my way, uh, you ain't in a jam or somethin'?"

"Just the opposite, boy. Now get the lead out."

I hung up and went over to the desk. The night clerk woke up after ten minutes of shouting and pounding and I got a room, left him the keys to the rented car and hiked myself upstairs.

Jimmy was knocking on the door before I got my shoe laces untied.

"Hi, Mr. Mulcahy." He came in and shut the door.

"Here are your clothes and a little somethin' that I thought you might need."

He handed me the extra cartridges for the .38. I looked him over but I couldn't read him.

"I told you I was clean," I said. "Why the shells?"

"Maybe you wouldn't want 'em packed with your stuff."

"It's an idea. Thanks."

His eye caught the bloodstains on my shirt. I selected a twenty from my roll and tipped him.

"Forget about me, Jimmy."

"Yes, sir. Goodnight."

He went out without a question. A good boy, still young enough to be loyal.

I changed clothes, made a bundle of the suit, shirt and tie I had worn, and tiptoed out into the hall and down the back stair.

The night clerk had gone back to sleep. I found the door to the basement and went down.

This was a switch. With a hundred grand practically in my hands, I never thought I would be back down here. Sure, I had been here before.

I found the light switch and gave it a flick. The place was the same. Automatic gas furnace, newspapers still scattered around from last winter. I had spent cold winter nights here with other road bums. It's one of the oldest tricks of the trade. Find a place with automatic heat and a neglected basement and you can slide down the old-fashioned coal chute and keep warm for a few hours.

The incinerator was just where I remembered it. I stuffed my bundle into it and fired it up. What a laugh. Here I was doing everything in the book to get off of Bourbon Street and she was staying right with me.

Maybe I was only fooling myself. Being on the road had been a dirty, hard chore but here I was burning a two hundred dollar suit because it had a little blood on it.

The sound of Johnny's face breaking as Louis stepped on him came back to me. I caught the shivers going down my spine.

I looked into the incinerator. The clothes were ashes. Nobody would use it again until winter.

I found my way upstairs without seeing anyone. My window faced a brick wall only four feet away but the early morning light was filtering into the room. Another dawn. I had seen a lot of them, drunk, hot eyed and weary. It seemed like a long time since I had waited for a call from the man. This morning I felt more weary than ever before. I shouldn't be feeling this way. Everything was ahead of me now. Or was it? How can you ever be sure?

I woke with a start I got up and found my watch. It was run down. I had a bath and dressed in a hurry.

Downstairs I didn't stop to check out or ask if the man had come for the keys to the rental car. I had other fish to fry.

A ham and egg joint was open in the next block and I went in. The clock over the counter said ten o'clock. I could slow down. Only three hours sleep; well, it was enough.

The scrambled and ham went down fine and I was on my second cup of coffee when I noticed the counter waitress acting funny. She would kind of put her hand up to her face and her mouth would work in an agonized way, then her arm dropped lifeless to her side.

She was looking toward the front door and her face was very white.

I put my coffee down slowly.

"Sit tight, Digger," said a voice.

I put my hands on the counter, palms down, and turned toward the voice.

It was Leon. There was a two foot piece of sawed off baseball bat in his hands.

"What's the gimmick, Leon?"

His face twisted mean. On that good natured lug it looked terrifying.

"We're waiting for Ma," he hissed.

So they knew already.

She knew how I had crossed Johnny.

"Mind if I finish my coffee?" I asked.

"You stinking rat," he said softly.

I threw my coffee, cup and all at him and lunged for the swinging doors to the kitchen.

The baseball bat crashed through the round glass window in the door beside me as I slammed into the kitchen past the surprised fry cook and out into the courtyard.

I crossed the yard and vaulted a wall and found myself on Conti Street.

Maybe Leon had thought I would wait patiently to have my head caved in. He had another thought coming.

I broke into a run toward Canal Street. I was getting away from here fast. I had to see Epstein and have him arrange that loan from Mr. G.

I had to get out of New Orleans fast. And the place I was going was ideal for me now.

Grannado Island—a flat, arid, sun-seared hellhole.

But that was good. Ma wouldn't hunt for me there.

The skies were clear, the sun hot. The early morning smell of roasting coffee reached my nostrils. I wouldn't miss that. I tossed my new traveling bag into the back seat of the second hand Ford and got in behind the wheel.

I opened a new pack of butts and lit up. There wasn't any hurry.

I took a last look at Bourbon Street, deserted at six a.m.

I goosed the starter and slid away from the curb. A red light stopped me at Canal Street. I was impatient to get on the road. No more stops for Digger Mulcahy, President of Seismograph Services Incorporated. I had a hundred grand in the bank—less a couple for the second hand Ford. I was on the high road for sure.

The light changed and I headed for the Huey Long Bridge and La. 78.

I made the span from New Orleans to Raceland, down near the Gulf, in good time; had lunch and struck out again.

I drove along a hard top toward the island at a slower clip.

The road is narrow and plows through mile after mile of sugar cane fields. The cane grows about twelve feet high and visibility is limited.

I can remember wheeling around corners at sixty in the old days only to find a car left parked right in the middle of the road where a Creole had left it. The old boys don't seem to have caught on to these modern inventions yet.

I came out of the cane forests and on to the ridge over-looking the three quarter mile bridge to Grannado. It was dusk.

The bridge was as rickety as ever and the boards slapped and rattled under the car as I crossed over.

The island was the same too. A desolate seven mile strip, a mile and a half wide. A few palms, bent grotesquely by the wind, Spanish Dagger and a few other semitropical plants, sand, surf and heat.

I turned the car into a rutted lane toward the wharfs.

A few lights showed in the shacks of the inhabitants. The population is a mixture of French, Spanish, Portuguese and Filipino descent. The language is a French-Spanish patois.

I kept on past the shacks toward the wharfs at the end of the island.

The road was made of crushed coral and oyster shells. I could hear the wash of the surf and in the distance I made out the blaze of lights that would be Coteaux.

I wondered if Catlin would remember me.

A couple of pickup trucks and an old Cadillac sedan were parked in front of the General Store. I braked to a stop and got out.

From the front porch I could just barely see through the jungle of rope, fire hose, canvas, winches, pumps and canned foods to the back. Everything was dust-covered and rusty, but it looked like the old boy still carried most of what I would need.

The screen door swung open under my hand.

I made my way through the sea of marine equipment and canned goods to a rough plank bar at the back. Nobody was home.

I pounded on the bar until door opened and a Cajun came into the room. Before the door closed behind him, I got a hint of voices and the clink of chips.

The Cajun stood with his back to the door and looked me over.

"What you want?" he asked.

It was my turn. I let him wait.

"You want a drink?" he asked.

I didn't answer and it made him nervous. He gave me a dirty look and went back out. I didn't have long to wait.

The door opened again and the jamb made a frame hardly big enough to let the man get through.

"Hi, Catlin," I said.

He studied me, his brow wrinkling, sweat rolling off his three hundred pounds.

He recognized me.

"So you're still alive, Digger."

"Shouldn't I be?"

"No."

"Thanks."

We stood there eyeing one another.

"I'm busy, Digger. Come back in fifty years."

He had left the door open and I could hear the game going on without him.

"You don't have fifty years left, Catlin," I laughed.

"That's what I mean." He started to go back into the card room.

"Okay, I can buy hundred-foot crash boats anyplace. I would have bought yours."

That stopped him. He turned around and looked me over again, carefully this time.

He was still undecided. I fished out a fag, put my foot on the bar rail and lit up.

"Cash," I said.

That or my two hundred dollar suit impressed him.

He closed the door and came over to the bar, picked down a bottle of bourbon and poured us each a drink.

"It's always nice to see an old friend," he said.

"I'll drink to that," I said.

Later the Cajun helper drove back with me to the cabin I had rented. It was old—weather-beaten, two rooms and a bath, screen windows and a door that would lock. At that, it was the best on the beach.

After the Cajun had gone, I sat on the reed chair on the porch and looked at the sky.

I was the first to arrive. Tomorrow my boys would start coming in. Baptiste was out contacting them.

It had been a job running the guys down. It would be a bigger job getting the boats ready to sail.

Grannado Island was a perfect headquarters for my deal. Catlin could be handled. He was my boy for a price. Trade was poor, his poker game netted him peanuts and he was used to new, not old, Cadillacs.

It had been different here when the fishing had been good. Now there was nothing. Only a handful of natives remained. The wharfs were still good and there was even a little dry dock.

Catlin had owned the island. Now he was in hock to his ears and I would keep him there. Then I would own it.

I got up, stretched, yawned and felt some of the strain go out of my back.

A little driving had made me stiff. Work in the hot sun would fix that. I went inside and slept the deep sleep.

It took the pounding surf to wake me.

I walked out on the porch. The sun reflected hot off the white sand and hurt my eyes, but I felt good. A small breeze whipped up white caps on the Gulf and felt fresh on my skin.

I was wearing dungarees and a T-shirt that I had picked up at the General Store. I yawned and stretched but I wasn't tired.

The shacks around me were still with morning sleep. I jumped down from the porch, not bothering with the steps, and started walking toward the wharfs. I felt like working, working hard with my hands, and back and legs. It was that kind of day.

Catlin was waiting with a big cup of chicory coffee cuddled in his great paws.

"Good morning," I greeted him.

He grunted, got up and brought the coffee pot and a cup to the bar.

"I'll need more than that this morning," I said.

"Nobody up yet."

"You're up."

He was going to tell me that he wasn't my cook but thought better of it and went into the kitchen.

In a moment I smelled bacon aroma.

After breakfast, Catlin and I walked out on the wharfs where the three ex-Navy crash boats were tied up.

They looked terrible.

The Navy had used them for patrol and to pick up crashed pilots in the Gulf. They were about 114 feet long, and fast. Now they looked like something washed up on the beach at Iwo Jima.

"You're asking too much," I told him.

"You knew what condition they were in five years ago. They couldn't have improved any."

"How true." I vaulted the space between the wharf and the rail where a gangplank should have been. It had long ago rotted and fallen into the water.

I climbed over debris on the deck and stepped into the pilot house.

It was true. I did know what condition they were in but they weren't as bad as they looked.

The paint was flaking off everywhere. The hull was a mass of barnacles and the engines and equipment were a picture of neglect. But nothing was seriously wrong with them.

The hulls were true and strong and almost all of the equipment could be renovated. The three boats were a good buy, especially in a package deal, but I wasn't going to let the blimp know I thought so.

There was a loose plank lying on the starboard side so I picked it up, carried it around to where Catlin stood.

It wobbled a little on the uneven footing but he could cross on it.

"Come aboard," I told him.

"It doesn't look very strong," he hesitated.

"Come on, you've walked narrower planks than that." He started over, balancing, his arms out like a tight rope artist.

I laughed as he teetered and almost fell on the last step. He gave me a dirty look.

"Let's take a tour," I said.

We went into the pilot house. I swept debris away from the ladder leading to the forward cabins, galley and storerooms.

I started down but Catlin hung back.

"What's the matter? Afraid she will sink?" I asked him.

He followed.

Below decks it was as dark as a well digger's lunch bucket. The ports were too dirty to let in light and the electric system was long gone. I lit a match and a rat scurried over my shoes and between Catlin's legs into a dark corner.

I smiled to myself in the dark. He was scared, scared of mice and the dark and cobwebs and the litter piles under his feet. Good! By the time I took him over the three boats, inch by inch, he would be eager to sell and not as hard-nosed about price.

We combed the boat like monkeys looking for fleas. The galley, hold, quarters, mess, officers' quarters, then topside.

"We can't see nothing with matches," he said when we emerged from the murk.

"You got a better suggestion?" I asked him.

"Yeah, I'll get a flashlight. Wait here for me."

I smiled and let him go.

When he came back he was carrying a large kerosene lamp and flashlight. He was carrying fortification of another kind too. He must have downed a half a pint. "Let's go." I took the flashlight.

We went aft and I cleared the ladder to the afterhold and engine room.

I took a lot of time with the engines. They would be my biggest expense if I had to replace them.

We were on the last boat when Baptiste showed.

I could hear someone yelling from the dock. I climbed out of the galley leaving Catlin to find his own way.

"Ahoy, aboard."

Baptiste was standing there with Pete McShane.

"Ahoy yourself, you old bazoo," I yelled.

I jumped down and swatted Pete on the back. He feinted toward my jaw and tapped me lightly in the gut.

"You're getting soft, Digger," he said.

"You want to try me, boy?"

"No, I don't think so. Not after the last time."

We grinned at each other. It had been a good fight and as often happens, it had made us friends.

I looked at Baptiste. "Where are the rest of them?"

"They're comin'. Hank has a car now and he's driving down with the Early Bird."

"Are these the cans?" asked Pete.

He was looking the crash boats over and he sounded skeptical.

"Yeah," I said. "They look pretty rough but they're solid. Let's get squared away, then we can go over them together."

Catlin had come out on deck by then.

"Have you got a place for my friends?" I asked him.

"Sure, go on up to the store and tell the boy what you need."

"Go ahead," I told them. "I've got some unfinished business with the

Cat."

They took off up the wharf and I climbed back on deck.

"Let's go aft," I said.

"Look, Digger, you've seen enough."

"Do you want to sell or not?"

"Yeah, yeah!"

"Then come on."

"No."

"Your price is no good, Cat boy."

"For cripes sakes, then give me an offer."

"Half." I said it flatly.

"Three quarters?" he pleaded.

"One half. Take it or grow old poor."

His shoulders sagged.

"Okay, Digger. For cash I'll sell them for half."

"I'll drink to that," I said.

Hank Palermo was sitting across from me. He was as big and rawboned as ever. He was an electronics genius without ever having gone to school. We worked together before and I had seen him fix a complicated Sonar device with nothing but a soldering iron and a hunk of wire. He could survey, map and read the seismograph plus keep it in trim.

To my right sat Pete McShane, one of the best small boat skippers I had ever known. He had red hair, a ruddy complexion, and an Irishman's temper. A few fool-hardy souls had tried nicknames on him in his presence and he had lit up like neon before he tore them apart.

On my left sat Baptiste. Burl, the Early Bird, was conferring with Catlin about stores. He was to be the cook for boat number one.

I had been listening to the boys swap stories about way back when and looking them over. I had spent a great deal of time in picking my men. They were tough and knew their jobs but most important was the fact that I had to be able to trust them. In a sense I would be in their power.

Nothing would prevent them from picking up a good load and going south with it if they wanted to.

Burl was the only one I had doubts about. Baptiste had bailed him out of a seaman's sanitarium. Burl was nuts.

He had been on every dope and alcohol kick known to man and a few he had invented himself.

I broke up a story Hank was telling.

"How is The Bird, Baptiste? Can he pull his weight?"

"I don't know. All I can tell you is what the Doc at the rest home said."

"Okay, what did he tell you?"

"He only said that to his knowledge Burl wasn't getting any junk at his place but you know how that is. A rum-dum can find quart bottles in the desert."

"Anything else?"

"Only that steady work and responsibility could keep him straight. Mind you, *could* keep him straight."

I nodded. The last time I had worked with Burl he had been so far gone that you could talk him into doing anything just by repeating it fast enough to him.

It had been a game on that boat. I could remember how he would swallow the cigarette he was smoking if you told him to. Another time when Burl had been standing at the rail some punk had said, "Jump in, Burl, jump in," and he had gone. We had had to put about and go back after him that time.

"Well, Baptiste, it's going to be your job to keep him busy. I'm appointing you crew chief."

They looked at me in surprise.

"What the devil," said Hank. "I thought you were going to boss this caper."

"I am—from shore." How dumb did they think I was. If the patrols caught on and raided the boat I didn't want to be there.

"But that only leaves four of us. We need more crew," said Baptiste.

"No you don't. Pete is the pilot, you are the nurse to the diesels, Hank is the seismograph man and Burl is cook and bottle washer. I've got some surprises for you. A new seismograph outfit that doesn't need to be lowered to the Gulf floor. That rules out the deckhands. With only four men to feed, Burl doesn't need a helper. That cuts another guy off the payroll. It's safer with less men and we got a better split. Any questions?"

"Yeah, I've got one." It was McShane talking. "Is Catlin in on it?"

"No, and make sure he stays in the dark," I said.

"That's good with me. I never did like that fat yahoo," said Hank.

"And another little wrinkle we will have is radar," I added.

"Radar!" said Hank.

"How do we swing that?" asked Pete.

"Easy, we work close in to shore. There is lots of fog this time of year. The patrols will never question it."

"Great," said Hank, "I can rig it up along with our radio antennae."

"Yeah. The patrols won't be able to sneak up on us." Pete looked at me in admiration. "You must have the Chase National behind you."

Catlin served up a dinner of fried oysters, green salad and cold beer.

We had about finished when a few customers began straggling in. They bought red eye or chianti by the gallon jug, and the Cat always got it from the back of the store. There was no telling what was really in those jugs.

Pete and Hank Palermo went over to the pool table to start a game of eight ball. I declined and Baptiste and I sat at the bar while the little Cajun cutie cleared the table.

I had to keep my eye on The Bird. He was truly shot.

All his teeth had been pulled at that sanitarium and he flapped his mouth open and shut like a hungry turtle. Burl was only thirty-three but he looked fifty.

An old-fashioned gramophone stood in the corner so I called The Bird over and told him to grind us out some music.

He went to the piece and looked at it in a dumb way and I thought I'd have to show him how it worked but he got it started and a pleased look spread over his puss.

Pretty soon the people stopping in for their jug were attracted by the music and they stayed. A few of the Cajuns had brought their girls and they cleared a space to dance in.

Catlin was getting a load on and about midnight he started reminding me about the last time we had seen each other.

"Why aren't you playing pool, Digger?" he said.

I took another swallow of sour mash before I answered.

"I gave that up along with repeal."

"You used to be pretty good."

"Only fair."

"Yeah, a fair country player." His eyes turned in on themselves. He was thinking.

I could remember too.

It was after I lost my second mate's ticket. After that long wait between jobs while my reputation cooled, then the deckhand job, Grannado Island and Catlin's.

"Ten dollars a game," he said.

I smiled to myself. Ten bucks had been big dough then. "Ten dollars against drunks," he continued.

It was a mistake.

I put my foot on the bottom rung of his stool and pushed. He lit on his head.

"Forget about that," I told him. "When you want to moralize about how people make their dough take a good look at yourself. Where are your two daughters anyhow? Did they leave you and sell the towel concession to someone else?"

He rubbed his head, got up and sat down next to me again.

"You're right, Digger. Those girls never was no good."

He sounded like he might cry.

"You're the only guy that never had hot pants for 'em. You left those girls alone, Digger. I appreciate that."

"You're breaking my heart. Nobody ever had to chase them hard."

I glanced around the room. The French dolls and their boyfriends were doing some dancing that wasn't Arthur Murray.

The Bird was winding the gramophone like he was the leader of the band. He would play a record three, four times before he changed it.

Pete and Hank played their pool like no one else existed.

I was about to turn around when the screen doors parted with a bang and in walked a lug I knew. A guy named Rossetti, a Gulf man from way back. There were a couple of seamen with him.

He scanned the scene before him, giving special and appreciative attention to the girls, and then came over to the bar.

"Hi, Catlin. You holding an Elk's ball?" he asked. He laughed, then saw me. "For Christ's sake, Mulcahy. What are you doing here? I heard you were running a horse house in Orleans?"

He elbowed one of his cronies and guffawed again.

"Hello, Rosey. I see you're still hauling manure," I said.

He bellowed out a real laugh this time.

"Get this guy," he said to the seamen with him. "He must be physic or is it psychic. No kiddin', we got a barge of fertilizer tied up outside. We're hauling into Raceland in the morning."

"Is that what I smell," I said. "I thought it was your natural odor."

We looked each other over to see just how serious this was going to get but Catlin broke it up.

"You and your boys have a drink on me, Rossetti," he said.

"Sure thing," said Rosey turning away. "Make mine gin. It's hotter than hades on that tug."

"I think I'll join the game," said Baptiste.

Rosey and his boys dipped their beaks like old hands. They didn't buy it by the glass. Catlin set a bottle in front of each of them and they drank it like soda pop.

It wasn't long before McShane joined us.

"I'm cleaned," he told me, "Hank is playing like Hoppe tonight."

"Don't I know you?" asked Rossetti.

He was peering at Pete like he was puzzled about something.

"You're new to me, stranger," said Pete.

"My name's Rosey."

"Mine's Pete."

They shook hands and we all joined in a round.

Rossetti's pals were the silent type. They just looked at the girls dancing, smacked their lips and pulled on the bottles.

It dawned on me that the same song had been playing for the last half hour.

Rosey was looking at Pete uncertainly and taking long drags from the gin bottle.

I could see this might develop into an interesting evening. I could take my boys out of here; on the other hand some action might prove something. So I took my boys out.

PART III

I was stripped to the waist. The sun beat down on my back with the intensity of a crucible. But I liked it. It was pure pleasure.

The boat deck was a hive of activity. The Cajuns were glad to work. Catlin had rounded up a crew and they were busy chipping paint and sanding the decks.

The wharf was a maze of cables leading from an auxiliary power line on shore to the electric sanders and to the emergency lights below decks.

I could hear Burl cursing the crew trying to clean out the galley below me.

Baptiste came forward from the afterhold.

"What's the bad news?" I asked him.

He wiped the sweat from his neck and face with a large red bandana and smiled.

"She will need a valve job and the generator is burned out, but I'll make her run."

"Make out a list."

"What are you going to call her?" he asked.

What to name her? I hadn't thought about that.

"Boat Number One," I answered.

"Hell, man, you can't call a pretty gal like this by number."

I looked around at the flaked paint and the broken glass. Baptiste caught the motion and understood.

"In a week you won't know her," he said.

"Okay, what do you suggest?"

"Well, I figured *The Myrtle* would be a nice name."

"The Myrtle!" I must have shouted it.

"It's a pretty name, Digger."

"Okay, okay, *The Myrtle* it is. Get back to work."

He left, a happy, triumphant man.

"By the way," I called after him, "where does this Myrtle pull her weight?"

"Near Morgan City, on a farm. I ain't telling you which farm, either."

I watched him disappear down the after-ladder. *The Myrtle!* Well, leave it to the people to be sentimental.

Hank came up to me.

"Burl isn't making any headway below decks. The grease and dirt must be a foot thick on the bulkheads."

"Run a firehose down there and peel it off with salt water," I told him.

"We haven't even got a hose, let alone a water system," he said.

"You've got the whole Gulf full of salt. Go up to Catlin's and get a gasoline pump and the hose."

"Okay, Boss."

He smiled and jumped to the dock.

"It only takes ten minutes to walk up there, buy the hose and pump, and cart them back," I said. "I'm timing you."

"Ah, Digger, please, just one little beer?"

"You've got more dodges than General Motors, but they won't work with me.

"If you come back with beer on your breath, I'll stick that hose down your gullet and flush you."

"Mr. Mulcahy," he said, "you have a disgusting tongue."

And with that he headed for the Coteaux.

Maybe we were friends, but as the headman I knew that work had to be kept separate from pleasure. A boss can't be lenient with his help. That went double when the hired help were friends.

McShane was standing at the rail looking up the beach.

"Get to work," I yelled.

He motioned to me to look where he was pointing.

I squinted my eyes against the sun and sighted down the sand. About two hundred yards away sat a lonely figure. I couldn't make it out at this distance.

Pete came up to me.

"He's been there all morning. I noticed it right after we came to work," he said.

"Maybe you should do more work and less looking."

"And maybe we have company."

"No, we are clean up to now. Nobody would possibly be after us until we have made a delivery."

"Got any ideas?" he asked.

"It's probably a native with a throw line doing his daily surf fishing."

"Yeah, and I'm Marconi."

"Then get back to your wiring, genius."

He left and I went back into the wheelhouse to do some more figuring on the blueprints of the boat.

I had to figure the arrangement of the seismograph and place it in the right spot. The pilot house was best. Up under the front windows where Pete would be able to make land sightings at the same time.

The radar screen would go in here too.

Now I had to find a place that could be made into a hiding spot. That was a necessary item.

The Government Patrol men knew every trick in the trade. I didn't.

It would take careful planning.

I had been going over the blueprints, discarding one idea after another for about an hour, when a guy called to me from the dock. He was young, maybe twenty-five or so, and blond, big and blond.

"Are you Mulcahy?" he yelled.

"Yeah," I answered.

"I'm looking for a job. Can I come aboard?"

I glanced at the blueprints and the marks I had made on them.

"I'll come down," I said.

I left the pilot house and jumped down beside him.

"How did you know my name?" I asked him.

"They told me back at the store. My name's Larson."

"Okay, Larson, what can you do?"

"I used to work for the *Friedling Exploration* outfit. I know the Tidelands business."

"How did you happen in here, Larson?"

I was looking past him, up the beach. The sand was clear as far as my eye could see.

"You're a new outfit," he said, "and I know the business. I thought I could make Crew Chief on a new boat. If Seismograph Services is going to have three bo ..."

He didn't get any further, because that's when I hit him.

I could hear the jawbone snap as I smashed home with a follow-up.

He landed on the back of his head, rolled over and tried to get his hands and knees under him. He had guts. He wanted to come back, but I had hit him too hard.

His elbows gave out and he collapsed. Nobody knew about Seismograph Inc. yet. It was only three days young. The guy was a spy.

I walked to a water bucket and took a dipperful back to him. I poured the water over his head until the hair hung in his eyes and he started to come to.

I pushed him back on his haunches.

He wasn't pretty. I've seen jaws dislocated before, but this was a beaut. A clean double fracture.

"Take your face back to Twigg and collect your insurance," I told him. "If you show up here again, I'll kill you. And tell your boss that that goes for anyone else he cares to send next."

The boy sat up and took his jaw in both hands and twisted. The bones grating together sounded worse than chalk shrieking on a blackboard.

He held his jaw tight and cursed me through clenched teeth.

I had to laugh. I could have used a kid with his guts.

"I'm letting you go because I admire nerve," I told him, "now move."

He got to his feet still holding his jaw with one hand. He didn't say goodbye.

I went aboard and locked the blueprints in a tin box. It was lunch time, so I told the workmen to take a break; gathered my boys and headed for Catlin's and food.

I couldn't shake the thought of Twigg continually breathing down my back. It was a bad thing. That pink gink hated me and he was out to get my skin.

By the time I got back to the boat I thought I had an idea about that hiding place.

I called Baptiste aside.

"Look at these blueprints," I said. "These are three-inch steampipes running forward to the galley from the engines, aren't they?"

"Sure. You have hot water forward in the galley and showers."

"And they measure about five or six inches around with the insulation and wrappings added?"

"That's right. So?"

"So, what's preventing us from adding one extra one—a hollow one."

"I get it. A dummy steampipe that could be dismantled at one end."

"Right. Who would ever notice an extra steampipe? They are too much a part of the equipment to cause suspicion."

"Let's see the blueprint again."

He studied it and pointed to a spot that would be in the messroom.

"Put it right here. The tables would hide it."

"No, Baptiste, the best place to hide something is to put it right out in the open.

"Let's go below and pick our spot."

I led the way down and walked past Burl who was sitting on a crate and directing the Cajuns like an emperor from his throne.

I kicked the crate over and sent him sprawling.

"Get to work, you lazy, cotton pickin' no good white trash."

He grabbed up a wire brush and attacked the rusty bulkhead like a maniac.

We laughed and made our way aft to the bunkroom. At the deck level ran the steampipes. There were two of them.

"This is the place," I said. "Tear out the bottom one, and replace it with the dummy pipe. Set the real one back on top."

"That won't be easy. I'll have to elbow up with the steam and then down again into the next compartment."

"Then do it. If it's hard to do, then it will be all the more inconspicuous."

"You're the boss."

"That's right. I am."

When I got back on deck, Pete was waiting for me.

"The albatross is back," he said to me.

I sighted where he was pointing and picked out the figure a couple of hundred yards down the beach.

"Well, I'll be damned," I said.

"That blond kid must have more nerve than sense—er friends."

"I'll take care of him once and for all," I said, and jumped to the wharf.

"You want help?" asked McShane.

"Are you kidding?" I called back.

I walked to the head of the wharf and struck off down the lane that ran through the middle of the island.

I figured to go parallel to the beach for three hundred yards, then cut across and come up in back of him.

The beach was lower than the sand dunes behind it, and I was out of sight of my prey. But then he was out of my sight, too. We were even.

When I was twenty yards from the hard-packed sand, I got down on my hands and knees and crept along.

I got to the beach without anything happening and peeked over a dune.

Nothing straight ahead.

I looked to my right. Nothing.

I looked to my left.

Twenty yards away I could see the top of a head. It didn't move.

Staying on my hands and knees, I crept toward a dune opposite the spot where the guy was sitting.

When I thought I was there I took a deep breath and stood up. I saw the most beautiful sight a sailor ever saw.

She was sitting crosslegged in the sand with her dress pulled up over her legs and the sun flashed on the golden sweep and litheness of her thighs. Her knees were narrow but dimpled and her calves were full and rounded, tapering to tiny ankles.

She was a brunette with hair so black that it shone raven in the sunlight.

I did a funny thing. I coughed.

She stiffened, then slowly turned her face from the direction of the boats far down the beach and looked at me.

I got another shock.

She *was* beautiful. Her face matched her figure. Full lips, narrow jaw, fine nose, darkest eyes I'd ever seen.

Her skin was clear and it colored a shade as I stared at her.

She pulled her skirt down over her legs.

"Okay, sister, what's the story?"

She had a small pair of opera glasses in her hands.

I watched her as she wiped the lenses on the hem of her skirt and put the glasses in a tattered case.

She stood up and started to walk away without so much as a *by your leave, sir.*

I stepped in front of her, blocking her way.

Standing, the girl looked more like a kid. I'd guess sixteen at the most.

In height she couldn't have been over five feet tall in her stocking feet. Only she didn't have on stockings.

She was barefoot and her cotton print dress was five inches short and two sizes too small.

On most women such a dress would look like a rag. On this doll it looked good.

We stood staring at each other. She was defiant.

I wasn't so sure of myself now. Even Twigg wouldn't hire a kid to do his spying.

I motioned toward the glass case.

"What are you doing with these?"

"I was doing no harm."

Her voice had a musical lilt to it.

"Please let me by."

I grabbed her arm as she started around me.

She stopped and glared hate at me.

"Let go of me, sailor."

She made it sound like a curse.

I looked at the arm I was holding.

It was delicate, yet strong. There wasn't a hair on it any place. Come to think of it, there hadn't been any hair on her legs either.

I reached out with my other hand and ran it along her arm. There weren't any bristles.

No wonder she looked so clean and perky in that tattered little dress.

I let go of her arm slowly and stepped back. I had a funny sensation that I was confronted by a wild animal and if I frightened her she would bolt.

"Tell me your name?" I asked softly.

She massaged her arm where I had held her.

"You don't want to know me, sailor."

"I want to know the name of anyone who spies on my boats. Especially if they are beautiful."

She laughed bitterly, then stopped.

"Your boats?"

"Yes."

"And you are taking them away?"

"Yes."

"Then I hate you."

"Why do you hate me?"

She looked at the sand and I thought for a moment that she was going to reach out with her foot and trace a pattern with her toe like little kids do.

"The boats used to be so pretty," she said.

That was another curve. I couldn't make this babe.

"They were so clean and fast," she went on. "I used to watch them race down the channel and out to sea. Away from here. Away from the dirty land and dirty people."

It had all come out in a rush and now she stopped.

"They will be clean and powerful again," I said.

"And then you will take them away!"

"But they will be back. Often."

I don't know why I was trying to explain it to this slip of a girl. She had got to me in some way.

"Tell me your name. I'll put your name on one and when it sails it will be you."

She looked at me, unbelieving at first, and then very excited. That expression changed just as rapidly into one of abject apathy.

She sighed and said, "I have no name for boats. I am the daughter of the *Portegee*."

She turned and walked away.

Very dramatic, little wench. You'll get along.

I headed for the wharf.

The *Portegee*. She had pronounced it with a hard ending, making it rhyme with McGee.

A crazy kid. Boats were a symbol of escape to her. One of the tumble-down two-by-four shacks would be her home. I couldn't blame her for wanting to escape.

McShane and Hank were waiting for me by the pilot house.

"Well?" asked Pete.

"Well, what?" I answered.

"Who in the hell was it?"

"Only an island kid that likes boats."

Hank was watching me narrowly.

"What kept you so long? I'll bet it was a dame," he said.

"Dame, hell, she was only a kid. She's nuts or something. The boats are a kind of symbol to her. Get back to work, you lunks," I said.

Now why should I be sore?

The afternoon was going slowly. I looked at my watch—only two thirty.

I stole a glance up the beach. It was deserted again.

I told Pete I was going up to Catlin's.

"Yeah," he said.

What can you make out of that?

Inside the store it was cool. Catlin was sitting at the bar going over his books.

"It's hot," I said as I sat down beside him.

"Uh, huh."

He didn't look up.

"Think I'll have a beer," I said.

"Help yourself."

He kept on adding figures.

I uncapped a bottle and rested my arms on the bar facing him.

"You got a lot of Portuguese on the island?" I said it with the soft ending.

"Not many."

"Mean bastards, aren't they?"

"No worse than the rest of us," he said.

"I'm having trouble with a guy they call the *Portegee.*"

The Cat looked up from his books.

"He isn't in your crew," he said.

"He's not?" I said.

"The *Portegee* won't work for anybody. And he *is* mean. You've seen his daughter, huh?"

"Okay, so I have."

He laughed. "She affects all the guys that way." Then he sobered. "Leave her alone, Digger."

"Why?"

"She's poison, that's why. Her old man has cut more than one young Romeo."

"Tell me."

"There isn't much to tell. The kid's ma died when she was a baby. The *Portegee* raised her.

"She went to school for awhile but when she began to blossom out, blam! The old man took her out of school. Now she runs wild."

"Which kind of wild?" I asked.

"Animal wild. No, she doesn't duck out at night to meet the boys. She seems to hate everybody."

"Don't the authorities step in on a case like that?"

"Not down here they don't. Too far out of the way. Besides, the *Portegee* would kill anybody that tried to take her from him."

I finished my beer.

"Maybe if she wanted to go …" I said.

"Don't go calling. The *Portegee* has a shotgun loaded with rock salt all ready and waiting."

I walked to the door.

"By the way, what's her name?"

"Marguerita, but forget it, Digger. The old man wants her for himself."

That hit hard.

I went on out.

But, damn, she was pretty.

One day has a way of melting into another when you are stuck on a reef in the Gulf.

Wake up, eat, work, eat, work, eat, sleep and wake up again. What a routine!

But the job was getting done. Another few days and *The Myrtle* would be ready for the dry dock to have her bottom scraped.

And then to sea. I would be in business. Money would be coming in.

By doing one boat at a time, I could have number one in the water and producing while I got the others ready.

What the hell do they pay executives so much for? Anyone can figure these things out.

The door of my cabin opened and Baptiste walked in.

"Let's go down to Coteaux and have a beer," he said.

I closed the account books and got my hat.

Outside, the night air was cooler. I could hear crickets chirping and the wash of the surf.

City people paid money for the peace and quiet of places like this. I hated it.

"Walk or ride?" asked Baptiste.

"Let's walk. I want to talk."

We started off.

"Look, Digger, it's none of my business, but why don't you ease up? The boys are beginning to complain. They don't feel they should have to work so hard."

"You're right," I told him. "It's none of your business. I don't want them to think they have a free ride to heaven. Just because we are going to make more money than the law allows doesn't mean they don't have to do the regular job besides. If I eased up on them, they'd get out of hand—and careless."

"Okay, but one of them is likely to go off on a binge. There isn't much for them to do here."

"Don't I know that," I wanted to shout it, but I kept my voice down, "I get hot, too, Baptiste, but I'd rather wait a few weeks and be able to do it in style."

That reminded me of a girl with style. A girl I was hungry for. Eldeese. I hadn't been able to write or call her. There had been a chance Ma Vivaldi would find out where I was.

But now I was safe. Ma was in the north with her string of thoroughbreds. She wouldn't be back until winter set in and the New Orleans track opened again.

We walked on in silence. Just before we sighted Catlin's, I stopped and lit a fag. "I'll be leaving in a day or two. I want you to keep the boys in line. If they get too edgy, take them up to Raceland and find them some women. Use your head."

"Where are you going?"

"It's not for you to ask, but I'll tell you.

"I have to round up the crew for boat number two." I hesitated. "By the way, we're going to call it *The Marguerita.*"

At Catlin's, Hank and Pete were playing pool with a Cajun.

He was pretty sharp and I watched for a while, sipping a beer. When it looked like Hank would finally take the eight ball and game I got up and went to the bar.

"Give me some sour mash," I told the Cat.

He put a glass on the bar and poured one.

"And leave the bottle," I added.

"Sour mash ain't no hot weather drink, Digger. Try gin or rum."

"Try tending bar for a change," I told him.

It wasn't long before a couple of native kids came in with their girls.

The babes were dressed in matching halters and slacks.

The kids bought a gallon of Sneaky Pete from Catlin and sat down at a table.

One of the babes was pretty in a coarse way. Her high breasts swelled out around the tiny halter and her belly was smooth and flat below the knot in the cloth.

I turned around on my stool and stared at the wall.

Catlin was watching the kids and drooling.

"Does this go on all the time?" I asked him.

"Yeah. That's why I don't hafta hire no belly dancers."

"I can understand."

Pete sat down beside me.

"I'm eliminated," he said.

"Hank's hot, eh?" I asked.

"You can't beat him with a club."

I finished my drink and got up.

"See you in the morning," I said to no one in particular.

And Pete said:

> "Early to bed,
> Early to rise,
> You'll die young,
> And feed the flies."

I looked at him.

As I passed the lovers, I noticed that the better-looking of the two girls had dirty ankles. That made me feel a little better anyway.

I didn't need sleep, so I walked down to the dock and past the boats.

There was a moon low on the horizon and it made a path of silver right to me.

I shucked off my shirt and trousers and made a pile of them on the sand. I sat on the cushion and took off my shoes and socks.

The water was cool and refreshing on my legs so I strode out in my shorts and started swimming.

I swam a long way, a quarter of a mile out maybe, and lay on my back floating.

It was dangerous, sure, but it was night and I had a good tan from working in my shorts on the boat. No shark was going to pick me up.

I started a steady crawl back to shore and found that the tide was carrying me to my right, away from where I had left my clothes.

It was a damn good thing I was a good swimmer or I would have been swept past the eastern end of the island.

I swam against the current and felt my feet touch bottom a mile below Catlin's.

I crawled up on the sand and lay there getting my wind.

It wasn't long before I got up and headed back for my clothes.

A couple of side windows at Catlin's threw beams of soft light on the beach and I ducked under them into the shadows under the wharf.

It's funny how you can feel getting caught out in the open with only your shorts on.

In daylight, people go strolling on the beaches without any more on than I had now, but change that normal situation in the slightest and you feel naked.

I started to make my way under the wharf to my clothes and then stopped.

There was somebody ahead of me in the deeper shadows near *The Myrtle.*

He started to run and I went flying after him.

When I got close enough I dived and felt bare legs slip through my fingers.

I rolled fast and got up, ready to go again but I didn't have to.

I had tripped the other person and he was lying a few feet from me.

It was the daughter of the *Portegee!*

She started to get up, but I planted a foot in her belly and picked up the gunny sack she had been carrying.

It was full of junk from the boats. Nothing of value, just junk.

I reached down and pulled her to her feet.

"So you're a thief as well as a spy," I said.

She was breathing hard.

"Maybe I should turn you over to the sheriff." That didn't faze her. "Or to your father, which?"

That got to her. She was deathly afraid of her old man.

"Let's go."

"No," she cried.

"Why not?"

"He will kill me. He hates the boats, and he hates you."

"Me? What have I done?"

"I told him about you. I told him you were like the boats, strong and clean. He made me quit coming to the beach to watch you."

"So you came down here at night after he had gone to sleep."

"Yes."

"Why?"

She looked past me at *The Myrtle.*

"You are taking them away. I wanted something to remember."

I still had hold of her arm. It was smooth and warm and pulsing under my hand.

She noticed my lack of clothes for the first time and looked away, embarrassed.

"If you want something from the boats to remember them by and I am like the boats, maybe you want something from me too."

She said, "No," weakly.

I dropped the sack of junk and seized her.

"Please," she said and tried to pull away.

I tightened the hold.

There was only one word to describe her—ripe.

The alarm clock woke me at five. I stumbled around in the dark, throwing the last of my belongings in the traveling kit.

The sun was a pale streak on the horizon when I threw the bag in the back seat and prepared to get in.

I had one foot in the car when Marguerita ran around the corner of the building shouting my name.

"Digger, Digger!"

What now?

"Here I am," I called.

She came over to me panting and breathless.

"You've got to get away from here," she said, then saw the suitcase on the back seat.

"That's what I'm doing," I said. "Getting aw y from this hole."

"You were leaving without me?"

"Sure."

"You can't, you can't. Father knows. He was loading his revolver when I ran out of the house. He's coming to kill you right now."

"How did he find out?" I asked her.

"He found my torn dress and beat it out of me. Now he will kill me, too."

"Then I'd better get going."

I started to get into the car.

"Take me, Digger. Take me with you," she screamed.

I goosed the starter.

"Digger!" she screamed.

I turned my head and looked at her. She had undone the top of her dress and her firm little breasts were beautifully rigid in the cold dawn light.

"Get in," I said.

She climbed in front with me as I gunned the motor.

The wheels churned up dust as I got away down the lane.

The dust probably saved our necks.

Two shots rang out before I had gone twenty yards.

I ducked and poured the coal to the little Ford and I didn't slow down until we hit the bridge.

"Has your old man got a car?" I asked her.

"No," she was crying.

"Then this is the end of the line. Get out."

I pulled the car to the side of the road, leaned over her and opened the door.

"But why?"

"How old are you, baby?"

"Eighteen."

I wondered if she was lying. I wondered if she knew about the Mann Act.

"When were you eighteen?"

"Two days ago."

"What year were you born in?"

"1935. What does that have to do with it?"

It checked and she was probably unaware of the Mann Act.

"Nothing, honey." I shut the door and stepped on the gas. "We'll have breakfast in Raceland."

I could smell roasting coffee and chicory, shrimp, docks and river crap five miles before we reached New Orleans.

I didn't drive into the city but picked a tourist court on the edge of town near the Beverly Country Club and the Club Forest.

They were closed now and there wasn't much traffic out this way.

We got a cabin without any trouble and I signed the register, Martin Epstein and wife.

When we got in the cabin I called him up.

"Martin? This is Mulcahy."

"Hell, Digger. I expected you yesterday. Where are you?"

"On the edge of town."

"I'm anxious to see you. Can you come right to the office? I have the current bills to go over with you and you have to sign the checks."

Marguerita had found the bathroom and she wasn't wasting any time getting out of her clothes.

She had the water running in the tub and I could see her lovely body.

"I can't make it right away. Two or three hours, maybe," I said.

"I'll wait for you."

"Don't hold your breath," I told him, and hung up.

I walked to the bathroom door and stood looking down at her.

"Want me to wash your back?" I asked.

She looked around, surprised that she had left the door open.

"Please," she said shyly.

Epstein was sitting behind his desk with his feet up, dictating to his wife when I walked in unannounced.

It was hot in the office and Mrs. Epstein had her dress pulled up a bit with her legs crossed.

Martin looked from me to his wife and back again.

"Okay, honey," he said, "that's enough for today."

She pulled her skirt down, got up and went out.

As I sat down and lit up I watched Martin's red face over the flame of the match. He was sensitive about his lovely wife.

"What are you doing at a motel?" he asked me after a pause.

"I have company."

"Young?"

"She says she's eighteen."

He hesitated.

"The law doesn't care how old she claims to be. The law says a *legal* eighteen or else.

"It's sordid, Digger. After this, spare me the stories of your exploits."

That made me sore. I hadn't told him anything.

"After this, don't ask," I said.

Martin shuffled through papers and came up with the Seismograph Inc. ledger.

"You are right on the nose on your budget. I can say that for you," he said.

"What do you mean you can say *that* for me? Do you have any more sermons to read?"

I was hot now.

"Okay, Digger, I do have a few things to say."

"Save it."

"No, I'm going to tell you. Then we'll have it out of the way. I heard about the deal you pulled on Johnny."

He let it hang on air for a second, then went on.

"That was rotten, Mulcahy. You purposely got him in debt to you and then used him brutally to prove your allegiance to someone else."

"Who else knows?" I asked him.

"Probably no one. I like to keep track. I don't think anyone else knows who you are working with and they wouldn't put the two things together anyway. And the way you got control of that handbook. That worries me."

"Fatso fell down the stairs," I said.

"Yes, and you found him there. I understand he had a phone call just before he fell and some shouting was heard. You didn't call him and scare him out of his room and then help him fall by shouting at him from the foot of the stairs, did you Digger?"

"That's a lot of circumstantial hooey," I told him.

"Yes, it is. In all probability, you came along and found him there and gave him an extra clunk with your foot just to make sure."

"Whose lawyer are you, mine or the prosecution's?"

"Don't try to kid me into changing the subject. I have one more speech to make," he said.

"It's about a girl, a nice decent girl. She lives in Metairie and that should tell you who I'm talking about."

"You're quite a sleuth, Epstein, but this time you're going too far."

"I'm asking you to listen to me, Digger. This affects me as well as you."

I decided to hear him out. He knew so damned much, maybe he knew something I didn't.

"I've seen this girl and she's basically a nice kid," he continued. "I wouldn't say this if you were serious about her, but I know you and I know you're just playing.

"You are ruining her life, Digger. Your backgrounds are too far apart. She doesn't know how to take the rough element. She will crack and when she does she won't be worth the powder to blow her up. Let her alone, Digger. Let her go."

"You're breaking my heart. I don't care if she goes to hell or not. Nobody helped pull my car but Digger Mulcahy."

I walked up to him and put my face close to his.

"We're all in hell," I spat. "We were born in hell."

I straightened up.

"So let her rich father buy her an asbestos dress."

"That's just it," he said. "Don't you see? She has a rich father. Everybody has someone … Johnny has friends."

I knew it was coming now.

"Are they looking for me?"

"An old pug has been asking questions around."

That would be Leon.

Ma and Leon, a dangerous pair.

"And this girl you have now. If she isn't of age ..." He let it hang in the air like a threat.

I was beginning to see what he meant. Some morning I could wake up dead.

"It looks like you are in the clear on Fatso as you so graciously call him," continued Epstein, "but that Metairie girl's father has a couple of private dicks on your tail. All they want is to beat you up. That's all this ex-pug seems to want, but this new girl's father seems to want to kill you."

"Okay, dad, ease up. What do you want me to do?"

He pulled a ream of checks out of the ledger and handed me the pen.

"First of all, sign the checks, especially mine for thirty-five thousand."

Everything was in order. I have a memory for figures. I signed them.

"Now keep your nose clean. You know when to play it cool."

"Is that all, dad?" I asked him.

The *dad* was making him sore.

"That's all," he said.

I started for the door. I had my hand on the knob when he called after me.

"One more thing."

"Yes?"

"Don't get any ideas about me. I'm in this to stay. And, Digger, stay away from my wife."

I laughed at him.

"Even with an extra thirty-five grand you don't feel safe, do you?"

It was the last word but a weak one.

I found a dress shop and bought Marguerita some clothes and then picked up the car in the parking lot.

I made one more stop for a jug and beat my way out of the traffic toward the motel.

Martin was a nosey yahoo but he was right all the same.

I would have to ditch the little Cajun as bad as I wanted to keep her for awhile.

It wasn't quite dark when I pulled into the stall next to our cabin.

I got the packages out of the back and tried the front door.

It was locked.

I knocked and Marguerita opened it immediately.

"What's the idea?" I asked.

"I was frightened here alone."

Inside, I threw the box with her clothes in it on the bed and went into the little alcove kitchen to make myself a drink.

"Open the box," I called to her.

She gave a little cry of surprise when she saw the dress.

"Put it on. Go ahead, try it for size," I told her.

She slipped out of her dress and started to pull the new one over her head.

"Wait a minute," I said.

I rummaged around in the box and came up with a brassiere and panties.

She fingered the lace and her eyes were big and moist.

"For Christ's sake, don't cry," I said.

She got them on somehow. I don't think she had ever worn a bra before.

I tried the shoes on her while she sat on the bed. When she stood up I couldn't believe my eyes.

"You look like a lady," I told her solemnly.

When she started to walk toward me she killed the illusion.

"I'm afraid I don't know how to walk in high heels," she said.

"You'll learn."

We had a few drinks and a few laughs and then she went to the john. I made a phone call.

"Hello, Jack, this is Digger."

"Hi, boy, long time," he answered.

"You know it." I hesitated. It was now or never. "I've got a piece of property for you."

"No dice, Digger. I'm closed. My best girls are working the streets."

"Are you still exporting?"

"It's being done."

"This is for export only."

"What's the scoop?"

I lowered my voice. "This is prime stuff. A Cajun girl. I would prefer that she was out of the country."

"I would have to see her. How old is she?"

"Eighteen and a gorgeous thing."

"Young, huh? Well, that's the way they like them in South America. Bring her around. You know where."

"I'll send her in a cab, now."

"Anything you say. Uh, look, Digger, I can't pay as high a premium as I used to. Things are tough."

"Keep the dough."

"Well, okay," he said.

I hung up as Marguerita came into the room.

"Who were you talking to?" she asked.

"A friend. Look, baby, I'm going to have to be away for a few days."

"Oh, take me with you."

"I can't, besides we have to be careful. Your old man will be hot on our trail."

She blanched and put her arms around me.

"I'm sending you to a friend. He will take care of you and send you to me when the time comes."

"No, no. If you leave me I'll never see you again."

"Yes you will, baby. We'll be together again."

"No, Digger, no."

I detached her arms from around me and she threw herself on the bed, crying convulsively.

I called a cab.

It was ten p.m. when I checked into the Monteleone Hotel in the French Quarter.

I had my bag sent up to the room and went to the pay phones.

I dialed an unlisted number I had memorized and when I heard a click at the other end I said, "This is Smith. I am registered at the Monteleone Hotel."

I gave the date, the time and my room number and hung up.

Giannini was a smart operator. There was nobody on the other end of that conversation. Only a dictaphone.

Later tonight the record would be picked up by one of Mr. Giannini's trustees and delivered to him.

No one called on him to transact a deal. I would probably never see the inside of his house again.

I lay in the bathtub in my room letting the hot water soak the sand and grime of Grannado Island from my pores.

There was thinking to be done. I had planned to hold on to this deal for a year or more, then sell out and retire. But it could go wrong. I had to have an out.

I toweled myself dry, dressed and headed for a penny arcade on North Canal Street.

When I got back to the hotel I had a handful of cheap portraits of myself and the current airline schedules to Mexico.

I sat at the writing desk and addressed a letter to the Motor Vehicle Division, Driver's License Department of the State of Kansas.

In the letter I gave a true description of myself and explained that I was a traveling salesman who was opening a new territory in Kansas and that I would like a state driver's license.

I signed the letter with the name of my favorite composer, Giuseppe Verdi. Only I Americanized it into Joe Green.

It took a few minutes to decide which picture to use. One of the snaps didn't look like me at all so I discarded that one for a pic that looked like me and didn't look like me.

I enclosed it with the letter and mailed the envelope in the wall chute outside my door.

In a week or ten days I would have a new identity. Joe Green, Kansas, traveling salesman.

I ordered a bottle from room service and settled down with the airline schedules.

It took half the bottle in drinking time to memorize the departures of all planes from New Orleans and the cities nearby to Dallas, Texas.

It only required one more drink to memorize the departures from Dallas to Mexico.

Planes leaving Dallas for Mexico City are not checked by the U. S. officials. All you have to do to get out of the country is get on a plane in Texas and fly across the border.

All you need in Mexico to get a visa is a driver's license.

Once in Mexico it is a simple matter to buy an excellently forged passport and then you can go anywhere.

I took a last drink and got into bed.

The summer heat had tapered off since I had been gone. It was pleasant to sit in the Swan Room of the Monteleone and sip long cool ones.

And the heat was off me too. I had been back a week and nobody was on my tail.

I hadn't called Eldeese so her old man must have decided to drop his plans to have me beaten up.

I wasn't afraid of a beating. I could take care of myself. But like Epstein said, I couldn't afford trouble.

I took the *Times Picayune* from my pocket and looked at the society page for the tenth time that day. Eldeese's picture was there with half a dozen other people.

The story under the picture listed the society names who had reserved season boxes for the coming race meet at the Fair Grounds.

She looked good, like a million bucks. She was tan as hell and a little fleshier than I remembered her. It didn't hurt her any.

I tore her picture out and put it in my pocket and left the paper on the bar.

As I passed the desk the clerk called me.

"You have a message, Mr. Mulcahy."

He turned and pulled the envelope out of the pigeon hole above my room number.

"Thanks," I said as he handed it to me.

I sat down in a chair and ripped open the flap.

All the message said was, "Eight o'clock," nothing else. I glanced at my watch and checked the time with the electric clock above the desk. Seven thirty.

I went outside and got my car from the garage.

As I cruised along toward Felicity Street I thought about that ride I had taken in the sports car.

What was that guy's name? The Southern gentleman joker—Clairborne, that was it.

It wouldn't be long now before I called Mr. Clairborne and ordered the biggest damn car they had. Then I would call up Louis Pappas and take him for a ride around that dirt track out near the lake.

The thought of it made me smile.

I cruised down the ramp into the basement garage and drove down the line of cars to the back.

It was ten of eight. I glanced at the spiral stairs leading to the street level.

Nobody there. And there wasn't anyone in the cars parked around me.

I lit up and waited.

At eight sharp, headlights blinked across the entrance and a car nosed down the ramp and idled toward me.

It was Giannini's limousine.

The chauffeur swung in beside me and cut the engine.

I got out and went around to the rear door of the limousine.

The window was rolled down and the man inside said, "Good evening, Mr. Smith."

"Good evening to you, Mr. Vitolo Giannini."

"Take a walk, boys," said Giannini.

The chauffeur headed for the entrance and the hood that had been in back with the boss went up the spiral staircase to stand inside the fire door.

"Where is Bird Dog Pappas tonight?" I asked.

"Louis is in Havana for his health. Get in, Digger."

I settled myself beside him on the plush upholstering.

"How was the Island?" asked Vitolo.

"Hot," I said. "If the Devil owned Grannado and Hell, he would rent out Grannado and live in Hell."

He laughed and said, "You look fine. A good tan."

"What did you want to see me about?"

"How are you progressing?"

"One boat ready to sail. The lease contracts are signed and I have two men for the new boats out hunting down the rest of my boys. The initial work should be done on their boats by the time they reach the island. And I've just about spent the hundred grand. From now on I have to run my outfit on the lease profits and credit."

"Good. I have been watching you since you got back. You've worked hard and kept your nose clean. Now when can you have that boat in position?"

"Say the word."

Giannini was silent a moment.

"I have arranged a big one, Digger. Something that should get me in the clear. If it works out, I'm off the hook." He drilled me with his eyes. "I need that boat off the Florida Keys in three days to complete the deal."

"Three days! I don't know ..."

"You've got to do it, Digger."

"Okay, I'll try."

"No, don't try, do it."

I did some quick figuring. The island to the Keys, five hundred, maybe six hundred miles. The boat wouldn't be ready for another day.

But it could be done.

"It will cost you extra," I said. "I'll lose the bottom paint. It's not dry enough and the boat will have to go back into dry dock."

"If this works, I'll be glad to pay extra."

I looked at him. He was on my hook. I relaxed.

"Someday I will own a car like this," I said.

"Yes," he said, "you probably will. That brings up the second proposition I wanted to talk to you about."

"Shoot."

"I hear you have been looking for an apartment. You have looked at expensive places."

"So?"

"So be smart. Don't overspend. The worst thing you can do in this racket is become obvious and bring yourself to the attention of the Feds. Look what happened to Capone."

"Look at you," I reminded him.

"With me it's different. I've been going long enough to invest in a lot of legitimate firms. I can show an honest income. You haven't the resources yet. Wait till your boats are paid for."

"I'm tired of hotels. I'm sick of restaurant grease," I said. "I got into this so I could start living."

"Okay, okay. Take it easy. Tomorrow go see the Kumpf Real Estate people. You will get fixed up." He smiled, "I can guarantee it."

I thought it over.

"I'll do it on one condition."

"What?"

"Fix me up with a membership in the Club at the track."

I waited while he turned it over.

"How do you bet the horses?" he asked.

"I play it straight. A boat race or two at the start or finish of the season. I'm no scratch sheet bettor if that's what you mean."

"I didn't think you were. I just want to protect myself." He looked at his watch. "I've got another appointment, so let's finish our business."

He pulled a small nautical map out of his breast pocket. "Here is the rendezvous." He was pointing to a marked place off the Woman Keys.

"Memorize the longitude and latitude," he said. "The signals will be the ones we agreed on previously. This is a special pickup. Afterwards we will revert to the operating procedure we laid out."

"Where do we deliver the stuff?"

"Punta Rosa. Do you know it?"

"In San Carlos Bay."

"Good."

"This is going to set me back almost two weeks," I said. "*The Myrtle* will have to be taken back to Grannado to have her bottom painted."

"Is twenty grand enough?"

"I guess I can repaint her for about that."

"I thought you could. Good night, Mulcahy."

"Good night and good luck," I said and got out.

The chauffeur and the hood came back to the car and the limousine purred away.

I sat back in my Ford and lit a cigarette.

Twenty grand. That was a real pile to be laying out for one job. I wondered what the load would be.

The goods would be whatever Pappas was guarding down in

Havana, Cuba. I wished I were there.

That night I dreamed about stacks of one thousand dollar bills.

Usually, in the morning, I feel great. I can look forward to a busy day. I feel fresh; I can get things done.

This morning it was different.

I woke up late and lay in bed dozing before I cared enough to order coffee and toast from room service. While I waited I looked up the number of the Kumpf Real Estate Agency and made an appointment, then I placed a person-to-person call to Baptiste.

This would be the first test of my operation. I would have to give Baptiste the date, longitude and latitude and full instructions in the code we had worked out before-hand.

I was hoping he was smart enough to get it right the first time. The initial job had to be letter-perfect.

I had breakfasted, showered and dressed when the call went through. The connection was perfect.

"Hello," I said.

"Who is this?" he asked.

"This is the Marine Warehouse in New Orleans. About your order …"

He caught on quick.

"Let me get a pencil."

He was back in a flash. "Go ahead," he said.

I read off the figures I had memorized.

"On order number W. zero, eight, five, two, we have to back order. It will take a week or so. We are trying the warehouse in Punta Rosa."

"I got it."

"Order N. one, eight, three, eight is on its way. It should be there in seventy-two hours."

"That's fast service."

"Glad to oblige."

"I don't know if we can use it so soon."

"You had better use it. They are hard to get these days."

"If you say so."

"I say so. Would you repeat those order numbers to see if you have them correctly?"

He repeated all of the numbers and they checked.

"Thank you. We are glad to have your business," I said and hung up.

It was simple. The first order had been longitude and the second, latitude. Only backwards. Put them right and they spelled Lo. 25.80 North and La. 83.81 West. He was to be there in three days. Punta

Rosa was the delivery port.

If he navigated correctly we were in.

I put on my hat and left the room.

The Kumpf man picked me up in front of the hotel. He wore a toothpaste smile, a loud tie and an oily voice.

"Mr. Mulcahy?" he asked.

"That's right."

We didn't shake hands.

He drove me past a couple of large second class apartment buildings, but I declined to take a look-see.

"I want more privacy," I said. "These places are full of crying kids and nosey old maids."

"You want a smaller building? Something more exclusive?"

"That's the idea."

He took me to an address where a widow wanted to rent the second floor of her home.

Not to me.

"I have one more house on my list," he said.

He drove deep into the French Quarter and parked before a small one-story building set flush to the sidewalk.

There were two doors and two windows in front and the paint was peeling.

The effect was somewhat less than exclusive.

The sign down on the corner said Bourbon Street.

Now I knew why I was feeling depressed.

I was back on *The* Street. Hell, I had never left it.

Then I got that prickly sensation on the back of my neck. The Quarter may not be safe for me yet. Ma Vivaldi may not have forgotten.

And then I got it. I was running. Not from the cops but running just the same.

I would forever have to be looking behind me. Afraid of darkened streets and that slow moving car that could be hiding an assassin.

I took a grip on myself. A million dollars makes it worthwhile to the hunted man.

All I would have to do was not to be listed in the phone book and see to it that my name stayed out of the city directory. I would have to do that anywhere I hung my hat.

He got out of the car.

"Let's take a look," he said.

The salesman unlocked a high, solidly built gate at the corner of the house that opened on a cobblestone walkway.

"You can enter through the front but they are really the kitchens," he said. "The living quarters are at the back."

"Kitchens?" I asked.

"Yes. This is a duplex divided down the middle."

We went halfway down the walk and unlocked a large French door.

"This is the living room," he said.

I could see that much.

The joint was unfurnished and cobwebs hung from the ceiling.

There was a fireplace with a phony gas log in it and large book shelves on either side.

The floor was buried under a layer of dust but I could see the flooring. It was made of extra large-sized red cobble stones.

He showed me the bath, a tiled affair with tub and shower.

The kitchen had a gas stove, and old-fashioned ice box. There was a large linen closet and butler's pantry between the kitchen and bath.

We walked back through the living room to the bedroom. It was small but double French doors with a fan-shaped window above led out into the patio.

The grass in the patio was cut and trimmed and against the far wall flowers were blooming.

Somebody was taking care of the outside anyway.

"This apartment was under OPA during the war," he said, "and the rent was set too low. It was closed off. Nobody has wanted to fix it up after all the disuse."

He went back to the living room, still talking.

I stood at the French windows looking at the lawn.

There was a small banana tree in the far corner and it had miniature bananas on it, still green.

I was about to turn away when movement caught my eye.

A small kitten came into view on the lawn. The kitten was followed by a lovely young lady. I say lovely because I could tell. She was wearing a Bikini bathing suit.

She spread a blanket on the grass and sat down.

I watched her smooth suntan oil on her belly and legs. The sun glinted on her very blonde hair.

I went into the living room.

"The ceilings are high," I said to the salesman. "They would keep the heat down and I could add air conditioning. The floors would be very attractive if they would be cleaned and polished so that the red brick would show. How much?"

"Seventy-five a month. You pay utilities."

"I'll take it," I said.

He gave me a ride back to the hotel.

I had a few moments to think. Seventy-five was cheap these days. That pad, if cleaned and painted up, would be a very classy place.

I didn't have to give myself three guesses about who owned the property. I wondered if he owned the blonde also.

And I reminded myself to check the wiring for a dictaphone.

The apartment smelled of fresh paint and turpentine. I walked around, aimlessly, stepping over paint cans and tarpaulins and tried to keep from walking under ladders.

I yanked the covering from a new deep-backed leather chair and sat down.

What was up? What was going on? Usually I could second-guess these crises.

It had been two days since Baptiste should have picked up the junk.

I had haunted the lobby of the Monteleone waiting for a message.

No calls, no message.

And no twenty grand.

If the deal was completed why hadn't I collected? I couldn't reach Twigg on the phone and I had left a half dozen messages at the unlisted number.

Was I being thrown a curve? Was this a cross?

It couldn't be! Giannini had too much invested.

I threw my cigarette against the wall and it stuck in the heavy wet paint.

I felt defeated. I couldn't act. I couldn't work this off physically or hit out at someone. Wait. That's all I could do.

In my pocket I had five thousand bucks getaway money. Out of desperation for something to do I had come to the apartment to find a place to stash it.

I lit up another butt and let my eye wander over the room. The fireplace? No. That gas log was coming out and I would have to hide it all over again.

I got up and tapped the wood at the back of the bookcases. They were solid, showing they were built flush against the brick with an air space.

The kitchen, bath and butler's pantry were finished. Only the living room and bedroom remained to be painted.

I went into the bedroom and pulled the painter's tarpaulin back, exposing the floor.

The bricks here were not washed yet. Those in the kitchen glowed a deep red under the scrubbing and waxing of the cleaning lady.

I searched until I found a stone that was loose and then got a knife from the kitchen.

It took about an hour to pry the brick up without damaging it.

I scooped a hole in the crumbly cement large enough to hold the paper money, being careful to leave a ridge that the brick would rest on.

I went back to the kitchen and emptied the bread from a waxpaper bag, put the money in the waxpaper and placed it in the hole.

The brick fitted nicely on top of the package, not too low or too high. But it was a trifle wobbly.

I poured wet paint from a can around the edges of the seam, then rubbed dirt in it.

When I was satisfied that the work was invisible, I swept up the cement and plaster and replaced the tarp.

When the paint hardened it would hold the brick tight and the scrubbing and wax would make it even less conspicuous.

I stiffened. There was a noise behind me.

I looked over my shoulder slowly. It was the kitten, the little black kitten that belonged to my luscious lady neighbor. He was sharpening his claws on the screen door to the patio.

I carried the little pile of cement to the kitchen, dumped it and I opened the door of the new refrigerator.

I carried a dish of milk to the patio and set it on the grass. The kitten sniffed around the edges of the saucer before he got his whiskers wet.

"Do you like cats, Mr. Mulcahy?" said a voice behind me.

I liked the voice, low and husky.

I turned around.

"I hate cats and like blondes," I said.

Our eyes met. We both got a charge. She had on a white housecoat that was gathered by a clasp at the waist. She was exhibiting a long sweep of tanned leg.

"It's a way to get acquainted," she said, recovering.

I watched her stoop and pick up the cat.

"But he shouldn't have too much to drink on a hot day," she said. "He'll get sick."

She cuddled the black ball of fur against her.

The cat purred audibly. Who wouldn't?

"How did you know my name?" I asked.

"The cleaning lady told me. I was curious."

She was looking me over now. "I'm glad you decided to take the next apartment," and she gave me a big smile. "Pardon my appearance. I was getting ready to attend the races."

I had forgotten. It was opening day at the Fair Grounds.

"My, it's hot," she said. "Could I offer you a drink?"

It would be nice to tarry. It was plain she had more on her mind than whiskey.

"Not today," I said.

She was disappointed.

"All right, but I'll ask you again. I can be very friendly."

"I don't doubt it," I said and went back inside.

I locked the apartment and drove back to the Monteleone.

I should have accepted the drink. There wasn't any message. I thought of going back to the apartment but she would have left for the track by now.

So that's where I would go. They could come looking for me. I had done my part.

I took a cab to the track. It was less trouble than bucking the traffic on opening day.

The Club was on the third tier of the stands overlooking the finish line. The walls were paneled and the ceiling high and beamed, and there were large oil paintings of famous race horses.

It was still fifteen minutes before post time but the joint was jammed.

Everybody looked like a big shot, gabbing away and table hopping. I didn't spot a soul studying the chart.

I hadn't doped the races—I had been too busy—so I elbowed my way to the bar and ordered a shot and beer chaser.

"Shot? Beer chaser?" asked the bartender.

"Yeah, beer chaser," I told him.

He brought my order and said, "Buck fifty," and gave me a superior smile.

I gave him a five. "Keep it," I said.

He said thank you like he thought the money was no good.

The loud speaker was announcing the first race and I watched the parade to the post.

It was to be a maiden race for three year olds and I tried to pick them for fun. Sometimes you can spot a horse that has been fed a fast pill and make a few bucks.

Suddenly I had that feeling. Someone was drilling holes in my back.

I turned around.

It didn't take long to spot her.

Eldeese was watching me from across the room.

I stared as she came toward me. Her hips weaved and her thighs moved under the silk of her dress and I got that old feeling.

"Hi," I said.

"Digger, I've got to see you."

Her voice was low and controlled.

"You're seeing me."

"No, not here, in private."

"That would be very nice, but we would miss the first race."

"This is no joke, Digger. I'm pregnant."

We stood outside the Clubhouse on the ramp. She was crying a little.

"What am I going to do?" she said.

"Find a doctor."

"No, I can't. I'd kill myself first."

"Don't be dramatic," I told her. "Does your father know?"

"God, no. He really would kill me."

"Get him to send you away. Have the baby in Europe, then put it up for adoption."

She put her hand on my arm and looked at me.

"Marry me, Digger."

"No soap, baby. I'd never mix with your crowd."

"Why would it have to be my crowd? We could go away."

"I'm set here."

"You don't love me, do you?" she asked and bit her lip.

"No, I don't."

"How could I have ever thought you would change," she said and her voice was very low.

She buried her face in her hands and collapsed against a pillar.

I went down the ramp to the taxi stand. I wasn't in the mood to see the bangtails run.

I hailed a cab and was about to get in when I heard my name called.

"Mulcahy, wait."

It was Twigg getting out of a cab at the entrance.

He rushed over and grabbing me by the arm pulled me to a corner.

"Trouble?" I asked.

"Yes, Digger boy," he said wiping his red face, "and of the worst kind."

"The cops?"

"Don't be naive. It's Giannini. He's fit to be tied."

What could have gone wrong?

"Your delivery came out short, Digger."

"How do I know? I haven't heard from the crew chief."

Suddenly I had an idea.

I grabbed Twigg by the lapels.

"Where is Baptiste? What have you done with him?"

"Take it easy. We are looking for him, too."

"What do you mean you're looking for him? Tell me what happened from the start."

"You may as well know. If Giannini gets you, you won't be telling anybody. The load your boys picked up was money. Five million in small bills."

I whistled.

"It was dropped from a plane in a cork container and picked up okay."

"Get to the point," I said.

"We didn't get it until last night and we only finished counting it this morning …

"There's twenty grand missing."

"And you think I had my boys collect in advance?"

"That's what the boss thinks."

"He's nuts. I wouldn't touch a penny. It's probably hot anyway. Tell him I'll get the dough back for him and take care of the guy that's responsible."

"It's too late."

"Why?"

"That currency was counterfeit."

What a blow!

"Giannini was planning on passing that dough all over the country," said Twigg. "He had worked on it for months. He was going to pass it all at the same time before the T men could get on it. Once they see it they put out a description and you couldn't give it to a blind man."

If Baptiste had spent any of it I was sunk.

"Tell Giannini not to worry. I'll get that paper and I'll get the guy who took it."

I started to go back into the Club, then remembered they don't allow public phones at the track and signaled a cab instead.

"Where are you going?" yelled Twigg.

"Around the world," I said.

"You'd better hurry. Pappas got in this morning and he's already on the trail."

The cab took off and I left him standing at the curb mopping his brow.

In the cab I sat forward, thinking fast. Twigg was no friend of mine. Why was he doing me a favor. That's it! This was no favor. It was a trap. I was supposed to lead them to Baptiste and the bogus. I would see that I didn't. I would find Baptiste first and alone.

Where would he go? And then I knew. *The Myrtle,* a boat named after a girl, and I thought of an idea that would put me ahead of Pappas and his .45.

At the New Orleans airport, I arranged for a charter trip and called Grannado while I waited for the plane to fuel.

"Hello, Catlin?"

"Speaking."

"Is Baptiste there?"

"No. They pulled in at dawn. He gave the crew a four day pass, woke me up and bought a bottle."

"Any idea where he was going?" I asked casually.

"No. He took your company pickup and pulled out."

"Look, Cat. Was the dough he gave you for the bottle a new bill?"

"Why, yes, it was."

"Save it. I'll buy it back at two to one."

"Oh, will you? Well, I have news for you. I've already looked at it in the sunlight. Your boat is doing some night running, isn't it boy? Let me tell you something, Digger. I never did think you were on the square. A guy like you with all that dough to start a company. You're up to something and I want to cut in."

"Shut up, you fool. I'll talk to you in private."

"You'll talk with the green stuff, Digger. I'm on to you. I'll talk to someone else if you don't …"

I cut him off and went outside to the strip.

The plane was ready and we took off.

The pilot had said that we only had a couple of hours of daylight left and he would have to put down at dusk.

We got a tail wind and the light was giving out when he pointed below.

"There she is," he said. "Morgan City."

By the time we landed and I got a cab into town it was dark.

I had the cabbie make the rounds of bars but there wasn't a sign of Baptiste.

I had been sure he would try to blow up the town to impress his farm girl.

A guy with twenty G's in his kick isn't going to sit out the night on the front porch swing.

And then I got another idea.

Baptiste had never had a girl. He was too ugly. The only girls he had were shady ladies.

"Is there a house in this town?" I asked the cab driver.

"Why didn't you tell me what you was looking for in the first place?" he said. "I could have saved you a five buck fare."

I let it go.

"Take me there," I said.

"There ain't any in this town but down the road a piece."

"Okay, okay," I said.

"I can't take you there, mister. I'd lose my license."

"Well, for Christ's sake, can you tell me where it is?"

"Sure. I'll take you to the city limits."

We cruised along the dark and empty streets.

It was getting late.

The driver stopped at the edge of town and I got out.

"Just keep following this here road till you come to the railroad tracks and then turn down the dirt lane. You can't miss it."

"Thanks," I said and gave him a ten spot "How far is it?"

"Only a piece, five, six mile maybe."

He drove off. I guess he was used to a guy who was eager enough to walk five, six mile to tip five bucks.

I got to the tracks and found the lane.

And I felt like I had walked a hundred miles already.

It was pitch black and the crickets, frogs and birds back in the bayou set up a chatter that would drown out the whistle of a locomotive.

I walked and walked, stumbling in the ruts of the road, and I was beginning to think I had been taken for a sucker when I tripped and crashed into the brush at the side of the road.

I lay there, still as death, not daring to move.

I had tripped over something soft and human.

A body.

The crickets suddenly became still and I could hear my own breathing.

I lay for a long time and nothing stirred.

I inched to the form in the road and felt it for a pulse.

I knew before I struck a match that it was Baptiste.

He was alive but sodden drunk and beaten up.

I searched him frantically, even taking off his shoes. He was clean.

He didn't have fifty cents in change on him.

He used to joke about his ugliness and how he couldn't make out in a cathouse with a fifty dollar bill.

I had laughed then but now I was getting sore. I was going to find out just how well he had made out on twenty G's and I was going to bust that place wide open.

I got to my feet. I felt better. It had been a long time since I had gotten mad.

Well, I *was* mad. Mad enough to kill.

I left him there to get run over. I wanted him to get run over. That would save *me* the trouble of taking care of him.

The house was set back from the road in a stand of slash pines. It was a one story job with a large main room which was probably a bar and dance hall, with a narrow wing leading off to the right.

The wing would be a row of cubicles where the girls did their work. Two cars were parked in front. A Buick convertible and the company pickup.

A shaft of white slanted to the ground from the shutters on the bar.

I eased forward keeping the slash pines between me and the buildings.

When I got to the window I looked inside.

There was a bar, a few tables and chairs and a poker table.

At the poker table sat a guy in shirt sleeves riffling a deck of cards. He wore a beard and a shoulder holster. The gun was a .38.

He laid out a game of sol. Nobody else came into the room.

I went to the door and opened it.

"The black seven on the red eight," I said.

He made a mistake. He glanced at the cards and I rushed him.

I hit him with a straight right and he bounced off the wall behind the table.

I got to him and pulled his gun and pistol-whipped him in the mouth. I gave it to him again just to make sure and the barrel buried itself in the crimson slit where his teeth had been.

A door behind the bar slammed shut and I could hear somebody scampering around in there.

I vaulted the bar and shot the lock off the door with the .38.

The door crashed open under the, weight of my shoulder and I almost fell as I went in.

A fat Creole was trying to get a scattergun loaded so I shot him in the shoulder.

He dropped the gun and I shot him in the leg and he went down.

I picked up his gun and chucked it out the window.

There was a girl in the bed against the wall. She didn't have her nightshirt on.

She was staring at me out of one big brown eye.

Where her other should have been was only a jagged scar that had healed in a grotesque pattern. She was screaming hysterically.

I raced out of the office and down the corridor, kicking open the doors.

I found one girl and a couple.

They weren't having any. And besides they all were naked.

Back in the bar the houseman was still asleep, swallowing his blood.

I went into the office.

The girl was kneeling beside the fat guy on the floor.

He was moaning.

I jerked the girl to her feet and sent her spinning across the room and started to slap the Creole conscious.

It didn't take long.

He started screaming for a doctor but I cut him off.

I put the still smoking barrel of the .38 under his nose and told him I was ready to press the trigger.

"I'm dying," he screamed.

"You'll die with no nose unless you shut up," I told him.

"Help me, help me," he yelled to the girl.

I waved her back with the gun and she buried her face in the pillow.

I cased the joint. There was a floor safe next to the bed. On top of the safe stood a bottle, two glasses and a lamp.

I took a grip on the guy's collar and dragged him over to the safe.

"You've got something that belongs to me," I said. "Open it."

He moaned.

I put his good hand on the dial and put the gun at his temple.

"Open it!" I said.

I didn't think he could really do it but the tumblers clicked over and the door swung open.

He tried to reach inside so I put my foot out fast and smashed the heavy door on his arm.

The bone snapped and his forearm came out of the safe at right angles.

The one-eyed girl was on my back, clawing like a wildcat.

She was hissing, "You killed him. You killed him."

I laid her scalp open with the gun barrel and shut her up.

She fell in a heap on top of the fat man.

I found a stack of new bills in the safe.

I didn't have to count it to know a few would be missing.

Back in the bar I frisked the bouncer. He had a couple hundred in new bills. His cut was pretty small.

I went down the hall to where the lone girl had been.

She was huddled in the corner of the bed with the sheet clutched to her skinny chest.

"Okay, Myrtle, I'm not going to hurt you."

Her mouth dropped open and she started to breathe again.

"Where's the dough?" I asked.

Her eyes went to the washstand next to the bed. There wasn't anything on it but a tin wash basin and a couple of small towels.

I lifted the basin and found five tens beneath it.

"You're a sucker, Myrtle," I said. "Your boss got two G's for the night's work."

I left her there with her hate and the rotten smell of a hundred antiseptic douches. And I left the barroom with its stale odor of beer and fresh smell of blood.

I got into the pickup and backed into the rutted lane.

I thought of the guy lying back in the office with his arm broken and two slugs in his body. I couldn't feel sorry.

I drove slow, watching for Baptiste. He wasn't where I had left him!

I cut the lights and engine and as I stuck my head out the window I heard a shout and a splash. I stepped on the starter, pushed down hard on the gas. I was getting out of here fast.

Someone was getting buried in the bayou.

At the head of the lane I saw a black Plymouth coupe.

I gunned the car past it and ducked. No shots followed me.

Louis Pappas was a fast worker.

It was almost dawn when I pulled up beside the plane at the airport, and it seemed like hours before we could take off. I kept my eye on the dirt road leading out from town.

When we were finally in the air I allowed myself to lean back and relax.

I pulled the wad of bills out of my pocket and counted it.

I had a surprise coming.

The roll was a thousand short.

I had forgotten to look under the one-eyed girl's pillow. And I couldn't go back.

I thought fast.

New Orleans wasn't safe now. I was washed up with Giannini.

Pappas had got Baptiste. I would be next.

But I had time in my favor. It would take Pappas seven hours to drive back to New Orleans.

I would go to Mexico as Joe Green and send Mr. G. his phony dough. Maybe he would forget.

Epstein could run the boats for me. There was still good money in oil exploration.

I wasn't licked, not by a long shot.

At the New Orleans airport, I got a cab and went directly to my apartment.

Nobody was on the street when I got out and paid the fare.

Instead of going down the short alley way to my place I knocked on the kitchen door of the blonde's apartment.

She opened the shade, recognized me and opened the door.

"You look great," she said. "It must have been a good party."

I fingered the stubble on my chin.

"Yeah, first class," I said. "Anybody been around to see me?"

"I can't say. The walls are too thick to hear anything."

Suddenly I felt let down.

"You look like you could use a drink," she said.

I followed her into the living room.

She poured a highball glass half full and I tipped it up.

It burned going down, then spread out and mellowed in my belly.

"Another?" she asked.

I nodded and dropped into a chair.

She brought the bottle over and put it on the end table beside me.

"Say, what kind of a brawl have you been in?"

I looked at my fists. They were swollen.

I closed my eyes and tried not to think.

"Class reunion," I answered.

She sat on the arm of the chair and stroked my hair. I could smell perfume and woman.

"A hot bath and a shave would help," she murmured.

"Great," I said. "The hot water heater isn't turned on yet next door and I haven't moved my personal things over from the hotel."

"I can fix you up," she said, and kissed me lightly.

"I'll bet."

"Not that way. I like my strong men strong."

I had a couple more drinks while she ran the water.

It must have been hours later when I woke up with a start. It was pitch black and the water sloshed cold on my chest when I moved in the tub.

I stood up and almost fell on the bathroom floor.

The light switch was over the basin and I flicked it on.

I tied a towel around my middle and opened the door.

The apartment was dark too.

Blondie must be taking a nap. That's why she hadn't called me.

I went through the living room into the bedroom.

Nobody home.

My clothes were on a chair with the pockets turned inside out.

The dresser drawers were pulled out and her clothes were scattered everywhere.

The little cheater had pulled out with the twenty thousand in counterfeit.

There was an afternoon paper propped up on my clothes. I carried it back in the bathroom and read about myself.

The headline I was interested in said: "Gunman Runs Amuck in Roadhouse."

The guy I had shot was in the Morgan City Hospital along with his bouncer. The proprietor's wife was missing and feared kidnaped. There was a description of her. She had a scar that disfigured her left eye.

And I had been identified by an anonymous tip. My pal Pappas, probably.

Another story caught my attention. "Society Girl Found Floating in River," said the headline. There was a picture of Eldeese, the picture I had torn from the paper only a week before.

The story started: "A beautiful young socialite was found drowned …"

I couldn't finish it. I knew they would perform a post mortem.

And she was pregnant.

If that wasn't enough there was a box entitled Political Notes. It said: "Congress Fails to Turn Oil Back to States." That was all.

That finished everything. Goodbye crash boats. So long Seismograph Incorporated.

As I got dressed in the dark I thought I would have to get out fast now.

With the five grand under the brick in my place, I could go far enough.

I opened the French door leading to the patio and edged along the wall to my apartment.

It was too dark to see inside, so I waited listening.

I would have to chance it. I needed that dough.

My key turned in the lock okay. The door hadn't been jimmied.

I stepped inside and the ceiling fell on me.

Somebody laughed as I went down.

When I came to the lights were on and I could smell cigarette smoke.

All I could do was lie there with my eyes closed, thinking about how hungry I was.

"Open your eyes, Digger," said Ma Vivaldi. "I know you're awake."

I opened my eyes slowly.

Ma was standing over me. Leon stood next to her and I could feel the pain in the back of my neck where he had rabbit-punched me.

"Listen to me, Digger," said Ma. "I'm going to let Leon kick your face in just like you did to Johnny."

Her eyes were on fire and her mouth had an evil twist to it.

"I'm not giving you a chance." She was out of her mind with hate. "You didn't give Johnny a chance. You—"

I didn't let her finish. I reached out fast and grabbed her ankle and pulled.

She fell into Leon and I was on my feet before they got untangled.

"Take him, take him!" she screamed.

Leon came at me fast.

I pushed my left out, he lowered his guard and I threw a right.

He came again and we repeated the maneuver.

He was old, too old to catch me.

I hit him harder this time and he came off the wall like he was using the ropes in the ring.

But he couldn't get to me.

He knew it too and his face set in grim determination. He was going to try to wrestle me down where he could get his big hands on my throat.

Ma stood hypnotized.

I moved around fast, keeping Leon in the center of the room. I couldn't afford to let him get me in a corner.

I could feel his face getting soft under my punches. There was blood on his mouth and we were both breathing hard.

But I couldn't put him away.

His rushes were slowing and his eyes were getting glazed and still I couldn't knock him out.

I snapped a look toward Ma. She could see it too.

"Stop him, Ma," I yelled. Then I had to duck and clobber him again. "Ma, stop him," I yelled again. "I'm killing him."

Leon was starting another run when Ma stepped in front of him. He stopped and looked at her dumbly.

She took him by the arm and led him to the door.

He stumbled out and she turned and looked at me.

"You're marked, Digger," she said flatly. "When you leave this apartment, you're a hunted man."

She went out and I locked the door, turned out the lights and collapsed in a chair.

I lit up and when I had caught my breath I went into the kitchen and got a knife.

In the bedroom I found the right brick and pried it loose. It came out easy.

I reached in the hole for the waxpaper bundle and opened it.

Empty. It was empty!

I slumped down with my back against the wall.

Who had taken it? The cleaning lady? The painters? Or my lovely blonde neighbor? And a thought struck me. I didn't even know her name!

I laughed until I cried and hammered my fist against the floor until it bled.

What a sucker. The prize fool of them all.

A month ago I had a hundred thousand bucks, three boats and the sweetest setup in the world.

Now I was broke and I had a half dozen killers on my trail.

I stopped laughing.

What could I do?

I still had the Ford in a parking lot at the hotel.

And I had my .38 detective's special.

I got up and checked the bureau drawer. The gun was still there and I checked the load and put on the hip holster.

I could cash a few rubber checks, get the car and still make Mexico as Joe Green.

What I did for a living after I got there was a problem.

Epstein! He would still send me dough. He would have to.

It would work! I was still living.

I went out my bedroom door and into the next apartment. I found the phone in the dark and called Epstein.

He answered on the third ring.

I didn't let him say hello. "This is Digger. I'm in a jam. I need money and a lift over to where my car is stashed."

"That's tough," came the answer.

"Epstein! You've got to help me."

"Not this time, Digger. You've gone too far."

"You've cracked tougher raps."

"Not this tough and not this dirty. You don't know what's been going on today."

"Tell it," I practically screamed.

"The Feds have picked up Giannini. Your operation is washed up."

"We can go it legit," I said.

"No, Digger, we can't. Dunbar canceled his contract this afternoon an hour after the Congressional announcement. All the private operators are pulling out until the question of ownership of the oil is settled."

That was the final blow.

"Loan me some dough to skip town," I pleaded.

"I can't help you," said Epstein. "The police have been looking for you. They picked up that Creole fisherman's daughter you tried to ship out of the country."

"I had to do it, Martin. You told me to ditch her."

"Not that way. Where are you?"

"In the apartment next to mine in the Quarter."

"I'll see what I can do for you," said the lawyer and he hung up.

I stood there looking at the dead phone in my hands. I didn't like the sound of that.

But I wasn't going to wait and find out what he meant by it.

I started to let myself out the side door. And then had a better idea. Why not go out the back way and over the patio wall?

I went to the bedroom and let myself out by the French doors.

I took one step on the grass and stopped cold.

Someone was back there. There had been a flash of light by the little banana tree. It had looked like moonlight on steel.

I turned and ran around the corner of the house and down the dark passageway to the street.

There were running footsteps behind me.

I reached the gate and fumbled for the latch.

It wouldn't open!

The footsteps came close behind me and then stopped.

I put my shoulder against the gate and reached for my gun at the same time.

Light from the street lamps splashed into the alley way as the door opened and I saw a face in front of mine. A face horribly contorted.

That face had only one eye and I could see a farmer's sickle clutched in the girl's hand.

I screamed as the sickle cut the air and sliced my throat.

I fell backwards pulling the trigger as I went but the bullets whined off into the empty night sky.

I clutched my throat with my free hand to stop the bleeding.

Help. I needed help but I couldn't make any sound come.

In the distance I could hear a police siren wailing.

That was Epstein's help. The rat had turned me in.

I lay on my side looking down the street but there was no one. Nobody on my side.

My eyes fastened on the sign at the corner. I could just make out what it said. In white letters on a black background the sign read, "Bourbon Street."

And my brain was seared through by a sudden clarity. I could see it all as if everything that had come before was paraded before my mind's eye in the flash of a second's hundredth part … Old Johnny, Eldeese, Marguerita.

I knew that I had asked for it.

This was my fate and I was suddenly crying.

With the tears came a terrible fear. A strength-shaking fear of my punishment.

Brakes screeched to a halt as the police cruiser pulled up in the street and the slap of feet on pavement hurried toward me.

I twisted my arm up and put the barrel of the .38 in my mouth.

Before my index finger could squeeze the trigger, I came to a new realization. I knew my strength. I could imagine my punishment. With a last effort I threw the gun away.

It was not in me to turn yellow.

Let my fate be my redemption.

THE END

HOT CARGO

G. H. OTIS

CHAPTER ONE

I was looking at her ass-end first. Her heavy stern rose high, full, and rounded to exacting proportions from the skimmed-off, oil-soaked dock water. A couple of grapefruit rinds and a patch of yellow scum foam washed lazily against her exposed rudder.

Riding so high out of water meant she had a long time before her belly would be full of the crude black. A tanker can soak up a lot of liquid.

I slowed my walk. Here I was, in plenty of time. And sorry as hell about it, too.

One good look cooled my already frigid interest. The stern lines of the fan tail of a tanker can be a beautiful thing. This ship had more dents, scales, and rust on her bottom than an aging madam. I wasn't sure, now that I had seen her, that a quick cruise south was better than ducking blackjacks at two paces.

But then again I was. Really, I was.

I walked along the mace wire fence until I got to the guard house, then let the heavy sea bag roll off my shoulder and fall six feet to the ground. The guard popped out of his little house like one of those wizened figures in a hand-carved weather box and stood looking up at me. He must have been a hundred years old.

He grinned. I grinned.

"By gum, big fella, ain'tcha," he said in a cracked voice.

I searched through the pockets of my tight-fitting, gold-buttoned jacket and found my card and papers.

"If you fell down, you'd be halfway home," he said.

I held the card up close in front of his eyes. Anybody who would use such an old gag must not be able to read good enough to keep up with the new jokes.

"Sailor, eh?" he said, squinting at the card. He took it out of my hands and compared the picture with the real thing. "Brown hair, brown eyes, scar on chin … that's you all right."

"For a moment I had myself fooled," I said.

"Comic, eh? Let me see your pass."

I fished out the hiring hall slip and handed it over.

"Brody's the name, eh? Knew a fella named Brody once. He died." The old guy was quite a talker. "You got the right place. Pier 6. The good ship *Patty Sue.*"

I hoisted the sea bag and retrieved the papers.

"Wait a minute, young fella," the old man said, and ducked into the guard shack. He was back in a minute with a dock badge which he pinned on my coat lapel.

"Just like wartime," I said.

"It is wartime, buddy," he said, "otherwise I wouldn't have a job."

I looked ahead of me at the tanker, at 129,000 barrels of highly volatile oil. "And otherwise they would have scrapped this heap," I said.

I walked down the pier. The closer I got the worse became that dreaded stench. I had known what it would be like, 129,000 barrels of oil smell, crude octane oil smell, oil tar smell, and more oil smell until that stench was in your hair, eyes, ears, pores.

But this one was worse than usual. There was more rust than paint on her plates; the barnacles were clear up her sides, halfway to the tank deck and all the way to her scupper holes. They clung sucking to her sides like a million newly born piglets at a massive sow's teats.

"*Patty Sue*, you are unclean," I said to her, and went up the gangplank.

No, sir, I didn't even hesitate.

There wasn't anybody in sight on the poop decks or catwalk, so I ankled my way to the monkey island amidships and looked for the best polished brass doorknob. There wasn't much leeway in my choice, but the first one I knocked on turned out to be the captain's cabin.

"Who the hell are you?" he growled.

"Who the hell do you think I am?" I answered.

"What kind of talk is that to a master?"

"Where do you get off cussing at a licensed third officer?"

"Third …"

"That's right."

He folded up in the fight department too fast. I didn't like that.

He put a finger in one of his splayed, moisture-shiny nostrils and left it there while he looked me over.

"You're too young," he said. "Where could you have got eight years' apprentice?"

"I could convince another captain easier," I said, and shouldered my sea bag.

Then he laughed in my face. He had me pegged.

I shrugged my shoulders and put the sea bag down. Then I laughed with him because I was so goddamn miserable.

"Let's see your papers," the captain said. It took him only a minute to check the license, my log, and ask me the question I was prepared to answer honestly.

"How honest are you?" asked the captain.

"Not very," I replied.

"We'll get along."

"Sure."

We stood looking at one another.

"Tell me," he asked finally, "how did you catch it so quick?"

"What skipper would take a guy off the beach with my record? You knew who I was when I knocked on the door."

"Sure. I know the guy at the hiring hall. You were made to order. A one-trip sailor because you can't let the booze and broads alone."

"Now tell me how you knew I would stick," I asked.

"What American sailor in his right mind would bother to even come on the pier? It's a war surplus T-2 tanker with more loose rivets than the law allows. A Panamanian flag-flying, tax-ducking, seaman-killing scow…. How long have the cops given you to get out of town, boy?"

"Time was up three days ago, but there weren't enough of the bums still fit to get up a gang big enough to take me again. I just got tired of waiting them out."

"Oh yeah?"

"Yeah."

"I believe you, boy," he said hurriedly. "We'll be out of here on the tide tonight. I'll get the steward to take your gear to your cabin."

Outside, I took a deep breath and let the tar oil air burn some of his stench out of my head. If I had been his father I wouldn't have hesitated. I would have turned the rock back over.

A mess boy, who was a young thirty-five, led me to my cabin. It wasn't much. There was a steel bunk suspended by chains from one wall—just like in a jail, I thought. The wash basin was corroded with a yellow stain under each faucet, and the floor underneath was gummy around it.

The one closet would hold all my clothes—if I could ever get it aired out—and there was a small wall desk and chair to round out the complement of furniture.

"How had I ever got myself in this spot?" I asked no one in particular. All the good intentions in the world didn't seem to help. You sweat out a trip on a lousy cargo, tramp or tanker, stay out of the poker game, remain sober, and say your prayers. You're going to bank your roll, save a wad of it so you can have something to show for ten years inside tin cans—and you do it, too—all except that last part.

When they put you ashore with cash in hand you start for the bank, a smile on your face, and a mental pat on your back.

Then it happens. It happens *every* time.

There she stands, a bit of fluff, silk, nylon, a smile, and thirty-six inch thrust.

You stop; she stops; you look her over. Ankles, calf, thigh, hips, and the juice begins to move; buttocks, waist so small, and that thirty-six inch personality.

She's looking you over, too. Her eyes are riveted on you. She knows; they all know. They must be able to smell it. And you wake up six days later with a headache, sore loins, and a sad, broken promise.

This time it had been worse. Six hundred dollars' worth of sour taste in your mouth.

Try to get even, you say. So you find a wide open game in a basement in downtown Houston where the cards aren't new and the faces are. You try to get even, and you get even worse.

What a laugh! Those guys cheated. So you cheated, too. Do unto others what they damned well did to you.

Then a fight and another fight until they had to drive you out of town before you became a successful one-man crime stopper.

I fingered the bruise behind my right ear. Well, I got a couple dozen before they got me. I'm not running—just recuperating. This was just a little pleasure cruise to get the Caribbean air.

And this time I was going to save my pay, bank it.

I laughed at that one. I'm not always so funny.

The captain had me pegged. The only difference between us was that I was dishonest with myself only. I wondered what his game was. He was probably breaking a couple of rules. Pay kickbacks, underman the ship, carry a packet full of uncut heroin ashore. He probably pulled them all.

He could have it. I never played it that way.

I went out on deck and headed aft toward the engine room. The mess boy was standing at the railing picking his nose and looking down the coast line.

I could see a rowboat out there with two people in it, fishing.

"If you haven't anything better to do, you can go to work on my cabin," I told him gently. "I want it clean—C-L-E-A-N—when I go to bed tonight."

"Yes, sir," he said, and looked up at me out of big, soft, brown eyes. He gave me a funny smile and moved away switching his fat hips. So it was that kind of ship. Well, everybody to his own taste.

The engine room was under the poop deck. I crawled down the ladder, noting the grease and waste littering the floor and the gook built up in the corners.

There were two sailors sitting on boxes playing cribbage on an orange crate.

"I'm Ed Brody," I said, "the new chief engineer."

They looked me over.

"I'm Harry MacGill," said one of them. He had red hair, freckles, and forearms like a wrestler.

The other guy said, "Francis Garcia." He was short, dark, and spoke with a strong accent. Probably one of the Panamanian hands.

We shook all around.

"What are we doing?" I asked, and nodded toward the pump controls.

"Bringing on fuel oil," Harry said. "Running it in full suction. We should be loaded by nightfall."

"When was the last time you checked the gauges?" I asked.

They looked at each other, silently folded the cribbage board, and got up.

"Get this stuff out of here," I said, kicking the boxes.

Francis started carrying them up the ladder.

"How many men in the engine gang?" I asked Harry.

"Sixteen, not counting you."

I had been afraid of that. It was the absolute minimum to handle the four shifts. One guy gets hurt or sick and we would have to double up. New tankers have an engine room that can be handled by one man, if necessary, but not this old tub.

"Where are the other two men?" I asked. "There should be four of you down here. Go get them … wait, get them all down here. I want this place cleaned up."

My method was to start tough.

Harry was back in two shakes, followed by a few of the most bedraggled specimens that I would care to describe. It didn't look like they could be capable of running anything but out of money.

Most of them were South Americans, but the States boys looked the worst.

"Where are the rest of them?"

"About half are on liberty; they won't be back till sailing time, if then. A few of the guys had to get dressed," said Harry.

"Okay, break out the gear and put them to work."

I looked over the oil burning furnace while the crew got busy. It was sound, thank God. There was an engineer check list book stuffed away in a drawer at the chief's table. I got it out and started going over the whole works. When we tried to pull away from the dock I would know that everything worked.

It had only been a few years ago that a tanker just like this was ready to pull out when something went wrong and caused the Texas City disaster.

I sent Harry up to the bridge to ring up the signals so that I could see they weren't reversed or anything silly like that, and then told him to keep the crew working. I wasn't going to depend on him for anything but the cleaning detail—not yet, anyway.

With the list of names of my crew, I went up the catwalk to make up the watch list.

There were a few men in sight now on the tank deck gingerly checking the valves to the various tanks.

The captain wasn't in sight and the second mate hadn't put in his appearance yet. It looked like I was going to have a lonely trip. A guy wouldn't have to be a snob to look down his nose at this tub.

Just before dark, I grabbed a bite to eat. There wasn't time to stop long in the greasy smelling galley. In another two hours we would be pulling out, and there was a lot to do.

When I went out on deck it was dark and the tank deck was deserted. I went forward on the catwalk first. I wanted to see how we were tied up all around, so I would know what lines were being cast off when I got the signals in the engine room.

I was bending over a stanchion counting the great hemp lines when I first heard it, and the hair went up on the back of my neck.

Christ, it was only a small, soft bump, bump—but it was enough.

If we were rubbing against the dock we could cause enough friction to generate a spark and blow us to kingdom come.

But it didn't sound quite like that kind of rubbing.

I got over to the rail and leaned out. The sound was less distinct here. I tried the other side. The sound seemed to come from directly below me. It was coming from under the pier.

Probably a floating log, I thought. Then I knew I was wrong. There at my feet lay a knotted rope.

I picked up the line and looked at it thoughtfully a moment, then made my decision.

I tossed the rope over the side, crawled under the rail, and started down, hand over hand.

Just before I should have touched water, my feet hit something hard. I got my balance on the object and looked down. I was standing in a small rowboat.

There were a couple of fishing poles and a creel in the bottom of the boat. They looked lonely, like maybe the owners weren't coming back.

And I knew I was right—somebody had pulled the plug and the rowboat was slowly filling with water.

I climbed back up fast. Whoever had come aboard was just ahead of me. The rowboat hadn't had time to sink yet.

All the way up that line, hand over hand, I kept wondering when they would cut the rope.

But they didn't.

When I climbed through the railing the bow was just as deserted as when I had started down.

I heard one or two more bumps and then a gurgling as the boat sank. Whoever had come aboard was still aboard. A picture of a small speck of a rowboat with two seated fishermen in it flickered across my mind.

I made my way over the tank deck past a maze of brightly painted valves and valve wheels toward the monkey island. I was almost there when I stopped and turned around.

The valve wheels are painted different colors to denote which pipes are which and what the oil is that the different tanks hold. There are usually thirty separate cargo tanks on a tanker so that it can carry several different types of oil at one time.

When people think of oil they usually picture the rich, black stuff only. In reality that's just the beginning. First come the "white oils," gasoline, kerosene, naphtha, and other refined oil products. Then there are "black oils," crude and various heavy grades of fuel and lubricating oils. Some of those are so thick that they have to be heated while at sea to keep them fluid.

And then there is casing head gasoline. The devil with it. When you see it through an open hatch it looks more like a bluish vapor than a liquid. And when it's loaded they have to use high pressure to force it through the pipes and into the tank. And under pressure it always leaks out somewhere.

Then it settles, colorless, odorless, in some remote cranny of the ship. It's the most volatile cargo a tanker can carry.

No wonder the crew was short. There weren't many fools who would sail with it.

Those painted valves of different colors told the story.

We were carrying gasoline, naphtha, fuel oil, crude *and* casing head.

Now I had two good reasons to talk to that sick, white crook of a captain.

It took me less than a second to get to his door. I didn't knock.

He was sitting with his back to the desk, facing me when I burst in.

"Since when don't you consider it important to tell your chief engineer that you've been pumping casing head all afternoon?" I yelled at him. "Why haven't the deck sprays been running to cool off the top plates? What the hell did you hire me for—to see how high I would fly when we went boom?"

The skipper went white before he turned red. One hand groped at his huge paunch that hung a foot over his belt. The other hand came out toward me and clutched spasmodically. He gurgled, then choked some.

Christ, I thought he was going to have a stroke.

Now I wish he had had.

Suddenly there was a gun in his hand, and it was pointed at my guts.

"Sit over there, Brody," he said, calm as you please, "and put your hands behind your head."

The automatic didn't waver. I pulled my eyes from the automatic and looked at his face. The color was a dead white again. It had been quite an act—all that clawing at his belly to get the gun, while the other hand had diverted my attention.

I went over and sat on his bunk like he said, but my arms stopped halfway up. Now I was looking in the direction that would have been behind me at my left as I had slammed open the door and walked in.

I was seeing what the door, swinging inward, had hidden. There were two people there; one, I vaguely noticed, was a guy, deformed. I don't know exactly what he looked like, because I was staring at the other person. And my mouth was probably hanging open.

"Shut the door, Sheba," barked the captain. "Do you want the whole damned world to know you're aboard?"

"It's okay," I said. "The rowboat sank."

Everyone gave me a sharp glance except the girl named Sheba.

"Get your hands up," said the captain.

I folded my hands behind the back of my head and concentrated my gaze on Sheba.

The girl was young. Awfully young—maybe eighteen. She had hair that was red-blond and cut short but feminine, like the fashionable girls do it.

It's hard to describe her. I don't think I had ever known a dame with real class; the kind that goes to private schools, travels abroad, and belongs to the country club don't hang out around the docks much.

And she was one of that kind.

Breeding, they call it. Oh, she had the rest—a shape, I mean.

She was wearing a soft brown cashmere sweater, a light wool skirt, and low heels. Her legs were bare.

I could see the full, yet narrow, pointed breasts modeled beneath the sweater, and the skirt was tight enough to show a good prat. Round and soft it would be.

I was dreaming.

"Shall we kill him now?" asked the third person.

I looked at him this time. He was short and very slight. Two thin arms supported his weight on those new-type aluminum elbow crutches. His face was drawn tight and at first looked mean.

Then I saw that he wasn't mean, or even angry. He was just a sick man who had always had to use brain power instead of force, and he was chiding the captain in his twisted, jaded way, for pulling the gun.

"No," said the captain. "We might still have trouble. I'll kill him when we're out at sea."

And he *wasn't* kidding.

CHAPTER TWO

Things were pretty quiet in the cabin for a few minutes. The captain sat there with the automatic held steady in one big meaty mitt and a sickening grin on his face.

The cripple relaxed in a straightback chair and pointedly disregarded us as if we were beneath his attention.

That kid of a girl was kind of flattened against the bulkhead like she was scared. She looked too nice to be in this mess.

But to hell with them. Brody was the yahoo I was worrying about.

I leaned back, hands behind my head, against the bulkhead and looked at the ceiling, but all I let myself see was the situation.

The captain was smuggling a couple of people south ...?

If that was the gimmick he wouldn't have a gun in his hand. Smuggling people on a tanker is bad business, but it had been done before.

So that was only a part of it.

If I could convince Captain Croup and the cripple that I couldn't see past the smuggling angle …

But that wasn't enough. People as coldly criminal as these needed more edge than the idea the competition was dumb. What they liked was a patsy or someone they could use or *had* to use. And that was it!

"You had better kill me now," I said to Croup.

His eyelids slid down a notch, and he looked at me narrowly.

"Okay, wise guy," he said, "tell us why."

"I'm just thinking of you. You still have a chance to get an engineer from the hiring hall while you are docked. I don't think they will service you a hundred miles out in the Gulf."

"You think I *need* an engineer," he laughed.

"Is there anyone in the engine room gang that knows a gasket from a casket?" I countered.

I wasn't watching Croup. Out of the corner of my eye I could see the cripple. He was the boy, the one I had to fool.

Croup was silent a moment. I started my pitch.

"You can get away from the dock … with my help. The tugs can do just so much. You can't be on the bridge and in the engine room at the same time and from what I saw of the rest of your employees there isn't enough brains among them to pull the plunger let alone take the signals from you that will get us away clean and afloat instead of in pieces."

The cripple was looking from me to the captain now. I had his interest. It was a good time to set the hook.

"If your friends wanted to fly south they would have taken a plane," I said. "And I suppose they want to land whole instead of all over."

"You have a point," said the cripple, "but I'm afraid you have forgotten one vital fact."

I hadn't, but the conversation was beginning to get around to where I wanted it. He was going to get his chance to show off.

"What?" I asked, trying to sound impressed.

"If the captain relented and let you help us away from the dock, what would keep him from killing you once we were at sea?"

"The same reason he can't kill me before we leave. When we hit port the tugs need our engines to put us at the dock. That means the captain needs me again."

"And if he killed you now he couldn't get another engineer before we sailed?" asked the cripple.

"He had trouble getting me."

I waited. There was one final barb to set and I couldn't chance bringing it up myself.

"Well?" asked the captain. He was looking toward the cripple.

"Mr. Brody is a very composed young man. He doesn't appear to be concerned that there are two illegal passengers aboard this ship," the cripple said.

"Why should I be? I'm an engineer, not an immigration officer." I wanted to say more, much more, but I couldn't afford to belabor the point. That cripple was sharp enough to catch me if I got too far off base.

"He isn't the most honest man I have run across," the cripple said to Croup.

"I told you he wouldn't be," answered the captain. "Well?"

"How about a hundred dollars?" the cripple asked me.

I wanted to say yes, shout it. I asked, "What for?" instead.

"To keep your mouth shut, you fool," whispered Croup.

"Two hundred," I said, throwing my life in the balance. This was the crucial point. Either they would think they had me fooled or they would quit playing games.

"Two hundred it is," said the captain, and I saw the two of them exchange an almost imperceptible wink.

"Well, I guess I'll go below and get things rolling," I said. I got up and took one step toward the door.

There was a click as a new shell went into the chamber of Croup's automatic.

"Why don't you stick around here until we are ready to sail?" he said gently.

"Is that a suggestion?"

"Definitely."

I sat down again on the bed.

This wasn't going to be easy after all. They weren't trusting me enough to let me get to the railing and jump ship. I would have to think of another angle.

"How long?" asked the cripple.

Captain Croup looked at his watch. "Two hours, maybe. They should be here now."

Someone else coming abroad? We sat around, on edge, waiting. I was right back where I had started when I had barged in.

"Haven't you got something to drink?" asked the cripple in his bored voice.

Croup got up and went to a locker. He kept one eye on me, although the gun hung limp in his hand. I thought about rushing him then, but the odds were bad. And I was getting curious.

What the hell was going on? Who were these characters? A cripple, the captain and a beautiful girl whom they both ignored as though she didn't exist. And who was that someone else due to show soon?

I was either going to have to make my play soon and get out or stick around and run my string.

"Make mine a double," I said.

Captain Croup poured four slugs of rum into four water glasses and passed them around. I could have made a try for Croup when he passed in front of me, but again I hesitated a split second. And that was long enough to kill a man.

Nobody said much so I let my mind wander back over what had happened. I had passed up two outside chances at getting the automatic, and I felt a growing sense of tense excitement inside my belly. I should have pulled myself together right then and started getting out of there.

But I stayed.

What was I waiting for? Well, first of all I'm curious, as I said before. What *was* going on? And then there was an angle that kept nudging at my mind like new money washing gently against a deserted beach. If Croup had a deal up his sleeve it meant big wads of undeclared, tax exempt greenbacks for someone. That someone could be Ed Brody.

When a guy has been as magnificently unsuccessful at saving money as I have, the idea of one big, fast killing has its allure. There's nothing as nice as money.

Unless it's a woman.

I looked at the girl they called Sheba. She was sitting across the cabin from me. She had her soft, little-girl legs crossed at the knees, and she kept her head down between sips of rum. The reddish-blond hair fell fluffily over her forehead.

She didn't talk or act coy or even seem aware that those legs of hers were capable of heating up a guy's temperature to ten degrees above danger.

She was like a kid you would show off for or maybe want to take care of in some way.

And her present company consisted of enough sharks that being taken care of looked imperative.

So maybe it was the girl that made me stick around in the face of

Croup's gun hand.

Suddenly my ears caught the faint sound of an engine. It was coming from the dock somewhere. A moment later the captain heard it too and, if human ears can prick up, his did.

"That's it," he said to the cripple.

They looked at each other as they listened to the sound get louder. Then the captain got up and handed his gun to the cripple.

"I'll take care of it. You stay in here out of sight and entertain our friend," he said.

The cripple hefted the gun in his hand and eyed me. "Before you leave I want Mr. Brody to know that I have experience in using one of these," he answered.

"I'll bet," I said.

My sarcasm was wasted on him. He turned back to Croup. "Don't let anything go wrong out there," he said in almost a whisper. "I'm telling you, get it done quick and do it right."

Croup colored some, then went out and closed the door carefully so that no one could see inside.

"Well," I said, "here we are. Let's get acquainted huh?"

The little guy gave me a pained look, and the girl raised her eyes for the first time.

"Tell me," said the cripple, "are you always such a fool?"

This time I ignored *his* sarcasm.

"You know my name," I said, "Ed Brody, merchant seaman. And you are …?"

He shrugged, then smiled a bit. "All right, my name is Ringle. That's all you need to know."

"And your, uh, daughter?" I asked.

He really smiled now. A very dirty smile. "No, Brody. Sheba's not my daughter. She is my wife."

I got a little sick inside.

I said, "Oh, pardon me."

The girl's head went back down and she nervously turned the water glass in her hands.

I had a feeling she was ashamed of it too.

The racket outside got through to me then.

I could hear voices shouting and winches being unlimbered. I tried to push ugly thoughts of the shy young girl and the twisted old man out of my mind. I didn't know if I would ever leave that cabin alive, but what I could piece together from what was going on outside might help.

Noises become familiar to a sailor. From the different rattles, clanks, and shouts I could tell that the forward cargo winch was swinging a cargo net overside. We were going to load something beside oil.

What could it be? Tankers don't carry just any kind of cargo like freighters do. All they have below decks are huge tanks that hold liquid, and you don't load liquid with a cargo net.

It would have to be something that could be stored on deck if it was large, and if it were a small item that could be hidden in a cabin they wouldn't need a winch to hoist it aboard.

Then dope or narcotics was out. That stuff was smuggled *into* the States anyway, not out.

Maybe they were taking hard-to-get machinery or black market goods to peddle to a close-pressed South American country. But letting it sit out on deck that way, it wouldn't stand a chance of getting by the inspectors in port when we dropped anchor.

Unless they had the inspectors fixed.

I couldn't figure it. This was a new one on me.

The three of us sat and sipped the rum in the hot cabin, breathing the tar fumes and trying to look like we weren't bothered by anything, anything at all.

Maybe Ringle wasn't nervous. He was a cool bastard. But the girl … well, I could tell she was as edgy as I was.

By the time I heard the winches stop groaning and the sound of that truck moving slowly off down the dock again I was in a sweat.

It had taken them a good hour to load up and we must have been pressing high tide and sailing time.

The pumps had been quiet now for a long while, so I knew we had our cargo of oil aboard.

What was holding up Captain Croup? Why didn't he get back here?

The palms of my hands were wet from more than the heat, and I was beginning to wonder if they were ever going to let me get to the engine room.

To shoot me in the cabin would be comparatively safe. You can even smoke in a closed cabin and not set off the cargo. Maybe they had me pegged as too much of a risk.

But they needed an engineer or Croup wouldn't have hired one. I had pegged my play on that. And then again maybe I should have gone for the gun long ago.

I looked at Ringle. He was watching me like a hawk, and he smiled like he knew what was going through my mind.

Then the door opened and Croup stood there.

"Let's get it over with," he said.

"Now?" asked Ringle.

"Right now. We haven't got much time," said the captain.

I swallowed hard and felt my stomach muscles tie up.

Ringle worked the automatic and another slug went into the chamber. He looked at me then, calmly ejected the bullet from the chamber and put the gun in a side coat pocket.

"Well, what are you waiting for," he said with a crazy leer. "The engineer's place at sailing time is in the engine room."

I got to my feet shakily and walked toward the door, hoping it wasn't a trick.

Croup stood aside and I passed beside him.

The air on the catwalk wasn't any better than it had been in the cabin, but it smelled sweet as heaven in my arms right then.

Nobody said a word behind me as I walked along the catwalk aft to the engine room ladder. I could have jumped over the side thirty feet to the dock, easy, and taken my chances on getting away, but I wouldn't have left that ship for a zillion dollars of honest money.

Anybody who thinks he can throw a scare into me like that and walk away is mistaken. Now I had a personal stake in this caper.

I was older and wiser. Hell, they wouldn't share any of the deal with me. Those boys were the biggest back-knifing combo I had ever run into.

Down in the engine room I found MacGill and Garcia and most of my gang ready. The pressure was up and as I made my check I realized that they had done a good job of house-cleaning. It looked more like a naval vessel.

I could feel it when the tug came alongside and nudged the ship, and in a few minutes we started getting signals from the bridge. The *Patty Sue* moved away from the dock nice and easy. The tugs helped us out of the slip and we turned in the channel a full one hundred and eighty degrees and headed out the way the ship had come in.

We would navigate the shallow lake waters of Galveston Bay near shore and hit the Gulf of Mexico just before morning.

I handed my watch list over to MacGill and told him to see that the boys were on the job. I was going to take four hours off and four on duty the first day or two. I like to watch oil-burning furnace-engines personally.

I climbed up the ladder out of the engine room warily.

Sure enough, Croup was at the top waiting for me.

"Nice job," he said.

"Thanks. Now if you will excuse me I'm going to hit the sack. I haven't slept deep for two weeks."

"Gave you a rough time ashore, did they?"

Considering what this was turning into it had been a picnic. I nodded and we walked along the catwalk to the monkey island together. He watched as I opened my cabin door and stepped inside.

I closed my door, slipped home the burglar catch and waited. In a second I heard his cabin door open, close and the bolt go home.

With a speed that belied my weariness I opened the closet and got out the sea-bag. Then I stuffed it into my bed and with a little arranging of blankets made a pretty fair dummy. I took off my shoes and put on a black sweater and cap and went back to the door.

I unlocked and opened the door and went out, over the rail in one step and dropped noiselessly to the tanker deck. I crouched there with my heart in my mouth waiting to see if I had been spotted.

The engine room crew hadn't acted as if anything unusual was up, and maybe I was the only one who had stumbled onto this caper.

Up forward I could make out two big shapes.

They puzzled me. Something was familiar about it but I couldn't make it out. The shapes were gigantic crates, one on either side of the center aisle between the tank valves.

Then it started to come through to me. I threaded my way forward, bending low to keep out of sight of a chance late-strolling sailor.

When I got to the first crate on my side I made my way around, looking for markings. The crate nestled on skid racks that had been installed during the last war to carry airplanes. And that's what these racks were carrying now.

I sat there on my haunches looking at the stenciled name of a big U.S. plane manufacturer.

And the whole picture began to take focus.

Old Croup and that crook Ringle were smuggling arms to some revolutionary-minded politico in South America.

It was being done all the time, and it was big money. They have revolutions down south like we celebrate birthdays.

But this was *real* good dough. Rifles, grenades, ammo—that brought heavy cash, but two airplanes was a high priority millionaire type operation. No wonder Croup had been trigger tight.

I heard a noise and peeked around the edge of the crate. There was someone standing at the bow.

I backed crablike into the shadows aft and kept on going. It took fifteen minutes to get back to my cabin without getting caught, and when I got there I was wringing wet.

I lay on my bed naked and tried to sleep, but it wasn't any use. There was still something wrong.

It was all wide open, too easy. Now, Croup knows I would see those crates in daylight, I thought. Airplanes are big objects, and these were big airplanes. Bigger than usual. And that in itself was odd.

He wasn't giving me any two hundred bucks to look away while he dropped the girl and her husband off outside a South American port. What about the rest of the crew?

And what about the crates forward on the skid racks? He knows that a guy who would take a bribe would up the ante when he saw the planes. And then he had the crew again to settle with on that score.

Croup couldn't be that dumb. Or was he so smart he could afford to act dumb?

I turned over on my side, found my cigarettes, and fired up. The Gulf heat made my skin sticky hot and a new realization was gripping my brain in a cold vise.

Those crates were oversize. In the late unpleasantness they would have been almost big enough to contain light bombers, but the way they made planes these days those crates could be holding fighters or interceptors.

And what kind of fighters were they making? Why, jets, of course.

Croup had been ready to kill me on the spot. No hesitation about it. They had needed an engineer, all right, but not for long. And I had been so co-operative.

Hello sucker!

They didn't need an engineer to dock with and they weren't going to pay me two hundred bucks. They weren't worried about the crew *or* me because they never planned to dock in South America.

This ship was destined never to see port again.

The U.S. government was offering one hundred thousand dollars to any enemy pilot who would deliver a jet into our hands. It was cheap at the price.

So I wondered how much the Russians were offering.

And how much dough did Ringle and Captain Croup plan to make if this was what I thought it was … an old-fashioned high-jacking caper.

I was fully awake now, and the sound of someone gently trying my locked door reminded me that I'd better stay that way.

CHAPTER THREE

At midnight I got up and put on a pair of khaki shorts, slipped into my special nailless shoes, clamped my third officer's cap on my head, and started aft to the engine room.

Going by the captain's cabin I took it easy. There weren't any lights from the portholes, but clear out here I could hear a rustling and heavy breathing. Light or heavy sleeper, I wondered?

Harry MacGill was on duty in the engine room with Francis Garcia and two guys I hadn't seen before. About half of my crew had been on special liberty up until sailing time. They were the men whose job it had been to go down in the tanks after they had been pumped empty back in port. The tanks have to be washed out carefully with sea water to clear them of dangerous fumes. It's a dirty job, one that tanker sailors like least.

So they had been given extra liberty to have time to wash the oil taste out of their mouths.

I relieved MacGill, but he stayed around to chat without my asking which was a break.

Right then I wanted to find out whom I could maybe count on when the fuse got short on the dynamite, and I didn't know which ones in the crew were on Croup's side, if any.

Garcia volunteered to go up to the galley for a pot of Joe, and the three of us sat around drinking the black, bitter coffee.

"How long have you been on tankers?" I asked MacGill.

"Fifteen years, not counting wartime. I've sailed in them all, but this is the worst."

He was about ten years older than me, and I wondered why he didn't have his mate's ticket. He knew enough. At least he was a better man than most of the engine gang.

"How about you, Francis?" I asked the Panamanian.

"Two trips," he said. *"Es bueno.* Is very nice."

Panama had experienced a shipping boom after the U. S. and Panama had agreed to a deal whereby American business men could escape heavy taxation by registering their ships in Panama and flying under that Central American flag. One of the rules that went with the deal was that a certain percentage of the crew had to be Panamanian.

That little country hadn't had too many experienced sailors and few training schools, but the recruits learned fast and were good potential seamen.

Anyway, this rusting sieve of a ship probably looked pretty good compared to what he was used to.

"What kind of a skipper is Croup?" I asked them.

"You should know," said MacGill.

"What do you mean by that?"

"Hell, you've spent more time with him than has anyone else. This is my first trip. Everyone else's, too, it seems. He hired me out of a Sneaky Pete dive in Galveston where I was in hock at a two-bit crap table. I'd never seen the tub before or I would have given the stick man my clothes like they had suggested instead of letting Croup bail me out. It's the same with almost everyone on board. Beach bums, rummies, has-beens, that's what most of us are. Almost as if the captain was selling last chance tickets to men who couldn't afford round trip passage."

He hunched over with the coffee cup cradled in two hairy paws and eyed me speculating. It was too early to take him into my confidence and he could be a stooge for Croup. I looked him straight in the eye and played dumb.

"What's our destination?" I asked.

"Nobody knows that I've talked to. South America they say. That doesn't mean anything."

"Maybe we'll hit Panama," I said to Garcia.

His eyes brightened. *"Ciudad Panama*, Aiee!"

"Y Balboa," I chorused.

"Muchachas, mujeres, y señoritas," said Francis.

"Girls, women, and ladies," I translated.

"Tambien espousas."

"Wives, also," I laughed.

"It may be a long time before we see Balboa," said Harry.

"Don't bother us, man, we're just getting warmed up," I said.

"Well, don't work at it too hard," he said, getting up and walking toward the ladder. "The only heat you're going to have for some time is that tropic sun."

"Don't bank on it," I said, and I was thinking of a redheaded kid called Sheba. Sheba Ringle.

I finished my coffee and went aft in the engine room to a steel door that was fastened with a big padlock.

Behind that door our spare parts would be stored. I should have a key to it, and I didn't see why Croup wouldn't give me one. But if he refused … Padlocks aren't much. They serve only as a minor deterrent to amateur crooks. A professional can open any of them and so can a crowbar. People buy padlocks because it gives them a feeling of security.

When I turned around I caught Garcia watching me.

The men in the new watch had come on and were busy wiping down and working good, so there wasn't much reason for him to stick around.

But there he was.

I walked back and stood above him.

"Let's get some air," I suggested.

He got up without hesitation, and I let him go up the ladder ahead of me.

We walked to the poop deck and stood against the rail looking down into the dark at the foam churned up by the tanker's twin screws.

"Do you like the sea?" I asked him.

"*Si. La mare es una mujer hermosa.*"

"Speak English, Francis. You can speak good English if you want to."

"Yes. I learned English in school. It is taught there."

"Where did you hire on? The States or Panama?"

"In Panama. It is unlawful for the company to fire a Panamanian in the States. If that happens they must give me passage back."

"Then you have sailed with the captain before?"

"No," he hesitated, and I could feel him watching me.

I didn't think Croup would take the chance of letting me wander around without some kind of check. Garcia or MacGill or any one of the crew could be put to watch me.

I didn't say anything else, and pretty soon Francis began to talk. He spoke with a strong accent, but he had a good vocabulary for a guy who learned English in grammar school.

"Captain Croup is new to me. We sailed from Panama six months ago with crude oil for the refineries and docked here a long time ago. There were sixty men on board. Now we have thirty-five. The Americans were fired; only the Panamanians remained. Finally the captain left. No one gave orders. Each day I go to the commissary on the docks and draw food and supplies. It is charged, and one day I see a new name on the books. From that I know the ship has been sold. Every two weeks a man comes with our pay, and I keep on buying supplies at the commissary. That is all we hear from the new owner. The men get restless, they drink, they gamble, there is no work to do.

"Two weeks ago Captain Croup comes. He looks at the ship and goes away. Two days ago he comes back, and we start getting ready to sail. The men have not worked for five months, they grumble and are slow. All they want to do is get drunk here on the after-deck and play the drums and dance. We will have trouble with the crew if someone does not use the strong hand. They are homesick for the country we have not seen for half a year."

We stood silently for a moment.

"Where were the first and second officers all this time?" I asked.

"They were American and were discharged. You are the first officer we have had."

"You mean we don't have any other officer beside the captain and myself? No first officer?"

He looked at me. "Have you seen a first officer, a navigator, anyone?"

"How could I? I was in the captain's cabin until we sailed and then down in the engine room. Don't we even have a radio operator?"

"*Si*" he said calmly. "He came aboard by a rope and is crippled from the waist."

I stared from him to the monkey island and then let my eyes wander up the tall mast into the star-flecked night sky to where the radio mast disappeared into the dark.

Well, well, well. Things were taking on weight.

Then Garcia broke the silence.

"*Señor*, my people are not wise in many ways. Sometimes they are like children. When there is much whiskey and little work it is bad. There could be trouble. *Señor*, is this a bad ship?"

It was candid. A little too pat. I felt that I was on dangerous ground.

"Is there whiskey aboard?"

"*Si*. Among the supplies was much cheap rum."

"Then it's a bad ship."

"I hope you are wrong, *señor*," he said. He wished me a good night and walked off toward the crew's quarters.

This was a crazy bunch for sure.

The educated Latin; MacGill, who had probably lost more mate's tickets than I had years at sea; one cripple who was among other things a radio operator; a captain who looked like he grew up in the woodwork; one little girl who was tongue-tied, red-headed and stacked like a brick shipyard; and a mutinous crew.

It was going to be interesting when we began choosing sides.

I caught myself just in time with a cigarette between my lips, ready to strike a match. "You've been away from tankers too long," I told myself. "Hell may be close, but you don't have to rush it."

I flicked the unlit cigarette away and went back down to the engine room. The men in the new watch were dressed in shorts. It was dead-air hot down here without a breeze. I found an old beat-up fan in a locker and sat down to repair it.

This trip was a bad deal in more ways than one. We were dangerously undermanned, and in a crisis that would be fatal. Besides that all the advances that had been made to protect the sailor under the Seaman's Act of 1937 were being disregarded. No first officer, half a crew, bad food, dirty quarters, no ventilation. It was a throwback to sweatshop labor.

After an hour of tinkering I got the fan so it would work and plugged it in to the electrical system. It squeaked and clanked but stirred up the air some. With a little oil I made it run better yet, and the Latin sailors gave me a big smile of appreciation. All except one, that is.

He was a big Panamanian, darker than most of them, and I guessed he had a little rum in him already.

While the rest of the sailors grinned and stuck their sweaty faces up to the cooling breeze he just kept on wiping down the machinery with a handful of rag waste.

On my way out I looked over my shoulder and our eyes met. His eyes dropped a second before mine and he turned and spat contemptuously, then went back to his wiping.

It was okay with me. He was big, but that made him just my size.

I climbed the ladder out of the engine room and went forward to the monkey island, then up another ladder to the bridge.

The side windows were down and the door open to the pilot house, so I walked in. There was a Panamanian on duty at the wheel and no one else in sight.

"Buenos noches," I said.

The helmsman jumped but recovered himself fast and stood sideways at the wheel so that his body shielded the illuminated compass that stood there.

That was okay with me. I had already seen what our heading was. And it wasn't one I liked any too well.

"Vamos," he said with a hiss. *"Es prohibido sabre puenta."*

So Croup had given orders to keep the crew off the bridge.

"Para los officiales, tambien?" I asked.

"Si, for officer, too. You speak Spanish?"

"Un poco."

"Por favor, señor, vamos!"

The guy was scared. He was actually pleading with me to scram. I started to pass around him and go out the door across the wheel house, but he let go of the wheel and put his arms out.

"No pase," he cried.

For Christ's sake, he didn't even want me to cross the room.

"You heard him Brody," said a voice behind me.

I turned around and confronted the jelly mass that was Croup.

He stood aside, waiting for me. I shrugged and went out past him and stood at the railing.

"You're pretty busy," he said, when he joined me on the bridge. "Up at all hours, chatting with the crew, making fans work, inspecting the bridge. I never know where I'll find you next."

"You get around yourself," I answered.

"I'm supposed to, it's the captain's job. You are the engineer, your job is below deck. Let's keep it that way, okay?"

"Just getting the night air."

"I recommend the stern," he said.

"It's pretty dark back there. Lonely, too."

"That's what I mean, boy, that's what I mean."

We looked at each other a moment, then I went down the ladder and walked aft. Before I went into the engine room I stopped and studied the sky.

We should have cleared the Bay of Galveston by now and be out in the Gulf. I made a fast check on the north star, then sighted back forward to the bow. The catwalk made a fine straight line to sight by. I was giving the compass a double check. Croup could throw the compass off ten degrees to fool the helmsman, and from what I had learned so far he probably had. The crew is usually well informed as to their destination, and they would learn fast if the ship was going in the wrong direction.

I was making guesses again, but from what I could figure we were headed east southeast at about 110° or less. That made the figures on the compass read about what I figured they should, give ten degrees one way or the other.

I tried to remember all that I knew about navigating these waters, but it was hopeless. My job had always been wet nurse to Diesels, oil burners, and coal smoke engines.

One thing was clear; we certainly weren't going to stop at any of the Mexican ports. To hit Tampico we would have to be sailing due southwest.

It was beginning to look like a long trip.

I went below and watched the engines and dials and pressure gauges, but I didn't have anything to worry about. No matter what else was wrong with the ship she had good machinery in her insides.

I caught cat-naps until early morning and got to know the next two gangs as they relieved each other.

All things considered, I felt I could handle them, and we got along. They weren't such bad guys.

About seven o'clock I went up to the galley and sat down at the officers' table. This ship wasn't big enough for separate wardrooms for officers and men, and everyone ate in one big mess room.

I heard the door open onto the catwalk, but I didn't look up. It isn't very democratic, but you don't mix with sailors at chow time, and if it was Croup I wasn't going to say hello anyway. He took my appetite away.

Then a tray crashed, and I swung around and saw the rolypoly mess boy who had carried my sea bag into my cabin the day before. He was standing over what had been my breakfast all scattered around on the deck.

His mouth was hanging open, and he looked too stunned to talk. I looked back toward the open door and there stood the girl, Sheba.

She was wearing a full embroidered skirt and sandals. Her legs were bare and so were her soft shoulders that rose out of a peasant blouse that just barely managed to cling to her arms and cover her breast.

The red-blond hair was framed by the rising sun from behind, and it was as if she was wearing a flaming halo around her head.

I was pretty well stunned myself.

"May I come in?" she asked hesitantly.

I jumped up and pulled out a chair for her. Just for a moment I was thankful that there weren't several other mates occupying the other seats.

She came toward me with a nice swing to her walk and sat down. I hadn't noticed the way she moved before, and I don't know how the importance of Croup's automatic had obscured it. I think she was the most graceful girl I had ever seen.

The mess boy was still standing, gaping.

"Turn that hash in on a new model," I said, pointing to my spilled breakfast. "And make it two orders of everything."

He bent over the tray on the floor and started to pick up the broken dishes.

I looked at Sheba, and she returned my gaze for a moment before she smiled.

"Sleep well?" I said, and it came out in a croak.

It startled her.

"Wonderful. I love the ocean. But everyone acts so strange. I passed a couple of sailors outside, and I thought they were going to faint. What's wrong with me? Do I *look* strange or something?"

She had a low husky voice. It was pleasant. I wanted to tell her more than, no, she looked fine, but I probably wouldn't have many chances to be alone with her and there were more important things to talk about.

"You look pretty good to the men. They act that way because they didn't know you were aboard. Women never travel on tankers. It's not only impractical, it's against the law."

The mess boy came with our coffee, and Sheba pretended to be very busy measuring sugar into the cup.

Finally she said, "Why is it impractical?"

I reached down and lifted one of her pretty ankles into view. The sandal came off easily before she could wriggle her foot out of my grasp.

"See the nails in the heel," I pointed out. "It seems like a small thing, but you could set this ship ablaze in one gigantic burst of flame by kicking up a spark. We carry 129,000 barrels of highly volatile cremating potential. Have you ever seen a man burned alive? Besides being a gruesome, hideous sight, it smells bad."

I put the sandal on the chair next to me and grabbed her wrists before she knew what I was doing. There were about five silver bracelets there.

She wasn't quite as astonished when I slipped them off and put them next to the sandal on the chair.

I kept hold of her arm and with my other hand turned her wrist over and looked at her fingers.

I had a shock in store for myself. There was no engagement ring, no wedding band.

"Well, that's one piece of jewelry you won't have to quit wearing, anyway," I said.

"No, I guess not," she said, as composed as you please. "And I won't mind going barefoot either. In fact I'll love it."

We ate our breakfast in silence. She wasn't going to tell me anything even by accident, and I was more curious about her than ever.

Was she really married to Ringle?

Every time I looked at her round soft shoulders and the swelling under her blouse where her young breasts nestled, I hoped not.

And sometimes when she looked at me in her curious way I had the feeling that she wished not, too.

"Hang up, Brody," I said to myself. "This lady is out of your league."

CHAPTER FOUR

Neither Croup nor Ringle came in for breakfast, and that was okay with me.

I finished eating, said adios, and went out on deck. We were sailing under a full head of steam which would mean twelve knots maybe. That isn't fast, but it would get us there.

The sky was azure blue and the sun beat a hot tattoo off the steel plates of the deck and was hard on the eyes.

Altogether it wasn't unpleasant. When you are under way in the Gulf you get a fine moist, cooling breeze, and you can still get a tan. I like the Gulf weather. After the heat has sapped your strength the first few days out you find yourself coming back, and when you get used to it and the appetite returns you feel strong enough to kick donkeys to death.

I headed toward my cabin. There was a glimpse of white on the bridge that could be Croup. But I forgot about that when I saw the small group of men hanging around my cabin door.

Some of them I recognized from the engine gang. There were one or two new ones who were probably deck hands. I walked up to them, stood with my hands in my pockets, and waited.

"What the hell's going on, Brody?"

That was MacGill.

"What the hell you mean, what the hell. You ought to know better than to talk that way to an officer."

"Okay, okay. Do you mind if we ask what a dame is doing on board?"

"That's no dame," I said quietly, then caught myself. I had no call to get sore, and I had to be careful about this. I was in a spot. The men had come to me because I was the only officer who might set them straight. They couldn't just walk up to the captain this way. And I was going to need the crew on my side. Here they wanted info, and I had nothing to give them. Not yet, anyway. I had to handle this slow, delicate, and sure. "I don't know what she's doing aboard," I told them truthfully.

"Where are we going?" another sailor asked. "What's our first port of call?"

"I don't know."

There was some grumbling and a curse or two.

"What kind of ship is this, Brody?" someone else asked. "The deck gang is at half strength and we don't have a mate with a ticket or a licensed navigator aboard."

"I know it," I said. "The engine gang is small, too. I'll speak to the captain and try to get some answers. That's all I can do."

The guys all looked at me and I looked back. I was hoping they would believe me and give me the time I needed to find out what the score was.

They drifted away one by one, talking among themselves.

I went into my cabin, locked the door, and opened my sea bag. Down at the bottom I found a few maps and shuffled through them until I found one of the Gulf.

Over at my desk I spent an hour drawing as accurately as I could a compass on the map just outside the Bay of Galveston. Then I took a straight edge ruler and laid it on the compass so that it pointed along the heading we had been sailing early this morning.

It was going to be a shock when I told the boys. The ruler pointed out into the Gulf at an angle that would clear the lower point of Yucatan by thirty degrees. We sure weren't going to South America.

Ordinarily a ship leaving Galveston Bay and headed for Central and South America beats a path across the Gulf and swings around the tip of Yucatan, follows the coast line so it can put into small ports and unload its cargo. Then it returns the same way.

From what I figured a heading of south, southeast would do it. That would be 135° or thereabouts. We were sailing at 105° or 110°. There wasn't anything out there that you could sell fuel oil to. Even Cuba and the Caribbean islands were not in our way.

Out there was the Caribbean only, and beyond that the Atlantic Ocean. For some reason in that hot, sultry cabin I got a chill.

I put the map away and went out on deck again.

The bow was rising and falling with a steady plunge, and there was a taste of real salt air on my lips from a fine spray.

A couple of sailors were lounging on the tank deck watching the bridge. I looked up and saw Sheba standing there.

She made quite a picture. The breeze gathered her hair and held it back from the good lines of her face and whipped her skirt up around her bare legs.

Someone else was watching, too. It was the big *mestizo* who had ignored my fixing a fan for the engine room gang.

He was on the tank deck back toward the stern, and clear from where I stood I could tell what he was thinking.

He was naked except for a loin cloth, and there was a strong primitive air about the powerful way he was built and the way he stood.

I looked back at Sheba Ringle and saw that she was watching him, too. There was an expression on her face that stirred me.

If she hadn't been dressed in that pretty little peasant blouse and skirt then I would have sworn she was straight from the jungle herself.

High above her flapped the big red flag that tankers fly when they are carrying explosive oil.

The red of the flag didn't quite match the color of her hair, but it meant the same thing so far as I was concerned. She wore her hair like a signal, too. It was red for hot.

I shrugged and went to hunt up Garcia. There was a sailor sitting on a hatch by the ladder leading to the crew's quarters, and he put something behind him out of sight when he saw me.

I walked up to him and lifted him to his feet by his shirt front without saying a word and slammed him up against the bulkhead.

The bottle he had been nursing said *Rum* on the label in big, bold letters.

"Where did you get it?" I asked.

He was scared pop-eyed.

I gritted my teeth and tightened my grip until his feet left the deck.

"Come on, sailor. You're in trouble, real trouble. You know what it means to be caught drinking on a tanker."

"Let me go," he squeaked.

"Sure. Just as soon as you tell me where it came from."

"I brought it aboard with me."

I let him down and he took a deep breath and smoothed down his shirt.

"If I don't believe you it could mean prison," I said, "and I don't believe you."

I picked up the bottle, plugged it with the cork, and heaved it overboard.

"Well, imagine that," I said surprised. "I went and dropped the evidence."

The sailor sighed with relief. He knew I couldn't put him in the brig and prosecute him without the evidence.

"Thanks, Brody."

"Don't thank me, just think about it. If you remember where you got it, come see me."

I went down the ladder. I couldn't beat it out of him without losing the crew's confidence, and I didn't have time to search the whole ship.

Garcia was sitting on his bunk reading a manual on marine engineering.

"Hi," I said.

"Buenos dias."

"You were right last night. It is a bad ship."

He put the book down and looked at me.

"What do we do?"

"We tighten the screws. We put the crew to work. Hard!"

"Let's go," he said. "Where do we start?"

"Get the engine room gang together. I want you to pass the word around that the next man I catch with whiskey on his breath, whether on duty or off, is going to get my personal attention. From now on a guy who is dumb enough to drink around casing head oil is also headed for trouble. And tell the boys to wear clothes above deck. No more jock straps. The lady may be on board illegally, but she's here, so we have to act like gentlemen. I'll see you later in the engine room."

"Where are you going?"

"They say a woman on a ship is a Jonah, and it usually turns out to be true. I'm going to start pulling the plunger and try to find out who our Jonah is unlucky for."

He gave me a funny look, but I didn't have time to explain.

There were four cabins and the radio shack on the monkey island. I knew the captain's and mine. Ringle and Sheba would have one cabin, and the fourth should be empty. No one was in sight as I sidled past it and tried the door. It was locked.

I went on to the captain's cabin and knocked.

"Who is it?" came the captain's voice.

"Brody."

"Just a minute."

I cooled my heels for two or three minutes before Croup unlocked the door and let me in.

"What is it? I'm busy," he growled.

"Good. I like to see a man earning his pay. I need the key to the engine room storehouse."

"Why?"

"We have a loose gasket in number one. I need tools. What did you think I wanted to do, build my own boat?"

He was watching me closely. "I was down there half an hour ago," he said. "It sounded good to me."

"Look, pop, I don't care especially what your big deal is. My job is to keep the engines going. I hope you don't have a schedule to keep, because if we have to lay over while I take that engine apart after it busts a gut it will take a day and a half. Like I said, I don't care. I'm getting paid by the month."

He walked back into the cabin to his desk for the keys, and I was right behind him on my tip toes.

When he turned back with the keys in his hand he almost ran me down, and we stood there looking cross-eyed at each other with our noses touching.

"What the hell," he breathed.

He jumped backward fast, and when I brought him into focus again he had the automatic palmed. I laughed.

"You are fast for a big man," I told him. "Did you ever think of competing in the Olympic broad jump?"

"Get out," he shouted.

"The keys?"

He looked down at his hand where the keys hung from a ring. He tossed them to me. I turned and walked out and shut the door.

That had been a silly stunt. I could have paid a big price for one quick look at his desk.

But I had seen enough.

The edge of a navigating chart and sextant told a lot. Croup wasn't checking and double-checking our position for practice. A slob of a skipper like him wouldn't ordinarily be this careful about navigation.

And he had given me the storeroom keys because he was afraid of being slowed down.

I ducked down into the engine room where my fifteen grease monkeys were waiting. They really raised hell. Someone shouted, "How come a work party? What do you think this is, the goddamned Navy?" One guy in particular wanted to heckle. He kept chanting, "Captain Bligh, Captain Bligh."

I let them rave. Then when they got quiet I just told them to get busy. That's one redeeming feature of being over six five and ugly. Most people don't care to argue.

I didn't have much thought out in the way of jobs for them to do, but I got half of them started on chipping and painting, and the rest, except for the four who were on duty, were set to odd jobs. I didn't know how much time I had, but I wanted my boys to know they were a unit. It was the only chance I had to hold the ship together against the captain, if he pulled the deal I was certain he had in mind.

I got Garcia and MacGill, and we unlocked the storeroom and went inside. It was damned hot there and dirty. You could tell that the previous engineer had been proud of his profession. Just about every tool that was needed for minor repairs was there and in a special place.

But we were short on parts. It looked like Croup hadn't invested very much toward keeping the engines running for more than a short trip.

I cleared a place on a work bench, hopped up on it, and sat down. Harry and Francis found places and got comfortable.

I looked them over. A little steel-muscled Panama sailor and a stateside oldtimer were the two I had chosen as my right and left hand. Here it was. I had to trust them both, although I knew someone in the engine room watch was Croup's paid man. Was it Francis Garcia, or Harry MacGill, or that big Panamanian who hated my guts and showed it, or one of the other men? I didn't have time to find out. I just had to take my chances.

"Well, what is it?" asked Harry.

"I'm not sure I know," I said. "But I'm expecting trouble by the minute. I found a sailor with a bottle of rum sitting right out in broad daylight. We have an unauthorized radio man aboard and a girl. I thought at first the captain was taking a bribe to drop them off in South America. It wouldn't be the first time that a couple of hot articles flew the coop this way."

"Maybe that *is* what's going on," said Harry.

"I don't think so. Why don't we have a full crew? Why has the ship been stripped of everything but the bare necessities? What is that cripple doing in the radio shack? Who gave that sailor rum so that he thought it was safe to drink it in public? And why are we headed out to sea instead of to South America?"

"What?" shouted Francis.

"That's right. If we hold the course we've been sailing all morning we'll wind up in Africa. And there isn't one port along the way."

"Are you sure of that?" asked Harry.

"As best as I can judge."

"What do *you* think is going on?" he questioned narrowly.

"How should I know. I'm a sailor, not a goddamned detective."

"Please," said Francis, "let's keep this from the crew. If the South Americans thought they weren't going home they might riot. I hate to think of a riot aboard a tanker. What do you have figured out?"

"It has something to do with the airplanes up forward on the skid racks," I said.

"I've been wondering about those," grumbled Harry. "Just like wartime, transporting airplanes, walking around waiting for the plates to blow off the deck from carelessness. Never seen a worse run ship. It's almost as if the captain didn't care whether he docked us again or not."

"I don't think he intends to," I said.

They looked at me wide-eyed.

"Look, what *could* be his game. If he's running ammunition the wise deal would be to transfer his cargo at sea. Ordinarily that would be too expensive, but not if the planes up forward are brand new U.S. jets worth a couple of million bucks."

"Holy Christ," murmured Harry.

"But what about our fuel oil?" asked Francis. "You say the ship will never land. They wouldn't throw away a ship full of oil."

"For a pretty smart cookie you are missing a pretty obvious solution. Somewhere in the Atlantic we tie up to another tanker that has been carrying salt-water ballast. They pump out the sea water and suck in our oil, load the jets, sink this tub, and who's to know?"

They sat there letting it sink in. Finally Harry roused himself. He looked younger and tougher now that he saw the possibility of a fight. "What do you want us to do?" he asked.

"First of all I want to be sure. Get someone you can trust to open those crates tonight and see if they are really jets. Listen to the crew's talk. I want to know who is in with Croup. Francis, I want you to poke around and find that rum. Smash every bottle if you can. If this gang gets away from us once we're sunk. I'll bet there isn't a gun on board that isn't in the captain's cabin."

"Maybe no guns, *señor*," said Garcia, "but sometimes this is better."

He flicked his wrist, and a throwing knife with an eight-inch blade appeared in his hand.

He smiled a wicked smile as he put the knife back up his sleeve and went out.

Harry looked at me and shrugged. Then he produced a pair of gigantic brass knuckles from one bulging pocket and tried them on for size. With one lightning-like movement he put a three-inch-deep dent in a steel locker.

"Everyone to his own taste," he said, and left.

I shuddered. It was nice that they were on my side. If they *were* on my side.

I got up and rummaged around until I found what I wanted. It took me fifteen minutes to grind into dust a small pile of the metal I had found. I put the dust in a piece of paper and turned out the light, locked the door, and went over to stand near one of the huge twin marine engines.

There was an oil can equipped with a compression plunger standing on a shelf. I reached over, unscrewed the lid, and looked in like I was checking the load.

Nobody was looking, so I took the paper out of my pocket and dumped the emery dust in the oil can.

Then I screwed back the lid and replaced the can on the shelf.

When that engine was oiled a little emery dust would work its way inside and come in contact with a few ball bearings. It wouldn't hurt things bad. Just stop us dead, that's all.

I could repair the engine because I had noticed plenty of ball bearings in the storeroom. But Croup couldn't repair that engine and neither could anybody else. Only I would know where the trouble was. It was my insurance.

And it gave me time.

Just then a sailor came over to me.

"Hey, Brody, the captain wants you," he bellowed above the engine room racket.

I looked up the ladder and, sure enough, there at the top stood Croup. He jerked his head for me to come over, and he looked plenty annoyed.

I waved okay and told the sailor to get busy and oil up the engines. It appeared that I hadn't taken out my policy any too soon.

I went up the ladder to where the captain stood.

"It's time we had a talk," he said.

He led the way to his cabin and let me in.

The first thing I saw was Sheba stretched out on his bed. She raised up on one elbow and smiled at me.

My answering smile was half wiped off my face as Croup's blackjack klonked off my skull. The next time he hit me it sounded more like "plonk" … squishy, like an overripe melon, I thought, as I hit the deck with my face.

CHAPTER FIVE

It was hot, murky, and dark. There was somebody a long way off moaning, and I felt foolish when I realized it was me. I opened my eyes and let the Gulf sunlight sear my brain back to consciousness.

Croup was standing over me, hands on hips, legs spread far apart. He looked bigger than two mountains.

"Congratulations," I said.

"Why?"

"You have the real artist's touch with a sap."

"Yeah, I do it good. Just hard enough to make the head mushy and I don't even break the skin."

"Takes practice."

"You bet."

"What now? I'm too stringy for shark meat."

"Oh, I'm going to see that you stay alive. This was just a warning."

"Gee, thanks."

"But you gave me an idea, and to see that you know the warning is going to be backed up I'm putting a man outside the radio snack with a gun and another up on the bridge where he can watch the whole ship. Yeah, that was a good idea you had that we had joined the Navy. I'm passing the word down to the men that we are transporting government property and I am taking security measures to guard it. That settles the question of them asking where we're going and why the show of guns."

That settled my hash so far as trying to sneak into the radio room was concerned, and it would help him keep the men under control. Guns can make a guy hesitate.

He helped me to my feet, and I walked on rubber legs over to the bed and sat down. A strange notion kept nudging my mind, and then I remembered that Sheba had been lying here when I came in. That was a worse jolt than being dusted off. Up until now I had hoped she wasn't too much a part of the dirty work, that she was what she looked like, a nice kid.

"Where's the lady?" I asked.

"I excused her so we could have a little talk."

"What do you want?"

I pretended to concentrate on rubbing my swollen cranium back to life, but all the time I was studying Croup. What most interested me was where he was packing the automatic.

"I thought you wanted to play a hand in our little venture," he said.

"I do."

"Then why can't you keep your nose clean and stop bothering me? Every time I turn around I find you breathing down my neck—on the bridge, in my cabin. What do you think you are? A goddamned spy?"

"Don't cuss at me. You invite me in for a talk and then abuse me. Christ, my head aches."

"It should. I admire you, Ed. First time I *ever* had to tap a fella twice."

"Don't, I'll cry."

"To hell with you," he said, exasperated.

"I'm fed up too." I was sore now myself. "Why don't you tell a guy the score. I want to make a few extra dollars myself, but I still have my job to do. This tub is ready to come apart at the seams, and the crew acts like they want to jump overboard and swim for it. Some of the men may be dumb, but you can't fool them all that this cruise is kosher. How do you expect to deal with them and still keep the engines running?"

"It's all been thought of boy."

"Go on, tell me."

"Okay," he said, and as simply as that he opened up and told me the story. Part of it at least. "I have you to run the mechanical side. I handle the navigation and steering. We stay sober."

"So it *is* you that's passing out the rum."

"That's right. I'm giving out a few and only a few bottles a day, then more as we get close to our destination. By the time we're ready the crew won't be in any condition to say aye or nay."

"Some of them will be sober."

"Okay, but only a few. They will be taken care of."

That meant he had a couple of hired goons aboard that would materialize as gun hands when the time came.

I hesitated before I asked it, "It's the airplanes?"

"That's right."

We stared at each other. There was prickly sweat standing out all over his bloated face.

"You in or out?" asked Croup.

I shrugged, "What do you think?"

"I think not," answered a voice from the door.

I turned to see Ringle standing there supported on his aluminum elbow crutches. He closed the door and came across the room with that crablike swing that people who have lost the use of their legs are forced to effect.

He stood over us, glowering.

"What is this?" he asked. "Who told you to start spilling your guts?"

"We need him, don't we," complained Croup.

"You fool. We can use him, but we need him like an extra hole in the head."

"Now wait a minute. You may be a big operator where you come from, but you don't know a bathtub from a boat," said Croup. "You always need an engineer, and on this ship that goes double."

"Then it's your fault. I told you to pick a sound ship and a cheap one."

"That's like shopping for a virgin in a whorehouse. They don't exist."

I sat back and enjoyed myself. Maybe they would wind up killing each other and save me the trouble.

"I should have got a man for the job," Ringle said. "A two year old could have handled it better."

"You should talk, you gangster."

Ringle's metal crutch whipped around with a snap and caught Croup alongside the head. The blow smashed him to the deck where all his lard bounced once. Then he lay still, out cold.

Ringle looked at him a moment, then sighted along the crutch to see if he had bent it any.

"I hate myself at times like that," he murmured.

"Croup probably agrees," I said.

The cripple put the captain's chair back on its feet and sat down. "I dare say," he said pleasantly.

"I'm surprised you could do the job with that thing," I said, pointing to the aluminum crutch. "Looks pretty light."

"Combination of strong forearms and lead in the tip of the crutch. Here, feel the weight."

He handed me the crutch and I hefted it. Well-balanced weapon, that. Made a better club than a policeman's billy.

I gave the crutch back and he put it on the floor beside him. He unlimbered a king-size cigarette and lit up.

"I caught polio as a kid on the east side in Chicago. In those days they didn't know how to treat it the way they do today. Both legs were paralyzed. But it didn't hold me back. Lot of good men got to the top with a handicap. Franklin Roosevelt, for instance."

"What field were you in?" I asked.

"Bootlegging."

"Oh!"

"It was a long hard pull. Even the end of prohibition didn't stop me. What with one thing and another I managed to do all right. But I'm getting old, be forty-nine next month. I want to retire, settle down in some nice place with the wife, and raise a family."

"This is your last job, then?"

"That's right. You can't save much in the rackets. Don't you believe what they tell you about all of us big shots having trunks full of greenbacks. Big payrolls, grease the palm, fix the judge. I've made a lot of cops rich and never saved a dime."

"Tough," I sympathized.

"It sure is," he said, warming up to the subject. "Why do you know I had only a one million net on a nine million gross business in fifty-two. Hell, legitimate business men do almost that well."

"And the risk!" I exclaimed. "Tell me, how *did* you get hold of those planes?"

He smiled a secret smile. "Well, I'll tell you, Brody. Most people think a crook has got to be clever and have all kinds of fancy plans for a caper." He laughed. "But it's simple, just like swiping apples off a peddler's cart. Just put yourself in the way, that's the angle. Don't go where the apples are, wait for them to come to where you're standing and pick one off. What I did is get in touch with a friend in Washington left over from the last administration. We beat around the bush for months waiting for something worthwhile to come along.

"Finally we heard that a couple of new Army combat planes were going to be sent to one of the South American countries participating in the U. N. defense set-up. It took a lot of finagling to get the airplanes shipped by a new line that I had originated but then it's influence that counts. That's all there is to it. I stand to make enough profit to keep me the rest of my years. Not as much as I'd like, but enough."

"Too bad you couldn't steal the H-bomb."

"I looked into it," he mused.

Croup was stirring, and I shook my shoulders to try to rid myself of the hackles that had risen on the back of my neck. What he had said was probably true.

"Get the bottle of rum in that desk," said Ringle. "I think my partner is about to arrive."

I went to the desk and opened the top drawer. There was a bottle of rum lying on top of some papers. When I lifted the bottle out I could read what was printed on the top paper. It was the ship's manifest listing our cargo and registered destination. A while back I would have been interested because the papers would have confirmed my suspicions. All I could learn from them now was where we weren't going.

I took the bottle over to Croup and gurgled three or four fingers into his open mouth.

He sat up slowly and shook his head.

Ringle got to his feet and looked at us. "Let me give you a bit of advice. There is someone watching my back every instant. Even if you killed me it wouldn't do you any good. We are all in it together now, and that's that. I won't hesitate to have you put out of the way if you give me one more reason."

He hobbled out leaving two true believers behind.

I looked at Croup sitting on the dusty steel deck. There was an ugly purple-green welt rising on his cheek bone.

"What's the matter," I asked, "too old to duck?"

"He cheated," said Croup. "I thought he would hit me from behind."

We were silent for a while. Croup rubbed his face and drank rum.

"Has he got help?" I asked.

"Some of those sailors I never hired. They just showed up."

"I think I'd like a drink," I said.

"Sure, we have plenty of it aboard."

"Where?" I asked, after I had choked down a mouthful.

"In the extra cabin. But don't get any ideas. Ringle has the key, and he only gives me a bottle or two at a time."

"You don't trust me, do you? You think I'm going to try and stop you?"

"Uh huh," he answered, and took the bottle from me.

"Well, you're right. I'm going to stop you if I have to blow up the goddamned ship, you fat son of a bitch."

"Okay, okay, but just don't call me that."

"What?"

"Fat. I can't stand it to be called fat."

"Pardon me," I said, "and give the bottle back."

We drank our lunch and generally let our hair down. It was an armistice. We both knew that when I walked out of his cabin we wouldn't be able to turn our back to each other.

But Croup had the best of it. He also knew I wouldn't blow the ship up. There's only one thing worse than hell and that one thing happens right here on earth.

I once watched my best friend burn to death as he tried to swim away from a burning tanker. Cremated his head clean off.

I couldn't take that again, no matter what.

When I left Croup he was still sitting on the deck, drinking out of the rum bottle.

"Hey, Brody," he called after me.

"Yeah?"

"Stay out of the engine room from now on. You're through down there. Understand?"

"Sure, I understand."

I had missed noon chow and my stomach was doing flip-flops what with being sapped and swigging sour rum. I went forward on the catwalk and down to the tank deck, past the jets sitting snugly on their racks and stood on the bow looking down at the water. There was a good breeze and my head cleared in no time at all. In fact, I felt pretty good when she came to stand beside me. But I was still sore. I pretended she wasn't even there.

The prow of the ship cut the water nicely and laid a green phosphorous wave to either side as we steamed along. A porpoise and his mate appeared off the starboard side and they began playing around the ship, cutting back and forth so close that each time they passed it looked like we would hit them.

"Look at the big fish," said Sheba. "What are they?"

"Porpoise and they're mammals, not fish. Graceful, aren't they."

"Oh, yes. I've never seen anything like it. They swim like seals. Can we catch one?"

"Sailors don't fish for porpoise. They're supposed to be good luck. If you fall overboard and one of those giants spots you he will pay you a call. A lot of sailors have been pushed to shore by a playful porpoise."

"That's romantic."

"And mostly bosh. They will play around with you and have the power to toss you ten feet in the air. Probably fifty drowning sailors have been butted to death for every one that's been saved."

"Good heavens, what are those?"

I looked down in time to see the porpoise high-tailing it out of there. We were entering a sea covered with tens of thousands of Portuguese Men of War. They're ugly sea animals, like huge jelly fish.

I told Sheba what they were, and we watched them float by on all sides with their ugly, dangling, pink tentacles trailing slowly behind them.

She shivered, "I don't like them."

"Nobody does. If you touched one you would get a bad sting wherever you came in contact with one of those little red spots on their bodies. Enough stings and it would kill you. That's why the porpoise took off."

"You like the ocean, don't you?" she asked.

"Sure, it's my job."

"No, I think it's more than that. When you talk of the water and the animals in it you become serious. You really do care."

"Okay, have it your way."

"Now you're becoming nasty again."

"Is that any skin off your nose?"

She looked away from me. In a few moments I felt her hand on my arm. "What's the matter, Brody? What have I done?"

"Do you have to rub it in?"

"Rub what in? I had the idea this morning that you liked me. I felt you were the one man on this ship that I could be friends with. Now you've gone male on me."

"Gone male, hell," I said. "I've never been anything but male in my whole life. I'm talking about how pretty you looked as bait when I walked into the cabin ahead of Croup and gave him a chance to sink his blackjack three inches into my skull. That's what I'm talking about."

Sheba turned and looked out to sea.

I had her there, I thought.

She kept her back turned, and when she spoke again her voice was soft and troubled. "I didn't know that was going to happen. You don't have to believe it, but if I had known I would have warned you. When you fell all limp that way I thought he had killed you, and I screamed and jumped up and stood between you and Captain Croup. I was afraid he would hit you again. Then I stayed until you started to come to and then that awful man told me to go get my husband. I wanted to come back and help you. I don't know how, but I would have done anything for you. I can't stand to see brutality.

"My husband wouldn't let me go back with him. We had an awful fight about it. He doesn't tell me anything, and I'm afraid."

She sobbed and turned and threw herself against me.

"Oh, Brody, what's going on aboard this horrible ship?"

"Baby," I said truthfully, "I wish I knew."

Her little-girl body was soft against me, and I couldn't resist the temptation to put my arms around her and give us both a little comfort.

Then somebody whistled shrilly, and I saw MacGill and a couple of the Panama sailors watching us from the catwalk.

I shoved Sheba away from me a bit too roughly and coughed a couple of coughs to get my heart down out of my throat. All the time I was wondering just how good a marksman was her unbalanced husband with a pistol at sixty paces.

We were in plain sight of the radio shack and he could be watching us from the porthole at that very instant.

"I guess I'd better be getting to work," I said, forgetting that Croup had taken my job away.

"Do you have to?" asked Sheba. "It's boring alone. I don't have anything to do."

"You'll find something," I said and had a feeling she would, given enough rope. "By the way, what *were* you doing in the captain's cabin?"

"My husband told me to go there and stay. Some of the sailors had been standing on the deck below the catwalk and they whistled as I went by overhead. It made him mad, and he said he wanted me to stay out of sight."

"He's jealous, huh?"

"Not at all," she smiled. "It's just that with so many men around he doesn't want trouble."

If she had been a few years older I would have taken that smile as an invitation. The kid just couldn't know what it did to men.

And then again ...?

"Will I see you at dinner?" she asked.

"It's a date."

"Thanks," she murmured. "I don't know what I'd do if it weren't for you."

I watched her run to the ladder and across the catwalk and disappear into her cabin.

I walked aft and approached the engine room just to see what would happen.

I didn't try to go down the ladder, not right away. I stood there studying the sound of the big marine engines. Was that a slight grinding noise I heard already?

A sailor appeared on the ladder and passed me going to the crew's quarters. It was the very one I had told to oil up number one.

"Good man, good man," I said as he passed, and patted him fondly on the head.

He looked at me like I had a touch of the sun and hurried away.

I stood there humming and rocking back and forth on the balls of my feet.

"*No pase,*" said the big native that Croup had posted as a guard.

At least one of his boys was out in the open, and I was glad that it was one I could naturally dislike.

"Is that so," I replied.

"*No pase,*" he said again.

"Must be the salt air."

I went up to my cabin, and just before I went inside I noticed a gang of sailors back on the poop deck. They were playing cards and sitting around in small groups shooting the breeze. I recognized most of the engine gang.

So Croup had told them to take a holiday. No work and all play makes Jack a restless boy.

When the time came to start giving orders again I would have a hard time making them listen. In their eyes I had lost my authority.

I crossed my fingers and prayed that when the engines conked out I would be able to fix them.

That would be my one chance to win back their confidence.

I opened my cabin door and stepped inside. Garcia was sitting on my bed cleaning his fingernails with his big knife.

"Meet the new engineer," he said.

"So you're one of them," I said.

The knife whistled past my right ear and embedded itself in a wooden coat rack.

"You missed," I said quietly.

"No, *señor*. I never miss," said Garcia. He lay back on my bed and put his feet up. "You made me mad. If you call me that again I will miss you right between the eyes."

I let my breath out. My head was throbbing and I wanted to sleep.

"Why did Croup make you engineer?"

"I read the manual. He comes into the crew's quarters. He sees me reading the manual. He says, 'You there, do you know anything about engines?' I say, 'No.' He say, 'Good, I make you new engineer.'"

"So you told the crew to knock off?"

"No, Croup tells them, 'No more work today.'"

"So now you think you're going to move in here."

"No, I just come with news. I'm waiting for the MacGill now before we tell you."

I was just about at the end of my patience with him.

The door flew open with a bang that set my head to ringing.

"It's true," shouted Harry. "Every goddamned word you said."

"No," I said, holding my poor head in my hands.

"That Ringle ain't no radio operator. Not a real one anyway. He doesn't even have a license. I think he's some kind of a crook."

"Gee, Harry," I told him. "You may have something there."

Harry yelped, "Well, what are we waiting for?"

"Go take a look in front of the radio shack and up at the bridge," I said. Harry went out and then came back in fast. "Guys with guns. The ship is crawling with guys with guns."

"That's right. And Ringle has a lot more where they come from. Do you want to try and take this ship now?" I asked.

"No," he said, deflated.

CHAPTER SIX

After Harry and Francis left, I stripped and lay on the cool sheets of my bunk. The question seemed to be, "Where do we go from here?"

Neither one of my conspirators had been able to come up with an idea. We had discussed trying to storm the bridge, but with only the three of us and one or two others it was out of the question. In the first place it would be necessary to control the engine room, too, and while that could be done it wouldn't leave enough of us to take over those guys above decks. At the same time without guns there wasn't any way to keep the opposition from walking right down to the engine room and reclaiming it and our lives as well. It would take hours before the engines conked out, and that was our big hope of stopping the ship and throwing Ringle off schedule. But the longer those engines ran the worse beating they would take. It wasn't a pleasant thought.

The radio was a worry, and I wondered if Ringle really knew how to operate it. Either he was in touch with another ship that was standing out in the Atlantic or he wasn't.

That other ship was important. It could be a big, fast tanker belonging to Russia or a satellite country, and the crew would be large, well armed, and sailing under strict military rule. I wouldn't have a snowball's chance in hell if we got that far. A little checking with a navigation map and the proper instruments would tell me how much time we had before the rendezvous, but I didn't have the right map or instruments.

I dropped off into a fitful sleep.

I woke up in a sweat and it was dark. My watch read seven o'clock and I was still alive. A shave, cold shower, and fresh clothes brought the color back to my face, and I noticed I was getting my tan back after those idle weeks on the beach. I headed for the mess hall.

It was an odd kind of feeling I had, but if her husband and Croup would get themselves lost it would be enough like a dinner date to satisfy me. There's nothing like dinner with a beautiful girl to set a guy up right.

But I was all alone at the officer's table again. Either she had eaten early or she was late.

The roly-poly mess boy brought me a dish of chilled canned fruit, and

I spooned it in listlessly keeping an eye on the door.

"What the hell, Brody," I thought, "you sure are getting yourself in an uproar. She's married. Any babe who would cheat on her husband would cheat you too. Now here you are getting hot for a girl fresh out of finishing school with a husband who doesn't need an excuse to start shooting. Use your head, man."

I tore my eyes away from the door and concentrated on dinner, but the mess boy kept hanging around my table, giving me a lot of extra service and being generally annoying.

A couple of the sailors were watching from the end of their long table, and one of them yelled, "Give him a tumble, Brody. He's in love with you."

I picked out a banana from the bowl in the center of the table and threw it just as he turned to laugh with the others, and it bounced off the back of his skull.

"One more remark like that and I'll come over there and make you eat more than words."

They all got very, very quiet and I turned to the mess boy. "Go ahead and serve my dinner," I told him. "But cut out the fancy stuff."

He was a little scared, and he hurried away to do what I told him.

From then on the only stir in the room occurred when the door opened and Sheba came in. She was in a white, tight-fitting dress that emphasized her slim hips and round buttocks. There were hundreds of little pleats low on the skirt of the dress that moved subtly when she walked and made her hips and thighs come alive sensuously.

Behind her Ringle stood supported by his crutches. I could tell it was the first time he had come into the mess hall by the curious way the crew studied him.

He had guts, I'll say that for him. He stood there and let them examine him. It was as if he were saying, "Here I am, you peasants. Take a good look, and when you're through you'll know I'm a better man than you."

Then he swung crablike across the room and lowered himself clumsily into a chair.

One of the tough looking U.S. sailors followed him and stood near our table with his arms folded. There was a bulge inside his shirt. This was probably his personal body guard and one more face to put on my mental list. A few more days and I would know who all of them were. If I had a few days.

Sheba greeted me bashfully and Ringle didn't say boo.

We ate in silence. The other sailors drifted out gradually, foregoing their usual coffee-time conversation and evening card games. It was plain that the little cripple and his beautiful woman made them feel self-conscious and uncomfortable.

I finished ahead of Sheba and leaned back to fire up a cigarette. The mess boy hustled in with a fresh cup of coffee for me, and I sat and studied Ringle.

He kept his head lowered over his plate and shoveled the food in automatically without any apparent savor. Fuel, that was all it was to him. Fuel to run his warped mind and heavy muscular shoulders. Years of hoisting his body around on crutches had made his arms, shoulders, and neck as big and powerful as a wrestler's. He could probably crush a man to death with those arms.

"What's the news?" I asked him.

"How's that?" he said, looking up.

"Over the radio. Usually our radio operator monitors the air-waves and posts the news each day: baseball scores, juicy murders, that kind of junk."

He just lowered his head and went back to shoveling in the fuel.

Well, I had failed to find out if he could operate the radio.

The mess boy fussed around the table, but I caught his eye and he faded into the background.

When he was gone Sheba stared after him and muttered, "I hate him!"

I was surprised with the vehemence of her tone.

"Why?" I asked.

"He is unnatural. Now I've lost my appetite."

From outside came the faint sound of a guitar and the wail of someone singing a South American love song.

"What is that?" asked Sheba.

"I suppose the boys are getting together back on the fantail for a South American jam session. They have to make their own entertainment out at sea."

"I'd like to hear them," she said. "Can I?"

"I suppose so."

Ringle wasn't paying any attention.

I knew that the songs would be plaintive and sad at first; then as they got warmed up the narrative would get rough and finally downright vulgar. There would be a little solo dancing to the solid beat of Afro-Cuban rhythms drummed out on the long, cylindrical tom-toms that always mysteriously appeared on ships manned by natives. It would be exciting for Sheba, and since she didn't know the language she wouldn't be offended by the songs. I could make some excuse to take her away before the dancing got too dirty. Her beauty wouldn't be any calming influence on the imaginations of the men.

We got up from the table and went out into the balmy tropic night. The sky was star-studded and a big yellow moon threw a splash of yellow on the water toward us from the far horizon.

It was romantic, all right, romantic and exciting and a helpful nudge at all the primitive urges that push men and women toward each other.

We walked toward the fan tail in step, and it seemed natural that our arms touched and I found her hand gripped in mine.

The men were grouped around a guitar player who was singing a ballad about an unfaithful woman and her lover's undying devotion. Most of his attentive audience was South American and they wore singlets, loin cloths, and as few clothes as possible. I could see that all my orders were being systematically disobeyed.

Moonlight glistened on dark bodies as the men swayed to the music and murmured encouragement to the vocalist.

Sheba stood close beside me and watched with rapt attention as one man after another took the floor and sang a song native to his tribe or region.

This went on and on until at what appeared almost to be a preconceived signal we heard the soft tattoo of bongo drums, and the men parted silently to reveal a seated figure. He was beautifully built with strong, clean limbs and a fine head. He was crouched cross-legged on the deck and between his knees was gripped a wooden cylinder open at the bottom and covered across the top with a thin, tight-stretched piece of cowhide.

His fingers barely caressed the drum, but with an almost imperceptible tensing or relaxing of his finger tips on the cowhide he was able to bring forth a wide variety of sounds, now deep, resonant, demanding and then staccato, shrill in urgent tattoo.

Several men began to shuffle their feet to the rhythm of the drum. Another bongo player seated almost out of sight took up the basic beat and for a moment the two bongo players competed, throwing a variety of rhythms out at each other. The sounds began to be more intense, demanding.

Sheba, standing close beside me, was moving with the tempo, and I could feel it myself.

A sailor dressed only in a loin cloth jumped into the circle of men before us with a piercing yell and they fell back to give him room. It was the big native who was on Croup's payroll.

He began slowly to dance by swaying his body. I could tell right then he was capable of putting on a good show.

He moved up to directly in front of us. His body swayed and undulated, and his feet were moving under him at sixty miles an hour.

It was sex personified, no mistake about it. And it was Sheba he was dancing it to.

"Come on, lady," I whispered in her ear. "It's time I took you back."

But she didn't hear me.

Her body was swaying with the bongo rhythm in subtle, sure movements.

I took her arm and shook it. Then I noticed her eyes. They were riveted on the man dancing before her. It was as if they had hypnotized each other.

I put my arm around her waist. She struggled forward, but I lifted my arm until her feet cleared the deck and carried her away from the circle of chanting men. Her body didn't stop moving even when I carried her all the way to the bow and set her down.

Finally I had to slap her face.

She came out of it and fell against me, panting. I put my arms around her again, only gently this time. She shivered and caught her breath, then looked up at me. I bent my head to kiss her, but she pulled away.

"Please, Brody," she said.

I felt like a high-school punk who had just got the shaft from the home-coming queen.

"Okay," I said. "I should have known better."

"Don't be mad. I wanted you to kiss me, but it's wrong. You don't know anything about me."

"What's there to know?" I asked. I leaned my arms on the railing and looked out at the dark rolling sea.

"I know how you hate my husband and all he stands for."

"I don't see how that affects you. Somehow I can't believe you are a part of it."

"But I am."

I looked at her, getting a little sick inside.

"Not a part of what he is doing aboard this ship," she continued. "He forced me to come with him on this trip." She hesitated for a long moment. "But my father is a man just like Ringle. They were partners in the beginning. Ringle went on to be a sort of Mr. Big. My father did well enough to send me to good schools and give me everything I ever wanted. About a year ago they got together again in a meeting in Miami. Father wanted something from Ringle, and when Ringle saw me, I was what he wanted."

"And your old man didn't kill him?" I asked, aghast.

"On the contrary, my father was honored. To him it was like marrying me to royalty."

"Christ!"

"That's how I was afraid you'd feel," she said, and turned her back.

I put my hands on her shoulders and turned her around. "I think you've had a bum deal."

"I don't need your pity."

I looked at her soft pretty face and the wind-blown red-gold hair. I wanted to believe her story more than anything. "It's not pity that I feel."

We melted into each other and her kiss was full, mature, and exciting.

She pushed me away suddenly as if she were afraid of herself.

"Maybe we had just better talk," she said.

We stood arm in arm and watched the bow cut the waves. The foam that swirled back from the prow was white in the moonlight and gleamed brilliantly with millions of phosphorescent specks.

"What is that?" asked Sheba.

"I've never known for sure, but it must be minute particles of minerals. Pretty, isn't it?"

"Beautiful, the ocean is friendly and exciting when you share it like this."

We were silent for a while, until I felt Sheba's back quiver under my hand.

"What are you thinking about?" I asked.

"That dancer and the drums. It was tremendous. I love dancing. It's probably the only thing I know."

"Do tell."

"Don't make fun of me," she pleaded. "I can dance."

The bongo drums were still beating out back on the fan tail, and Sheba cocked her head to one side and listened to them. Then she smiled devilishly and said, "Shall I show you?"

"Sure," I said, preparing myself for at best a pitiful hop-skip and one-hip-hula routine.

Sheba moved away from me and stood, head down, arms relaxed. She stayed like that about six feet from me for what seemed like minutes.

Then slowly her hips began to sway, ever so slightly, and her feet started a quiet shuffle. Her head remained down, but I could see her eyes pressed tight closed and strain building up around her soft mouth.

Her arms began to rise, palms caressing her legs, thighs, and belly as they rose.

The rhythmic switching of her hips became more pronounced, and her feet moved faster as the arms came higher. Then her head came up and the tense look was one of complete, happy, yet sensual detachment.

Jesus, I was beginning to get interested.

Her arms went high in one spasmodic movement, and she paused there, head high, with eyes that looked far away beyond me into the moonlit sky.

The pose was tremendous. Her back was arched, and the thin cloth of her dress stretched tight across her breasts and thighs.

I was swept back in time to an era of worship to gods we had long forgotten.

How long the young girl hung there, paying homage to an unseen queen of love, I don't know, because I was caught up in her emotion too. It's hard to remember in what sequence things happened next, because when she came down off her toes and straining thighs she did a dance of sex to end all dances.

The next thing I remember was her in my arms, moaning and clawing at my back.

"Let me go, please let me go," she begged.

I had to shake my head to remember where we were.

We were both wringing wet, and it wasn't the salt air that had done it.

"Oh, please, Brody," whispered Sheba.

I could have kept right on, but I released her and she stood there panting and trying to catch her breath.

Finally she said, "Well, did I show you?"

"Yes, you showed me."

"Am I bad, Brody?"

"No, I don't think you're bad."

She gave me a quick peck on the cheek and whispered, "I couldn't live if you thought that." Then she was gone.

It was almost unbelievable that there was so much power crammed into that little girl. And I knew how she had developed such a terrific figure. A dance like she had done would have knocked me out, and she was just breathing good when it was over.

She was a human powerhouse, and it scared me a little to think what she must be like in bed.

And if she was a powerhouse, did that make Ringle a dynamo? He couldn't be.

That thought was comforting. It was doubtful if there was one man any place that could take care of all of that, let alone Ringle.

In fact she probably didn't make life any more easy for him.

When I started for my cabin I found that my legs were a trifle shaky. Hell, she wasn't making *my* life any easier either.

CHAPTER SEVEN

The noise that woke me up scared me half to death. I thought the sea was opening up.

Then there was complete silence as I sat up in bed. Somebody started pounding on my door again and yelling their head off. I got up and asked who it was.

Some sailor screamed that Croup wanted to see me right away and to get dressed.

I smiled. Above all that racket outside, I noticed the absence of one sound. No engines. We were floating free with the current, and our forward up and down roll was gone. In its place was a lurching sideways motion that made you want to grab out to keep your balance.

"Well," I thought, "it sure had taken long enough. That bone-headed captain probably let the laboring, grinding engines run until they just couldn't run any longer." And suddenly I found myself feeling glad that I was going to be elbow deep in engine grease again.

I put on my oldest pair of khaki pants and my old weathered, beat-up mate's cap and went out on deck.

It looked like the whole crew was up. Men were scurrying up and down the engine room ladder in the ghostly light of lanterns. Black smoke poured up from the engine room, and Croup stood back there by a fourteen-inch search light bellowing orders.

I walked back and stood beside him. "What's the matter," I asked. "We run out of gas?"

"You crazy Irish bastard," he screamed. "What have you done to those engines?"

I looked wide-eyed and innocent. "Who, me? I haven't been down there since early yesterday morning."

"You sabotaged me, that's what," he yelled, but in a somewhat quieter voice.

"How could I," I pointed out. "It was your orders that I stay out."

He stared at me while he tried to make up his mind. Now he was undecided.

"If I hadn't been told to stay away maybe I could have prevented it."

"So help me, Brody," he breathed, "if I thought for one minute that you had anything to do with it, I would kill you on the spot."

"But you can't. Then you wouldn't have a mechanic left good enough to get you sailing again."

"You have me in a fix. I don't really know you didn't wreck us, and still I have to send you down there to work on the engines. But so help me, I'll be looking over your shoulder every minute, and if you make a false move I'll put my gun to the back of your head and pull the trigger. You're going to work, Brody, like you've never worked before. You're not going back to bed until we are under way again if it takes you sixty days and sixty nights."

"Not just yet, I'm not," I said as calmly as the butterflies in my stomach would allow.

"And why not, big boy?"

"If I'm going to get my job back as engineer I want things my way. I give the orders in the engine room."

"Fair enough. Let's get started."

"Okay, tell your boys to turn off all unnecessary lights and then get out of here. I need elbow room."

I went down into the engine room while Croup was still giving orders. It smelled bad down there from the burned-out bushings and rubber-wrapped wiring that had got hot enough from friction to heat up and smoke.

Harry MacGill was standing before number one with a dejected look on his face.

"We'll never get her going," he moaned.

"That's bad?" I asked.

He gave me a surprised look. "Did you ..."

"Now would I do a thing like that?"

He laughed, "I never would have thought of it myself, and if it was your idea, why I might say we still had a chance."

"Have you found any guns," I asked, moving close so we wouldn't be overheard.

"No, and neither has Garcia. Even the captain's boys have been going around clean. But we know who most of them are now. I say to hell with trying to fix the engines until we've cleaned up on Croup, Ringle, and their mob."

"That's just what we won't do. The sailors don't bunch up where we can take them all at once, so there'll always be somebody to warn the captain. And we don't have enough men to try and overpower them separately. Besides, once Croup starts throwing lead there's a good chance a stray bullet would ricochet off the plates and blow us all up. We have to think of something else."

"Have you any bright ideas?"

"No."

"Well, you'd better. We don't have much time."

Croup came up behind us, and I saw the warning in Harry's eyes.

"Get Garcia," I told Harry in a business-like voice. "Turn out all the lights on the ship that aren't absolutely necessary. Check the storage batteries and come back and tell me how long we are going to have power without a generator. Then break out every piece of manually operated fire-fighting equipment you can find. It would be just our luck to have a fire while we don't have the pumps working."

"Anything else?"

"Yeah. Put some of the wipers to work spreading out all the tools we have and get plenty of waste here. And I want an inventory of all the spare parts in the storeroom. I'll bet there hasn't been an inventory taken in six months on this tub."

"Right," said Harry, and hurried off.

"What do you think is wrong?" asked Croup.

"Come back in ten hours and maybe I can tell you."

"Ten hours," he exclaimed.

I could have laughed, because he looked worried sick.

With the help of a couple of my wipers I got the heavy cowling off number one and took a look. Without even tearing her down I could tell she was through. At least, I thought, I'd never have the time or tools to fix her out at sea on this trip.

"Okay, clear this junk away and open up number two," I said.

"What's up?" bawled Croup. "Aren't you even going to try that one?"

"No."

"Come on, Brody, I wasn't kidding about what I told you topside."

The crew stopped working to listen. Sailors can smell blood trouble, and they aren't above watching a man get killed. They were just curious enough to want to see which one of us it was going to be.

"Which would you rather have," I asked, "some power from one weak engine or no power from two dead ones?"

"Can you get number two working?"

"Maybe."

"No maybes about it. And after you get us moving on number two you can stay down here and play nursemaid to number one."

I motioned to the boys and they started unscrewing the bolts that held the cowling over number two.

This one didn't look so bad. There was still insulation on most of the wires indicating she hadn't heated up so bad. I tore into her like a madman, dismantling everything that would come loose and handing it to a wiper to clean in kerosene and oil.

It took hours to get down inside the engine to where the trouble was, and by that time I had parts spread out around me on rags until it looked like a secondhand junk yard.

Croup was getting bored, and he was on his third pot of black coffee trying to keep awake.

I was just an anxious as he was to get one engine working, because a tanker without power is no place for people to be.

All we needed was a high sea, and the *Patty Sue* would jump around like a frog on a hot frying pan.

A T-2 tanker like this one has a bad habit of letting its back end come around in rough water anyway, and sometimes these equatorial storms are enough to split bigger and better ships that breach the waves and catch one amidships.

"Say, tell me," I said to one of the Panamanians working beside me. "When is the rainy season off Yucatan? I've forgotten?"

"Last month, this month, and next month," he said matter-of-factly.

"Oh!"

I hurried the work along. You don't get much warning about storms this far out in the Gulf, because they shape up too fast. And Ringle probably had the radio tuned into some stateside jazz band instead of monitoring the coast guard weather station wave length.

All we needed was good old number two. That would give us steering power and not much more. Croup wouldn't be able to go to the races on just one engine.

Things were getting to the point where I could take a breather and let the helpers do some of the reassembling, when Croup gave up and decided that he'd had enough.

"Satisfied that I didn't wreck the engines myself?" I asked him with a grin.

"You're okay with me, boy, but I'm going to have some explaining to do to Ringle."

"Why do you let him tie cans to your tail?" I said.

"Nobody does that, Brody. I'm master of my own ship."

"And Ringle cracks the whip at the pay window."

I poured myself a cup of his coffee and weighed my next words carefully before I spoke.

"You know, captain, you may have a real sweet deal in this and again, maybe not."

"What do you mean?"

"If that tanker you plan to rendezvous with belongs to the country I think it does you may not get the welcome you expect. From what I've heard they don't live up to their bargains."

"You trying to scare me? I wasn't born yesterday. Ringle has it fixed."

"So do a lot of people who go over there and are never heard of again."

"We don't make the whole trip," said Croup. "North Africa is where I'm getting off. I like you, Brody, sometimes. You're smart. Why don't you start co-operating with us, and maybe I can get you a big cut. Ringle will listen to me."

"But I'm already in," I said in mock surprise. "I get two hundred bucks for keeping my mouth shut."

"To hell with you," said Croup, and he stomped out.

After he was gone I went to the head of the ladder and stood letting the fresh air brush my face. It was dawn, and although it was cool now I could tell that this day would be a scorcher.

"Look," said Garcia, who had come up the ladder behind me.

Off the starboard side the full, white moon was just sinking. There was a clear ring of haze around it.

"Monsoon weather," he said.

I shrugged. Not much could happen now that could make things worse. In fact a hurricane would be a more welcome sight than a tanker flying a Russian flag.

I felt like going to my cabin for some shuteye, but I wasn't sure how serious Croup had been when he told me to work on number one.

Anyway, it would be a good idea to stick around when I had the engine room to myself.

"How many men do you think we can trust?" I asked Garcia.

"Not many in the engine room. He put most of his men down here with us, because it is the most important part of the ship. The deck hands did not count for much, so they are not killers. But of us there are only five or six."

He sounded discouraged, and that wasn't like him.

"Okay, spill it. What's up?"

"Croup has promised every man who will not make trouble a fat bonus and safe passage to North Africa."

"And you believe him?"

"No, but what can we do against guns? They outnumber us three to one, and every day more go over to their side."

"It looks grim all right."

"And I was walking by the radio room when I looked through the open porthole and saw the cripple Ringle and two others oiling what you call Thompson machine guns."

"Yeah?" I was interested in that. "Which porthole was open?"

"The one forward on the port side."

"Now if we had one of those, things would be different."

"*Si*, but ..." He shrugged his shoulders dejectedly and did not finish. I guess he realized that his throwing knife was now out-gunned.

"Let's go below," I said. "We have work to do."

MacGill and a couple of others were still assembling number two, and the rest were lounging around and acting bored.

Garcia, MacGill, and I got the engine running, and we could feel the ship take hold and start sailing on course again. Croup wasn't going to make many knots, but then maybe he didn't have to.

We spent the early morning hours sweating over the other engine to see if we could possibly ever make it run again, and I gave it a fifty-fifty chance. I told my boys to turn in, then went up on deck and stretched, looking into the hot sun and wishing I were a cowboy or railroad gang foreman. I had probably been one kid in a thousand who had never wanted to be a cowboy, but right then I was seriously considering it.

When I turned around and headed for the ladder that led to the monkey island, I stopped and rubbed my eyes.

Sheba was standing outside her cabin door at the rail. She was posed for me so that I would full appreciate the costume she had whipped up. She was barefooted and barelegged and just about bare all over.

The shorts that she wore were tiny and tight. They rode high up the side of her leg and just covered her buttocks. The top barely reached her navel, and from there up there wasn't enough to blow your nose on. She had made a halter out of a shirt that was tied in a knot below her breasts. The way that halter gaped open you could see all the cleavage there was and the material was just thin enough to let you know that her breasts were pink-tipped and luscious.

She watched me approach with a devilish grin on her schoolgirl face, and when I stood glaring down at her she still managed to look innocent.

"How do I look?"

"Like Bubbles la Tour without the rhinestone in her navel."

"Come off it, Brody," she laughed. "I was hoping you would take me to see the men dance again tonight."

"In that costume?"

"Why not?"

Why not, she asks. I'd be busier than a one-legged man at a pants-kicking contest keeping everybody's meat hooks off her.

"I'm going to be occupied," I said.

"Well, then maybe I'll let Captain Croup have a date," she said pouting.

"Croup!" I said. "Has that big gorilla been making passes at you?"

"Not passes. I've known him almost as long as I've known my husband."

"What does that mean?"

"You figure it out," she said, and flounced off.

A couple of sailors grinned at her as she passed and she smiled back, then looked over her shoulder to see if I was watching. One of the sailors acted drunk. He *was* drunk.

A squatty rum bottle swung by the neck from his hand. He offered Sheba a swig, but she kept on going, hurrying a little.

The sailors had me worried. When I looked again I noticed that all of them had bottles. Ringle knew what he was doing, and he wouldn't have given out liquor before he was ready. That meant that even with our slowdown we must be near the rendezvous.

Evidently he wasn't taking any chances on getting too near the crowded shipping lanes around Cuba and the Caribbean islands.

He wouldn't want any interruptions while the other tanker was sucking our tanks dry, even if it only took a couple of hours to do it.

My best guess was that it would happen at night, and with the liquor being passed out freely that meant tonight. And what could I do about it? Nothing.

Even wrecking the engines hadn't helped. All we had done was float for a few hours while Ringle had radioed our position to the other ship, so that it could close in on us instead of our going to it.

And then I got another one of my bright ideas accompanied by hot flashes and cold chills.

It could get me killed and still not be any more successful than my other attempts. But I had been lucky so far.

I forgot about sleeping and headed back to the crew's quarters.

Harry and Francis had both turned in, but I rousted them out and we went to the engine room together. I told them my plan as we unlimbered the tools again.

"You're crazy," Harry said.

"Do you have any better strategy," I asked.

"No."

"Then let's get at it."

"I don't think we can ever fix the engine," Harry said.

"Okay. Take off and hit the sack," I told him. "I don't want anyone looking over my shoulder who is going to gripe all day."

"I'll stick."

"That's better. Hand me that Stilson wrench."

We were tired but we tore into that engine like college boys going on a panty raid. It looked impossible, but if we could make it run for just a few moments at the right time somebody would get a big surprise. All we needed was a one-shot chance.

"Garcia," I said.

"*Si.*"

"Is there one man you could trust your sister with?"

"*Si*, I don't have a sister."

"Get him up on deck and have him watch the radio shack. I want to know everything that goes on up there."

He left and Harry and I went on with the work. It was a hot day to spend in the engine room. The little fan I had rigged up only stirred enough air to keep you from losing your mind.

When Garcia came back and reported that our lookout was in place, he brought some news.

"The sea is running high. The monsoon is near."

"Maybe they will have to lay off tonight and not risk tying up to us," said Harry.

"And maybe it will hurry them into pulling the job sooner," I reminded them both.

We kept at it through lunch, and as much as I wanted to go topside so that I could see Sheba when she went to the mess room I stayed below and fought the grease, oil, and worn parts that had been an engine. I wanted to talk to Sheba. Sure, I had no strings attached to the girl, but she was headed for trouble, dressing that way and fooling around with men. There were other reasons I didn't like it, too, but I wasn't letting myself think about them.

Harry went up and brought back some chow, and we kept on working. Croup looked in later in the afternoon and tried to oil me up again by telling me he sure had me all wrong. The way I was working proved it.

I let him talk.

From the sounds above deck we could tell the crew was getting out of hand, and about five o'clock when I went up to take a breather I got a shock. About half the men were loaded with rum and raising hell.

And the other half were gathered around the bridge radio shack and airplanes in small grim groups.

Most of them wore forty-five service revolvers, but one of the boys on the bridge and another at the door of the radio shack held Thompson sub-machine guns.

Ringle wasn't taking any long-shot bets that I could cause trouble this late in the game. But he was tipping his hand to me also. This made it positive that tonight was the night.

This wasn't going to change my plans any. Only one thing would be different. I didn't know how the hell I could get through that gang around the radio shack to wreck the radio. Maybe I wouldn't need to. The place where Ringle had made his mistake was that he didn't know ships. There were ways of fouling him up that he would never guess.

Ashore, Ringle would be the man to fear. He was heartless, cruel, and smart about his gangster profession. But aboard ship it would be Captain Croup who would ruin all the marbles in the end. I looked out at the tossing sea that was growing rougher by the hour and prayed that Ringle would go on playing it close to his vest.

Because if Croup caught on to what I had in mind the armed guards would be re-deployed.

What the hell did I care about those airplanes sitting up on the bow? They could have all the guards there that they wanted. Before I went below I glanced idly at the auxiliary steering station on the poop deck.

It was out of sight of the bridge, behind the hatchway leading to the crew's quarters. From where I stood I could see the big wheel and the emergency signal box that could send signals to the engine room and control the motion and speed of the ship.

Ringle hadn't thought to put guards there.

The number one engine still looked hopeless. We were cruising along at the three or four knots that number two could produce, but for my plans we needed a good twelve knots of thrust. Even if it was only for a couple of minutes, we needed that power.

So that's the way Harry and Francis and I patched and improvised and put her back together. We wouldn't even be able to test. If Croup heard one peep from number one he would use it himself, and then we would be lost.

Somehow we got it back together in the next couple of hours and just said a prayer. I told the boys to leave the cowling off and all the tools scattered around as if we were still working on it.

Harry and Francis were beat and so was Brody. I told them to turn in so that they would be some good to me when the time came, and we put one of the few men that we could trust to watch the engine so that no one would accidentally try to start it up. Then I went out on deck myself.

The sun was a red ball on the horizon. It was a tropic sun that looks like a big hot balloon and it just hangs there for what seems like hours, then drops out of sight fast, and it's dark.

It wouldn't be long now until the light failed, and when that happened more things were going to be rough than the sea. I looked around at the drunken, unsuspecting sailors.

Some of them had passed out from too much rum and no food. They were sleeping it off on the deck and in passageways, oblivious of the watery fate that awaited them. They were a sleazy lot, and I doubted that any of them would have been any good to me if they *had* known what the score was. Even if they had tried to storm the bridge and got themselves shot it wouldn't be any worse than if my plan failed. Right then I didn't know whether to feel sorry for them or myself.

I climbed the ladder to the galley and got a plate of chow and steaming mug of coffee and carried them back down to where some of the sailors still sat drinking.

CHAPTER EIGHT

I sat down right in the middle of a group of the passed-out warriors and started to eat.

The aroma of the coffee and the click of silver against plates woke one or two of them up, and they sat there rubbing their eyes and yawning.

I ate with as much gusto as I could muster, and pretty soon they got the idea all by themselves and went up to chow.

One oldtimer woke up and looked at me with disgust. "Never did think you was a real sailor," he said. "Too young." He fumbled around until he found his bottle, took a healthy swig, belched, and went back to sleep.

But pretty soon I had most of them on their feet and going after dinner. Those that came to had a chance of surviving if we sank or caught fire later tonight. The others would die in their sleep.

I hadn't finished my own chow when one of Ringle's boys came down from the monkey island and stood in front of me, but just out of reach. He kept one hand on the butt of his forty-five.

"Let's go," he said.

Now I'm very easy going. A guy my size has to be or he gets accused of being a bully. But I hadn't slept much, and I was cross and irritable.

"Are you asking me or telling me?" I said.

He decided that he would play tough. I don't look big sitting down; besides, he had that forty-five.

"I'm telling you," he bluffed.

He wasn't very good, that man, because he tried to duck the coffee cup when I threw it. He should have taken the coffee in the face and shot me instead.

I threw the plate next, then got up and gave him a left jab to get my weight set and let go with a short hooking right. He left the deck a couple of feet and bounced on his head when he came down.

And there he lay out cold with that revolver half out of the holster and no one to stop me from picking it up.

Could I use a gun?

Sure, it would be like having a flit gun in a school of sharks. Maybe I could get as far as Ringle with it, or even Ringle *and* Croup, but what good would it do? I would be dead, and our cargo, the ship, and the men would still wind up where they were going, with one of Ringle's men in charge.

I pushed the forty-five back into the holster with my foot, so that the boys on the bridge wouldn't think I was getting ideas and cut loose at me. Then I leaned over and picked the sailor up and put him on my shoulder and went up the ladder to the monkey island.

Croup was in his cabin, and I dumped the sailor at his feet. "Did you send for me?" I asked.

"You goddamned clown," said Croup.

"You want to go for a ride, too?"

"Take one step toward me and I'll put six holes in you before you take the second."

"I should have borrowed his gun," I smiled. "You wouldn't talk down to me then."

He laughed, shook his head, and sat down at his desk. "Come in with us, Brody. You and I could have a hell of a good time in Algiers."

"I don't think my ashes would look good in a jar on a shelf in Algiers."

"So you still think Ringle will cross me?"

"Sure. And the people he's dealing with will double-cross him."

"What else have you got to look forward to?"

"My face in the mirror when I shave every morning."

"You won't have one after tonight."

"Maybe. What did you want to see me about?"

"I don't want you sobering up the crew. It would be messy if they objected when we parted company tonight."

"Tell me, big hearted, are you going to sink this tub or let the others try to make it into Cuba on one engine?"

"So you know what our course has been?"

"Just about. Answer my question."

"What do you think?"

"That's all I wanted to know. Doesn't it make you sick to your stomach?"

"I'll tell you, Brody. I've been a sailor for twenty years and I've seen it all—guys chopped up by sharks and torn up by barracuda. They get burned alive on tankers and crushed to death on freighters and bitten by tarantulas on banana boats. A sailor is lucky to live as long as I have. Take a good look at the crew … has-beens, old-timers, and winos. You are here accidentally. It's about time they cashed in and what better way than dead drunk at sea?"

"What about the South Americans? They aren't old or has-beens."

"So what? They aren't white."

"It's always been my idea that essentially they are people," I said.

"Come off it, boy. What are you, a Communist? Now how about that engine? Ringle is in a tizzy to make contact."

"Do you mean you still want me to go down in the engine room?"

"Sure."

"Croup, sometimes I don't figure you. You still trust me not to wreck the other engine?"

"That's right."

"Why, for God's sake?"

"Because you are one smart cookie. When the time comes you will go along with me to save your neck. All heroes are dead men. You aren't that dumb."

"Maybe you're right," I said.

"Anyway, our speed is too slow. Can you fix it?"

"I don't know."

And that was the truth.

Outside it was still light, but the sun was ready to take its plunge. A few sailors were whooping it up on the tank deck. The food had only given them a second wind.

I went to my cabin and took a cold shower and changed into a fresh khaki uniform. Before I left I took my one good mate's cap with the shiny gold braid on it and put it on. I don't know why. Maybe I wanted to look good for someone besides Sheba. There was no telling where I would be when morning broke.

I went back to the engine room where I could smoke to stay awake and keep an eye on things.

Croup had a little surprise for me there. Two of his men, both packing rods, were keeping their eyes on things too. That's why he hadn't been worried.

I got out the engine room log book and pretended to enter the readings on gauges and temperature instruments. Things like that had been ignored on this voyage, and it didn't matter much any more. I was doing it for show.

It wasn't long before I noticed the change in the reading on the voltage gauge and knew that they had turned on our running lights from the bridge. So it was dark now.

We wouldn't have long to wait.

From above I heard the first few sounds of bongo drums and some scattered laughter. The boys weren't wasting any time beginning their nightly music session.

I piddled around trying to act as though I knew what I was doing for an hour and then started out to wake up Harry and Francis.

"Where you going?" asked one of Croup's guards.

"To wake up the engine room watch. It's time we got back to work on the engine."

They were stumped because they both knew that was what Croup wanted.

When I got topside the sound of bongo drums almost knocked me over. The crowd was jam-packed on the fan tail, and they were whooping and hollering to beat all hell.

I went down to the crew's quarters and roused MacGill, Garcia, and three other men that were in with us and had stayed sober.

"Go down to the engine room and pretend to work on the engine and wait for me. Don't let those guards down there become suspicious."

"So there are guards there, too?" asked Harry. "Does that change anything?"

"No," I shrugged. "It just makes things tougher. We'll have to jump them when the time comes."

I went back on deck to take a last look around. I had to know where Ringle's hoods were stationed and how many there were at each spot. And I wanted to know if he had put anybody back by the auxiliary steering station.

It was noisy and crowded back near the fan tail. The men were crowded around the bongo drummers, and they were yelling like crazy. I edged over that way and saw that no one was guarding the wheel and started to turn back when my eye swept over the group that was knocking itself out there.

I stopped. For a bunch of boys living it up among themselves, they were riding high. Too high.

I went up behind them and looked over their heads into the circle of flickering light. What I saw there chilled my blood and heated my brain forge-hot all at the same time.

Sheba was in there dancing the dance I had seen her do last night. She was dressed in those tight shorts and crazy halter that she had worn earlier, but the look on her face was different. This time she wasn't dancing for that same imagined deity, but directly to the men straining and gasping around her.

The movements of her body were no longer innocent, but graphic and brassy hot.

I didn't think twice. I had to get her out of there before the men knew what was happening or …

I slammed aside the sailors directly ahead of me and stepped directly into the circle as Sheba turned in my direction. She had time for one bump and one grind before I picked her up under one arm and went away from there fast.

She kicked and screamed, and behind me I heard the bongos stop and an ugly murmuring begin.

I went up the ladder to the monkey island in bounds.

The guards stepped aside for me, and I didn't stop until I was inside my cabin with the door closed.

When Sheba was standing on her feet before me she swung from the deck and caught me square on the jaw. It didn't faze me, but everything else did.

For little Sheba was standing there with the halter half off from our tussle, and her deep breathing made those lovely breasts thrust out high and moving.

I put out an arm and pulled her close. She hit me again and again as I pressed my mouth to her throat. Her skin was warm and soft under my lips, and she moved against me every whichway as she fought to escape.

Then as my lips moved lower she quit struggling. And she didn't fight me that way any more.

I came out of the cabin an hour later with her promise that she would stay there and lock the door. It had suddenly become important that I save her, too.

But almost an hour had flown by and I was scared. I hurried by Croup's cabin like a kid past the farmer's house with his pockets full of stolen apples. Going past Ringle in the radio shack was even worse.

Christ, I felt guilty.

I only hoped that Harry and the boys were okay, and that we could still pull our trick play.

Harry looked at me questioningly.

"Where you been, to a party?" he asked.

"Shut up."

How long would it be before Ringle limped down here and gave his boys the orders to put the blast on me for cuckolding him? Those guards up above could guess what had gone on. Would they have the guts to tell him?

I waited for the action to start.

But when it came it sure wasn't what I had expected.

First I heard the drums start up again and I didn't think much about it. In fact I tried to shut out of my mind the noise of the hot Afro-Cuban rhythm and the dirty picture it created.

I got Harry and Francis over by the engine where the guards couldn't hear and explained my plan in detail.

"Here's how I see it. Francis, you know the engines good enough to switch the juice to number one when we're ready and get it started, so you stay here and run it from this end. Harry, you've done some piloting, so you'll take the wheel on the fan tail. Once you get there you'll be out of their line of fire from the bridge, and it should be fairly safe. Go up the ladder and start walking in that direction about sixty seconds before the time we are ready. They won't know what you're up to until you duck out of sight, and then it should be too late. Okay?"

"Sure, I can handle the wheel, but what's to keep them from just walking back there and blowing me off the fan tail with a Thompson?"

"We'll knock those two guards for a row of apples before you start off. Francis will take one forty-five and you the other. One of the extra men will stay down here and cover the ladder, while Francis operates the engines and one of them goes with you and covers you while you steer. It's risky, but they won't just walk up to you if your boy fires a warning shot or two in that direction."

"It may work," said Garcia. "They won't be expecting it."

"Those are the only odds in our favor," I said. "We need about ten minutes to close with the other ship, and I doubt if they can circle around and pick you off before it's too late."

"You make it sound like I'm a clay pigeon in a shooting gallery," said Harry.

"You will be," I answered.

"Do you still think we have to ram that other tanker," he asked. "We might both sink or catch fire."

"We sure as hell can't outrun it, and if the chances are slim that we can get away they're even worse that Ringle will let us live once they have the jets and oil."

"Where do we ram her?" asked Garcia.

"Aft. I don't want there to be so much steel above us that our bow gets stuck and keeps us from pulling away when we reverse engines. Besides, a good blow aft will knock their steering out and maybe disable their propellers, so if they don't sink we may still get away." I glanced toward the guards, but they weren't paying attention to us. I had noticed that about every fifteen minutes one of them blew into the speaking tube that led to the bridge, and when he got someone on the other end he would report that everything was okay. We would have to jump them right after they reported in. We'd have fifteen minutes in which to operate.

"I just thought of another angle," I said. "Francis, when you cut in number one, wait until it's turning over good then feed oil into the furnace that it can burn but not enough to flood it out. We'll make smoke like a destroyer, and it will help cover up what our angle is."

"Should help us to get away, too," he agreed. "There is moonlight tonight."

"Everything straight?" I asked.

"Yeah," Harry whispered. "I'm going to be aft dodging bullets, Francis is going to be down here pouring the oil to an engine that can explode easy, and you, Brody, where are you going to be?"

They both looked at me in a quizzical way and waited. I felt foolish because I wasn't just sure *where* I would be when the shooting started. I might be in the spot I had in mind, and on the other hand I might be putting on weight. Forty-five slugs weigh a lot.

"Well, I guess someone has to take that radio shack," I said.

Harry got real excited, and Francis started jabbering in Spanish.

"Shut up both of you," I hissed. "One look at your faces and both these guards will know something's up. I know it's risky, but we have to silence the radio to keep the other tanker from being warned."

They were silent now and embarrassed for having thought that I was trying to duck any of the dirty work.

"This has to be a split second caper," I continued. "We'll set our watches. Harry starts aft as soon as we have taken care of the guards down here. We time it from that moment. After Harry leaves I head for the monkey island. By then we should have the other ship in sight. At the right moment, I'll give that radio shack hell. Francis, when you hear the first shot that's your signal to cut all power to the bridge so they can't signal with the searchlights and can't steer from up there. Switch the power over to Harry on the fan tail.

"Harry, you will have to use your own judgment as to what heading to take to hit that tanker. We should be close enough so that they can't possibly get out of your way."

"What are you going to do up there," he asked softly.

"Don't worry. I'm not offering myself as a fatted calf. I'll live if I can. It's Ringle that had better look out." And as I said it I wished I felt as brave as I talked.

I noticed that Francis had one ear cocked to sounds from topside. I listened, too.

The bongo drums were almost drowned out by loud shouts and a strange screaming. "What the hell?" I said.

I got to the ladder in two jumps, with Harry and Francis right behind. When I got topside the whole scene was flooded with moonlight. Every drunken sailor aboard was on his feet howling and shrieking to the sound of drums and the chants of primitive man. They were being whipped into an orgiastic frenzy by the big sailor who had danced the mating dance for Sheba.

This was what the rum had been for. The bad booze and the drums were designed to make the useless crew lose the last of their civilized qualities when the proper time came. And it was working.

"Croup may be making a mistake," said Harry. "They may get out of hand and fire the ship."

"He has them herded back here out of the danger area," I murmured. "If they tried to go up forward he wouldn't hesitate to shoot them down."

Suddenly the air was rent with screaming. It was the same unnatural sound we had heard from below.

My attention quickened.

Then half the sailors began pushing and fighting each other to get at something, and Sheba Ringle appeared above their heads held in a dozen arms.

I started forward without thinking, but Harry grabbed me from behind and held me fast.

The sailors put Sheba on her feet on top of a hatch, and she stood there dazed for a moment.

If they hurt her I'd kill them myself.

The shorts were twisted on her hips and the halter was disarranged, but she didn't look beaten or hurt from where I stood. I tried to shake off Harry's bulk, but he tightened his grip.

"Let her be," he yelled in my ear. "Remember the rest of us."

My stomach was tied in knots, and I felt almost sick. "Why did she leave the cabin?" I thought. "To hell with our plans. I have to get her out of there."

I jammed an elbow back into Harry's ribs and broke free. I ran toward Sheba and I was almost there when she started to dance.

The sight of her wriggling her hips up there stopped me short.

I was close enough to see her face now. She wasn't frightened, scared, or hurt. She was enjoying this.

I started to turn away, confused.

Then that scream ripped the night again, and I wheeled back. If it hadn't been Sheba screaming, who had it been?

For the first time I noticed a small clearing in the midst of the wailing, chanting men.

I seized the guy right in front of me and threw him aside. It only took seconds to fight my way to the clearing, but it seemed like hours because Sheba must have seen me coming.

She screamed at me from the top of her lungs, and then when I didn't stop she shouted, "Kill, kill, kill," and the men fell on the object laying on the deck and began to beat it to death.

By the time I got to him there wasn't much left to save of the fat little mess boy.

Then I went a little berserk myself, and when I started to fight my way toward the crazy woman that had caused this gruesome thing the roof started falling in.

There were maybe twenty wild men against one, and no matter in what direction I lashed out I clubbed one of them. I fought with my fists and knees, and when I finally went down I used my elbows and teeth and feet.

A sailor's foot crashed off my jaw at the same time a pointed toe caught me in the groin, and I felt the damp black of never-never land closing in.

It was life or death now, and I rolled into their legs trying to get to my knees.

I was up, then down, and halfway up again. One powerful surge would get me to the grinning mask that was a beautiful, mad woman.

Then they hit me in the back of the neck with a canon. My eyes bulged from the blow and I caught one below the belt.

CHAPTER NINE

"He don't give up easy," said a voice.

"Hit him again," said some other guy. "I can't hold his arms forever."

"I'll kill him if this keeps up," said the first voice. "Croup says don't kill him, just make him safe."

"To hell with what the captain said," the tough guy growled exasperated. "He's tough enough to get loose right now and do the job on you."

"Okay, here goes."

I was scared, but I relaxed and took the blow, skyrockets, blinding pain, and all. It was just nice to know I was still alive.

The next time I woke up I was rational. I remembered right away that someone had hit me to put me out, and if I was alive it was just lovely.

Every bone in my body was sore, but I wasn't stiff yet. My mind was working so fast that I knew that I hadn't been out long or my muscles would be crying in pain when I tried to move.

First I flexed the fingers of my hands. Nothing broken.

Then I opened my eyes. It was pitch dark wherever they had put me. One eye was swollen but not closed yet. I ran my tongue over my teeth and found they were all there.

I didn't get any farther because there was a loud clanking noise, and before I could turn my head in that direction a door opened and flooded the room with light. It hurt so bad I had to close my eyes for a second, and when the voices started up I just left them closed.

"He's still out. Get some water."

That would be Captain Croup.

I heard footsteps hurry off, and there was silence for a couple of seconds.

Then, "What the hell are you doing here?" Croup growled.

"I just wanted to see how he looked. Please let me look at him."

That shy little voice belonged to Sheba. Her eager, breathless tone made me want to toss my cookies. It stirred up something evil in my memory.

"Get her out of here," said Croup.

There was scuffling, and I heard Sheba yelling obscene words. Then she said, "Oh, you're so strong. I'll go with you."

Croup cursed and a door slammed.

I opened my eyes to find myself lying on my back on the deck to the storeroom off the engine room. I recognized it right away.

"Welcome aboard," said Croup.

"Thanks."

"I was just about ready to splash you with water," he said.

"That's why I came to. I don't think I could stand another blow even if it was water."

I sat up, and Croup moved back a step. He was the kind of warden that would stay out of a prisoner's reach even if I had logging chains wrapped around me.

"How do you feel?" he asked.

"I don't know yet."

"Try your arms."

I did.

"Now your legs. But don't try to stand up. I have you covered." He did, too.

"How come I'm still alive?"

"I sent some of my boys down to drag you out of that rhubarb you started. I hated to break it up. Some fight!"

I looked at him, "But why?"

"Like I said. You're my kind of man. Why, you were still fighting when we carried you down here."

"Yeah?"

"I like you, Ed, but if you don't mind your manners and co-operate with Ringle and me you'll really get a chance to see how tough you are."

He was so deadly serious that it sobered me.

"What now?" I asked.

"I'll play square with you like I have done right along. We need you on this end when we begin to transfer the oil. The sea is running so high that we won't be able to rig a bosum chair and bring over a couple of their men like we had planned. It's going to be touch and go as it is to get the hoses across to let them suck out the oil."

"How about the planes?"

"That's another problem. I figure we'll have to take our chances on their swinging a boom out long enough to reach us and lift the planes off."

"You're going to need decent seamanship to stay abreast of that other ship while we do it," I said.

"That's right. And the moon has gone under so we don't have any light."

I let all this sink into my fuzzy mind. All I had to do was say okay and then go ahead with my plans.

"How about it?" asked the captain.

"Why not?" I said.

"Not so fast, Ed. I've played square with you, but you haven't done the same for me."

"What do you mean?"

Croup turned his head slightly and yelled, "Harry, come in here."

The steel door opened and I wanted to keep my eyes from seeing what I knew was true. But I had to look.

Harry MacGill stood there framed in the light.

I tried to get up fast and tear him apart, but Croup cocked the gun and I sank back down.

Harry, that bastard, had turned me in.

"I know all about it," said Croup.

I looked at Harry, and he tried to avoid my eyes.

"Don't be so disappointed," said Croup. "Harry has been with me from the start. He couldn't do anything else if he wanted to, could you, Harry?"

MacGill didn't even answer.

"Okay, Harry, scram," the captain growled.

The door closed and we were alone.

"Maybe I'm a sucker," said Croup, "but I've let you run all over this tub trying to sabotage me, and I'm still willing to give you a chance."

"What does Ringle say?"

"Nothing. I haven't told him. Christ, he'd have put the blast on you long ago."

"I can't do it," I said.

We were both silent a long time. I sat staring at my feet while Croup kept me covered and waited.

Finally he started talking again.

"You are the most ungrateful son of a bitch I've ever run across." His voice softened then. "I saved your life, Brody. Don't that mean anything to you?"

"Yeah," I answered. "But if you let me out of here, I'll still try it."

"Well, thanks for that much, anyway."

"Don't mention it."

He backed toward the door and I turned to watch him go. His face was all twisted up like he would cry or something. But he kept the automatic steady and pointed at my head.

"When we're through they are going to sink this tub with a six-inch cannon. Come over with us."

"No."

"I'd send somebody down to unlock this door at the last second, but if I did you'd climb out of the ocean right behind me in North Africa and we'd have it to do all over again. Wouldn't we?"

"I guess so."

"So long, you crazy bastard," he said, and slammed the door unnecessarily hard.

I sat there for a long time with my head down, staring at the steel plates of the deck.

How long it was that I sat like that I don't know. A guy can feel sorry for himself only so long. Then I cocked my head a little and listened. I shook my head to clear the haze and listened some more. Then I got to my knees and felt my way to the door and put an ear to it.

Once a grease monkey, always a grease monkey. While I had sat there the sound of the engines had come through to me unconsciously.

But it wasn't engines that I was listening to, it was *one* engine. Why hadn't they turned on number one if they knew all about it?

Just then somebody unlocked the door, and I scrambled back to where I had been sitting just in time.

Two burly sailors came in.

"We got some jewelry for you," one said.

They made me put my hands behind my back, and one of them tied them with wire while the other kept me covered.

I flexed the muscles in my wrists as hard as I could when the wire went on so that after I relaxed the muscles there would be a little play left over. I couldn't do anything like that when he wired my feet together.

After they left I sat and thought about it. Maybe number one just wouldn't turn over. That's why we weren't using it. I hadn't been too sure it would work anyway.

The wire had been twisted onto my wrists so that it cut in, and even with my muscles relaxed it was barely comfortable. I had to keep my fingers moving to insure circulation.

I wondered what had happened to Garcia. Was he dead or had he been one of Croup's boys, too? I must have looked pretty silly to everyone in the know as I ran around like a chipmunk in a wire wheel cake making big plans.

What a laugh.

There was a lot of noise outside the door, and then it opened and closed. The one person in the world I didn't want to see walked in and stood looking down at me.

I looked back at Sheba Ringle, and she was no longer beautiful to me. I must have been pretty far gone, because she didn't even make me want to puke. I just didn't care.

"Aren't you going to say hello?" she said.

"Hello."

"Not like that. I thought you liked me."

I turned my head away.

"I can help you. I want to help you. Please believe me."

There wasn't anything for me to say.

"Don't be mad, Brody. Ringle made me do it. I still like you best."

I looked back at her and shuddered. She still had the figure and the face to torment men, but I was the wrong guy. There was something terribly wrong with her to make her come down here and fool around with a dead man. That's what I was just as good as.

"Did Ringle make you come down here this time?" I asked.

"No, he doesn't know. I had to bluff the guard to let me in."

"Okay, get it over with. What do you want?"

"I'll help you."

"How?"

"I don't know," she said helplessly.

"Tell me something, Sheba. When I finally went down for the count back on the fan tail the last thing I remember seeing was that sailor carrying you toward the ladder leading to the crew's quarters."

She blushed, but there was an odd smile playing on her lips.

"You weren't struggling," I said.

"I don't remember."

It didn't make any difference any more. It was a fact.

"And the first night out someone tried my door," I continued. "That was you, wasn't it?"

"It was my husband's idea," she said, almost in tears.

"And later that same night when I went by Croup's cabin I heard a rustling noise. When you couldn't get into my cabin you went to Croup's. Was that Ringle's idea, too?"

"I told you I had known him for a long time," she almost screamed.

I was silent for a second or two, just looking at her. By then I was feeling sorry for her, because I knew the truth. The kid was nothing but an insane, desirable nymphomaniac.

"You'd better beat it, kid," I said. "I don't need your help."

"And I don't need you," she howled. "There are plenty of others."

"Scram."

Suddenly her face blazed and hardened. She jumped to the work bench and grabbed up a heavy wrench. When she turned back I could see the crazy light in her eyes.

She advanced toward me with the wrench held over her head in both hands.

I was going to be bludgeoned to death while I sat there bound hand and foot by a maniac in shorts and halter that couldn't look better on a burlesque queen. It was a fantastic and horrible way to die.

She raised the wrench still higher as she stood directly over me, and before I turned my head away from the blow I could see her smile.

But the blow never fell. The door flew open and Garcia bounded into the room and knocked Sheba to hell and gone over the head. She crashed head first against the bulkhead and lay still where she fell.

Garcia didn't waste any time with explanations. He found a pair of wire cutters and cut me free.

I sat there dazed and massaged my hands and feet to bring the life back, and he stood and watched. When I felt I could stand I put out a hand and he helped me up.

"How do you feel? Can you make it?" he asked.

I tried out my legs and found them wobbly but serviceable. My head ached like hell from the beating I had taken. "Yeah, I guess I'll live," I said.

"Then let's go. The other ship is just in sight."

"Go where? We're all washed up on that gimmick."

"No, *señor*, I have just started it off by taking care of the engine room guards."

I must have looked surprised. "I didn't hear any noise."

"Look, I make no noise."

I looked.

The guard outside my door was flat on his face, the knife handle sticking out of his back.

I wheeled back fast. "What about the rest of them?"

"I took care of them, too."

"You and who else?" This was making me dizzy.

He went past me into the engine room where a couple more men lay face down. I followed to the foot of the ladder where Francis stopped and made a hissing sound.

It just about knocked me over when Harry MacGill came hurrying down.

I started for him without thinking.

"Stop," said Francis, grabbing my arm.

"He is with us?"

"Sure," said Harry. "What kind of a rat do you think I am?"

"I don't know," I said, shaking my head.

"Well, I don't have time for it all now," Harry said. "I was with Croup, sure, but I couldn't go through with it. He has something on me. I can't tell you what. So when he wanted to know what your plan was I gave him a cock and bull story about how you planned to pull the plug on this tub and take the lifeboats while he sank."

I studied him and, by God, the man was telling the truth.

"How much time has gone by since you jumped the guards?" I asked.

Harry looked at the engine clock. "About five, six minutes."

"That gives us nine precious minutes to take this ship."

"Is it enough?" asked Garcia.

"What do you think?" I grinned.

"Let's go," said Garcia.

"Oh no," I said. "The monkey island is all mine. You stay down here and pour the coals to those engines when you hear shots. And remember to give us smoke. Harry, you'd better go first so you can get to the wheel before they spot me. You're safe enough on deck, but when I go out there all hell's going to break loose."

"I'm ready," he said grimly.

"What about those other guys you said would be with us. You'll need a man to cover you," I exclaimed.

They both looked away from me.

"Well?" I asked again.

"We lost them," Harry said.

"*Si*. That Sheba, she put on such a good show they go away and don't come back."

"Then it's just the three of us?" I said. "Are you still game?"

"Hell, yes," Francis whopped.

"Harry?"

"Right."

"Then get going. I'll be out of the hatch thirty seconds behind you so get ready to duck."

He went up the ladder fast without turning back for a last look. And that's a good way to go.

"Has he got a gun?" I asked Francis.

"*Si*."

I ran over to the guard by the storeroom door and turned him over. There was a police special .38 caliber revolver sticking out of his belt. I transferred it to my pocket, then turned him back and pulled the knife out from between his ribs. I wiped the knife blade on the dead sailor's shirt and tossed it toward Garcia who caught it in mid-air.

Then I crossed the engine room and went up the ladder. There was no looking back for me, either.

There was no turning back at all.

As my head came even with the deck the lights went out behind me for an instant and I made a dash for the monkey island on silent feet. There was a silent prayer on my lips for Francis' having that bright idea.

Instead of going up the ladder to the island I went in underneath the catwalk and flattened against the steel bulkhead. I could look up through the grating of the walk and see the feet of several men stand guard there. And if one of them looked down he would be able to see me.

I had two things going in my favor. It was dark, and if they didn't catch any movement they might miss me. The other thing was that everybody was looking out to sea. They were watching for the other ship. Francis had said that they had it in sight, but I knew now that that was premature. It was time that we should be coming alongside, but whoever had given out that false alarm had been wrong. We must still be minutes away.

And here I stood out in plain sight where I would have to stay until the other ship got in close. I would sure get caught here.

I moved cautiously aft around the corner of the island structure and started inching my way forward along the port side. There was an air funnel there sticking up out of the deck close to the bulkhead, and if

I could get next to it, the chances would be less of being spotted.

I couldn't take a chance on going for the engine room too soon or the other ship would catch on and make a run for it. If I waited too long they would be able to hear and see the shots that were sure to come, and then they could try to dodge us or stop us with the six-inch naval gun that Croup had mentioned.

I kept my back tight against the bulkhead as I moved. There weren't as many guards on this side, and I counted them as I inched along, head up, back flat.

One, two, three, four … and my foot touched something soft.

It was a body.

I didn't dare bend over to find out who it was lying there on the deck or if he was dead or alive.

It could be just one of the drunken sailors sleeping it off.

With my heart in my mouth and my eyes on the shadowy figures of the guards above me I started to step over the prostrate form.

I had one foot over and started to bring the other after it when a guard coughed and spit down between the grid on the catwalk. I froze.

The spittle hit the figure lying at my feet and the man moved and groaned.

I only had eyes for that guard.

But he didn't see me.

I started to bring my leg on then, but it wouldn't move.

The man lying there was holding my ankle in a grip of steel.

CHAPTER TEN

There just wasn't anything else to do. I jammed my foot down against the man's windpipe as he lay there on the deck and put my crushing weight on it.

All that time I prayed none of the gun-toting men above me would look down. The guy who had grabbed my ankle quit struggling in no time. When he let go I knew he was dead.

Then I inched ahead until I was in the deeper shadows of the air-conditioning funnel and sank down feeling weak.

That poor sailor had awakened from his drunken stupor at just the right moment to get himself killed, and there hadn't been anything to do about it.

This ship, its cargo of oil and planes and people was still more important than any one person. But that didn't make me feel any better for what I had done, and I knew that when things got rough up there above me at the radio shack I was likely to take it out on Ringle and his boys.

I settled down to wait. Eight or nine minutes is a long time in a spot like this. Harry would be tense back there on the fan tail wondering how long it would be before he was spotted and they started to throw lead in his direction. Forty-five slugs are big, ugly bullets, and those from a Thompson are worse.

Little Francis Garcia would be down in the engine room with a hand on the switches ready to cancel the juice to the bridge and cut in the other engine. He would have one eye on the hatch and a gun in his other hand wondering how long he had before one of Croup's goons blundered in and saw the bodies on the deck.

Right now we were all waiting: and praying and hoping that other tanker would hove into view so we could go into action.

We had seven minutes now or maybe six and a half and each second cut our chances like a meat cleaver chopping into a thin side of beef.

I got out the .38 special and checked it. The policeman's gun is like this, only bigger. Most detectives carry this type because it has a two-inch barrel and a smaller wood butt and can be concealed. Yet it does all the damage necessary, and I didn't bother much wondering how Croup's boy had come by it because it can't be bought by an ordinary citizen. I was just plenty glad he had carried it.

I could have kicked myself for not checking to see if he had any more ammo in his pockets. But then I doubted I would have time to squeeze off more rounds than she held. If I wasn't inside the radio shack and safe after six shots it wasn't going to make any difference.

Now we didn't have more than four minutes. Any longer than that and the bridge would wonder why those engine room guards didn't check in by whistling through the speaking tube. In that predicament Garcia would be in the hottest seat of all.

All he had was a gun, his knife, and guts. As far as guts were concerned I had an idea he was as well off as a guy could be.

Now I figured three minutes at the outside.

We were running without lights anywhere but on the bridge. It was dangerous, but Ringle was in a dangerous profession.

Then everybody topside started yapping and pointing and it caught me off guard. I almost squeezed off a round because I thought I had been spotted. But I could see them pointing out to sea, and I craned my neck around the corner of the funnel. The big black ship was almost on top of us, coming up on the starboard, aft side like a charging elephant.

She had come out of the night fast and didn't show one single light. Everybody had been watching ahead, and I wasn't the only one surprised.

I got to my feet fast and pressed up against the bulkhead with my back and watched the men above me.

Luckily the rendezvous ship was on the side away from me, and that's where all the excitement would take place. I was hoping some of these men would go around there to watch.

There had to be time for a few signals between ships so that other tanker wouldn't run off and start pumping shells into us. But I needed all that time to get started and make it around the rear of the catwalk watching the other ship come up alongside. It was now or never. We couldn't have more than sixty seconds before Croup sent someone down to help the engineer run the ship.

I stuffed the gun down in my belt. It was cool here on deck, but I was sweating like a pig.

I crouched, looked up to judge the distance, then jumped and grabbed the rungs of the catwalk above me. I caught and held by my fingertips, then got a better hold with one hand and pulled myself up. If I had missed the first time and fallen back to the deck everyone on board would have heard me.

I was halfway up and over the rail before I could count the guards for the first time. There were three of them, and they hadn't seen me. I got over that rail fast and went aft toward them, thankful for my big rubber-soled shoes.

I pulled the gun out as I went, holding the short barrel in my fist. They never saw me.

I clubbed one guy with the gun and one with my fist and switched the gun around and put it in the third guy's back.

Just then we were raked by a blinding flash from the other ship's search light and I said, "Stand still and don't raise your hands."

The sailor stiffened and I thought he was going to yell, but I jammed the gun a little harder into his spine and the cry died in his throat. The searchlight went right on past us and the two guys out cold on the deck, and we were in pitch darkness again.

"That was good," I said to the thug. "Very good. Now walk around the island toward the radio shack. Keep directly ahead of me and don't try anything. Play ball and I'll let you live. I'm a desperate man."

I prodded him and he went along. When we came out around the starboard side I glanced ahead and saw about five guys around the door of the radio shack. "Walk natural," I murmured.

Then I looked out to sea and saw that the other ship was about fifty yards away, traveling a parallel course. They had closed down on their engines to match our slow speed and were edging in slowly. It was perfect.

My prisoner was a big guy, and he hid me and the gun pretty well. It was a lot brighter here because the other ship had that spotlight trained on the bridge, but I was hoping the guards up ahead would recognize my boy and let him come up without questions.

And we almost made it.

"Hey Slezack," one of them called. "What the hell you doing here? Get back to your post."

"Keep going," I growled, and prodded him on.

"Who's that with you?" the same voice yelled.

Then, "Look out!"

"It's Brody, shoot!"

I pushed the guy ahead of me as hard as I could and went in low right behind him.

All hell broke loose as the punks at the radio shack door cut down on us, and the guy I was using as a shield screamed as the slugs ripped him.

Our lunge took us ten yards up the catwalk almost to the door, and when the boy ahead of me went down I cut loose with the .38 and swept the doorway. A bomb exploded off my temple and I fell sideways, scrambled to my knees next to the bulkhead; and poured two more rounds at the remaining two guys standing there. One went down and the other sighted his forty-five at my head and pulled the trigger.

The hammer fell on an empty chamber.

I got to my feet and charged again. He threw the empty gun and ran backwards. But I didn't waste my last bullet. When I got to the door of the radio shack I stopped short, wrenched off my shoe, and tossed it around the corner into the room.

A Thompson machine gun cut loose in there, and I stepped around the corner and shot Ringle between the eyes.

I watched the cripple try to swing the Thompson back toward me, but it was as if he couldn't decide which of his three eyes to use to sight with and he sagged, then slumped slowly toward the deck. His head refused to buckle.

He just couldn't accept the fact he was dead. There was a hiss of air from his clenched teeth and he lay still.

I slammed and locked the steel door behind me, grabbed up the Thompson and sprayed a burst at the radio panel.

It disintegrated like clay pigeons at a turkey shoot and I took the old drum off, clamped on a new one, and shot out the lights. Then I stood there feeling the ship lurch over on a new course with a tremendous surge of power.

Harry and Garcia were okay! We were picking up speed to ram that tanker. I could feel number one coughing and growling and vibrating the plates loose on this old tub, but it was sweet music to my ears. That steam turbine was working great.

I put a hand up to my head and felt blood running down my face. There wasn't anything I could do about it now. I still had work to do.

I went to the porthole on the starboard side and opened it wide. The other ship had tumbled to our trouble and they were lit up like two dozen Christmas trees. I could see men scurrying every whichway on the decks.

And I could see them unlimbering the big, black, potent muzzle of the six-inch naval gun.

Their captain had changed his course to get away, but it was too late. We had the jump on him.

Up above me I could hear Croup shouting over a dozen others. He couldn't figure out why he didn't have power and why he couldn't steer from there. It wouldn't take him more than seconds to figure it and send his boys down after Harry and Garcia.

But I could do something about that. From this porthole I could just see the entrance to the engine room.

We were closing fast with that other tanker now, and it was going to be close. I ran over where Ringle had stacked the ammo and grabbed half a dozen drums for the Thompson and got back to the porthole while we were only twenty yards from the other ship.

I leveled down on the bridge of that stinking big boat and cut loose.

They were shooting back before I got started, and I kept my head down. I could hear anguished screams as Croup's men were killed.

Then there was darkness as we cut in underneath the bigger ship, and all light was cut off. The two ships came together with more force than I had ever imagined it would be like. I was thrown against the bulkhead so hard that I almost broke a shoulder, and the place my head hit was covered with blood.

Garcia didn't even have to reverse engines because we had hit them so far back we sheared away half the poop deck and, I hoped, their rudder and screws. After a shuddering, grinding ten seconds we just kept right on going.

Now we were in their search lights again, and I went to the porthole on the port side and kept blazing away at them.

Above me I could hear sounds of gunfire, and I knew they were shooting at the other ship out of self-preservation.

I must have gone mad, because I emptied drum after drum into the tanker as we slowly pulled away. I was screaming and laughing and holding the trigger of the Thompson down like she'd never quit.

And then I blacked out.

When I came around I could hear hurrying footsteps on the catwalk outside, and I looked up to see a face at one porthole. I raised the Thompson on one elbow, fired a burst, and the face disappeared.

Then I dragged myself over Ringle's still warm body into a dark corner. I knew right away what had happened. I was losing blood from the scalp wound. It had only been a few seconds that I had been out, but if it happened again I would wake up dead. I put the Thompson on the deck beside me and ripped off my shirt. It was hard to make a bandage in the dark, so I just wrapped the strips of shirt around my head until I felt the wound was bound tightly. Then I tied the ends and crawled over underneath the starboard port.

I was in a bad spot.

They couldn't get me from the locked door, but if I stayed at one port they could get me from the other.

There was only one thing to do.

I crawled over to where Ringle lay and lifted him.

He was surprisingly heavy.

I carried him to the portside, stuffed his head and shoulders out the porthole, and pushed and shoved until he was wedged there tight.

Then I went back and took up a watch at the other one, where I could see the entrance to the engine room. "Poor Ringle," I laughed at myself. "It would kill him if he knew he was serving as my shield."

The little crippled was doing something for someone else at last.

There was a whoosh and a big splash about fifty yards away in the sea, and then came the loud report of the cannon. They had finally got the naval gun unlimbered on the other tanker and were taking range shots.

If that was an example of their marksmanship I wasn't worried.

But the next one was closer, too close.

Water cascaded up over the tank deck from the near miss.

The ship lurched, and I knew Harry had taken a new course.

I saw a couple of guys sneak up to the hatch leading to the engine, and I almost cut them to pieces with the machine gun.

They must have ducked below my porthole and sneaked by.

I fired an occasional round down there to keep them from trying it too often, and was cautious not to let the muzzle of the Thompson stick out where someone outside could grab it and jerk it out of my hands.

Those six-inch shells kept screaming toward us, but they fell on one side or the other. They only hit us once, up on the bridge. I could have cheered them myself, except I was worried enough to know that one good direct hit could blow us to kingdom come.

There was a crack and crash of sound as the shell hit the steel bulkheads of the bridge, tore its way through, and carried the superstructure away.

So I sweated it out. Garcia was pouring the coals to her, and the smoke helped a lot. Harry would tack off on a new course just before he thought they were ready to fire again, and that was often. It wasn't long before the sound of the cannon became softer, and I knew they weren't keeping up with us. It had worked. We were still afloat, and they had been crippled enough so we could get away.

We should be steaming out of their range soon, and I waited tensely each time I heard the high-pitched scream of the shell as it hurtled toward us, expecting the next one to fall aft telling me we were out of range.

Then I heard that lousy number one engine coughing and shaking below deck as it died and gave up.

We slowed down as the other ship fired faster and faster. But in their hurry they sacrificed even more accuracy, and we finally pulled away out of range at about four knots. That should have been the ball game.

But now I found myself in a worse spot than I had been in all along.

I sure as hell couldn't walk out in the open and neither could Croup. Harry was in a damned tight spot. Only Francis was relatively safe below deck. The big question that kept crossing my mind was, "Is Croup alive?"

He didn't leave me long to find out.

There wasn't any way out of the radio shack. Some of the hoods would still be there above me on the bridge ready to pump lead the moment I tried to step out on deck. Nobody was moving around much, but once in a while I could hear the scrape of a shoe overhead of a muffled whisper. When that happened I would flatten against the bulkhead next to the port, waiting for the shooting to begin.

But nothing happened.

My head ached and throbbed, and it was getting around to the time when I should have it looked after.

The noises on the ship settled down to an uneasy silence.

Our course was straight as far as I could tell. That meant Harry was okay. The lights stayed down in the hold, and the engine kept up its steady, slow beat so I figured Garcia was okay, too.

We had several hours of darkness left and we were safe till dawn. Then Croup could pick us off one at a time and take over his ship again.

My legs were weak, and I leaned against the bulkhead and tried to figure out how I was going to get back to my boys. Together we had a chance. There wasn't any speaking tube from the radio room to Garcia below, so we couldn't talk.

But there was one from here to the bridge, and I could hear someone whistling in it. I left them to whistle.

The one thing wrong with those speaking tubes is that you have to put your ear up to one to hear what's being said. All I had to do to get shot was to go over there and turn my back to the black night outside.

Then I heard the voice I had been dreading to recognize.

"Hey, Brody," shouted Croup from the bridge above, "can you hear me."

He had got tired of whistling. Now he was trying me out with a foghorn bellow.

Right away I got a small idea. I let him bellow.

"Brody! You all right?"

And I still kept my mouth shut. I wasn't talking for anybody.

There was silence for a moment. "I'll make a deal," the captain yelled. "Fifty-fifty. You killed Ringle, so you earned it. By the way, that was smart stuffing him out the porthole like that."

For my part, I wasn't trying to think about it.

"Brody, answer me. We have a good two, three million bucks here. You can make yourself rich. Call your boys off and we will go into Africa and make the deal work. You really powdered that ship. They were burning last I could see."

That was to take my mind off the fact that he was finished in the States as well as with his late partners. Yet I couldn't say I didn't feel sorry for those guys back on that other ship. There wasn't anything we could do to help them, either. I knew a lot of those sailors were innocent men.

"Yeah, Brody. A million bucks for you, a million for me, and one for the crew. You can't afford to pass it up. For Christ's sake, be sensible. Where is this going to get you? You can't steam into a port, because you can't navigate. At four knots it would take a week … and I'd get you in the end. What are you going to eat? Where are you going to get any water? One of my boys winged you, and tomorrow when it gets hot you're going to need water bad."

That woke me up.

I looked around the cabin, but in the dark I couldn't tell if there was any water in there or not. He was right. Without any chow we'd starve before we made port. It was just a choice between Cuba and S. A. The stars could tell us which. But food? Uh, uh.

"We'll just walk up to you in two or three days and blow you over, you'll be so dry," he continued. "Hey, can you hear me?"

That was what I had been waiting for. I gave him more of the silent treatment.

He called my name some more, and I could hear him saying some other stuff in a quieter voice between yells, and soon there were other noises near me.

"Do you need help, boy?" Croup started in again. He kept a line of chatter up to cover the other sounds. Who did he think he was kidding?

When the company came to call I was ready. I edged over to the door and put the lock off, then stood flat beside it. Croup was still calling to me when the knob turned slowly and the heavy door was thrown violently open. His voice was drowned out by the explosion of gunfire right next to my ear as the guy outside the door sprayed the guts out of the radio shack.

Most of the bullets were absorbed by the radio panel, but enough of them ricocheted around inside the little room to make it hot for me. I couldn't even tell if I had been hit by one, the racket was so bad. But the worst I got was two deaf ears from the concussion of the Thompson.

I could see the muzzle spurting flame less than a foot away, and when it quit I just reached over and grabbed the red-hot muzzle and yanked.

The guy came right in, and I shot him while he was still moving, then sprayed the doorway and went out after those bullets like I was one of them.

It seemed like bodies were piled up there like they had been storming a fort for ninety days and ninety nights, but I had forgotten the four men I had put down when I had entered. I almost tripped over the sailor I had used as a shield, and it saved my life. I staggered sideways and a burst from above caught the dead man and turned him over.

Somebody shouted, "I got him," as I skittered along close to the bulkhead and beat it down the ladder onto the tank deck.

"The hell you did," someone else said. "He's getting away."

I dived for the cover of the fan tail and the housing by the auxiliary wheel. I went in head first with a shower of lead kicking up rust behind me.

"Whew," I said to Harry, "that was close."

I could have saved my breath, because Harry wasn't there.

The auxiliary wheel was deserted. The ship plowed ahead on a straight course like a ghost.

This nearly had the effect that Croup was trying for. It almost killed me. Maybe he had planned it this way. Harry hadn't run out. He couldn't have. We had rammed that other ship, hadn't we? It couldn't have been done without Harry. The captain must have caught him napping and taken him prisoner.

That must be it.

And here we sailed along somehow, without anybody at the wheel.

Then I thought I knew what was up. They must have got Francis, too. The power had been switched back to the bridge and they were steering from there.

To do that they must have both Harry and Garcia.

CHAPTER ELEVEN

Up on the bridge, Croup bawled out obscenities.

"Flattery will get you nowhere," I yelled.

For an answer I got several stray bursts of gunfire. The harmless slugs whistled over my head and lost themselves out in the lonely ocean.

I had the Thompson with half a drum of ammo, and I still had my tongue. It was a comfort. The gun, I mean.

If I squeezed off one round at a time it would last a while. I put my back up against a bulkhead and caught my breath. The wound hurt from exertion, and my string was running out. Croup would harry me into a corner eventually like a treed 'possum, and that would be that.

I took a deep breath and got set to move out.

I peeked around the corner at the bridge and thought I saw a speck of white sailor's hat. There wasn't any use aiming, so I shot from the hip. Then I went around the corner away from the bridge and took a look from the other side of my shelter.

The answering fire was surprisingly light. The shot where they had seen the sharp burst of flame, and I counted them in return the same way.

Not more than six different men were slinging lead. But more of them could be lurking around in the dark near me.

I gave them a burst from this side, then ran around to where I had been and watched again.

Six men up there; I had been right. Then I repeated the gimmick of firing from one side and running to the other, until they caught on.

I fired once more and knew they were ready to be taken in, because they didn't return the shots but waited for me to appear at the other side. So I fooled them. I calmly sprinted across the open space and down the engine room ladder like a jack-rabbit.

I had caught them flatfooted, and they didn't see the move in the dark until it was too late.

Only one or two disappointed shots followed me as I clattered down the ladder into the engine room. The Thompson was cocked in my arms as I hit bottom. I brought it around ready to sweep the ginks who had taken my buddies.

Pure luck kept me from pulling back on the trigger.

Harry MacGill was sitting on the deck, crying. Beside him lay the body of Francis Garcia, and from the Panama kid's back stuck the handle of a twelve-inch screw driver.

My arms slumped and the gun hung lax in one hand as I walked over and stood looking down.

"Who did it?" I asked weakly.

Harry looked up at me with grief-stricken eyes. He nodded to the open door of the parts room, and I knew without turning my head.

Sheba Ringle.

"Where is she?"

He shrugged and let his shoulders slump.

I reached down, slapped him hard a couple of times, and then dragged him to his feet.

"Wake up, Harry," I shouted at him.

I hit him until the shine went out of his eyes and he began to fight back. Then I let him go. He stood breathing hard and shook his head a couple of times.

Finally he looked at Francis on the deck and turned green. He ran over behind the big steam turbine engines and was sick. When he came back he was okay.

I heard steps on the ladder and wheeled toward them to fire once. The footsteps went away fast.

MacGill and I got down behind the useless number one engine where we could see but not be seen and let ourselves relax.

"Do you want to tell me?" I asked.

He shuddered but nodded.

"I was back on the fan tail and it was weird. At first I didn't mind. I got there without any trouble, and when the shooting started I was too scared to think much. I thought sure you had got it up there on the bridge. Later when you were shooting back from inside the shack I knew you had made it. Then I thought we could pull it off. Christ, we could do anything.

"It was duck soup hitting that ship. All I had to do was pull the wheel over. Garcia had switched power without a hitch. But it knocked hell out of me, that collision did. I flew up in the air, came down on the back of my head, and I saw right away that we could go clean so I rang up full speed ahead and doubled in spades. Francis caught on fine and didn't reverse.

"I guess the blow did something to me though." Here he stopped and faltered.

"Whatever happened to him couldn't have been your fault," I said.

"I guess not, but it hurt. He was a good guy."

"That's right. He was."

"After the collision it was pretty dark back there. I got the jeebies. When you spotted those guys going down after Garcia and clobbered them, I knew they would try for me, too. Every little sound made me jump. I couldn't stand it.

"So I tied the wheel and sneaked forward. When Croup started yelling at you I took a chance and ducked down here. They were concentrating on you and they didn't see me. I got halfway down the ladder when I saw them."

"Them? Don't tell me ..."

"At first I couldn't figure it," he continued. "The girl's back was to me, and she was doing a kind of dance and backward shuffle, leading him on, like. Francis was coming after her slow, as if he were sleep walking. His eyes were glazed, and I thought he had gone nuts. I had my gun out and I said to them, 'Hold it.' Garcia doesn't stop, but the babe runs over behind the engines here and crouches down like a wild animal.

"I came on down and Francis is still plodding along. When I got behind him I see the screw driver in his back. I can't remember too clearly what happened next. I ran to the kid, and just as I got to him he went down. The first thing I thought of was helping him, but he had been dead on his feet, I guess. I got so mad I wanted to blow up that dame. I even knew where I was going to shove the gun. When I looked for her she was already halfway up the ladder. And I missed. I missed every time."

We were silent for a few moments. Finally he said, "I guess I was bawling because I missed."

Then the lights went out.

"What the hell," I growled.

"I've got you cornered now," came Croup's big voice. "I've cut the master switches and cables. You won't even be able to boil water for tea."

"We don't need light," I answered. "And I'll roast your carcass over the oil furnace when I get you."

"Don't waste your time bluffing, boy. You had your last chance."

"Come down here and tell me that."

He couldn't and he knew it. We didn't have any light, but we could still see out of the hatch. It was dark down here, but not as dark on deck, so anybody trying to come down would be spotted.

It was a stalemate. We held the engine room and he the bridge. With MacGill down here he could steer, but I controlled the power.

I got up and edged over to the one running turbine and shut it down.

"Okay, fat man," I yelled up. "Now where do we go from here?"

"I told you never to call me that," he answered.

But that was the end of the conversation for the time being. There didn't seem to be much else to say.

Harry still had his forty-five and a couple of rounds, so I left him to watch the ladder. I hunted up a trouble light and hooked it directly into the storage batteries. Then I got out the engine room first-aid kit and fixed up my head. There wasn't a mirror, so I couldn't tell how bad it was. I poured a bottle of iodine over my skull and let it burn the wound clean. I bandaged it the best I could, turned off the light, and went back to where MacGill sat.

"I'm sure hungry," he said.

"Yeah. I could use a steak myself."

"There's water down here," he said, contemplating our fix.

"You can forget it. We can't live on water."

"What are we going to do, Brody?"

"You don't have to do anything," I told him.

"But you have something on your mind," he insisted. "Will it get us out of this fix?"

"No."

It shut him up for a while.

I felt sorry for Harry. He hadn't been able to stand the gaff and had runout on his job, but then it didn't matter. Francis would have died anyway. Whose fault was it that we hadn't locked her in?

Nobody's, really.

Who's fault was it that we hadn't any chow? That was easy. Brody's.

So now it was a stalemate. But not for long. One day, two. How long would it take before we were too weak to fight back?

"I'm sorry I got you into this," I said to Harry.

He tried to look brave, but it wasn't any good.

"We could hold out down here for a couple of days," I said, "and maybe in the meantime another ship will come along, see the damage up above, and investigate. It's a chance in a million, but you can take it if you want."

"You're not going to?"

"No."

"Then what?"

"I don't feel like waiting till I'm so sick Croup can walk up and spit on me. I have an idea he doesn't like me any more … so when dawn comes and I can see what I'm shooting at, I'm going up there."

He didn't say anything, and he couldn't meet my eyes. He knew that was all there was left to do but it wasn't in him to say, "Okay."

We sat in silence, and after a while I could feel my head nod. It was such an effort to stay awake that I had almost decided to go topside when I noticed the gray light coming down the hatch.

Dawn.

I got up, went to the drain faucet of the number one engine, and washed my face in lukewarm water. It woke me up a little.

"Watch the ladder a few minutes," I told Harry.

Back at the rear of the engine room was a screened duct that led to the ventilating funnel on deck. I got a screwdriver and began loosening the heavy wire guard.

It took a while to get it off, and when it was done there was more light coming down from topside. Almost enough to see by.

Garcia's body was where we had left it. I went to it and got his knife and forty-five. It was hard to decide, but the Thompson gave me the most rounds so I slid the forty-five along the deck to Harry and put the knife in my belt. I checked the Thompson, then looked toward Harry. He was watching the ladder. He turned his head and said, "Good luck, Ed."

I nodded and climbed into the air vent. It was close quarters. By putting my back against one side and my rubber soles against the other, I was able to inch my way upward. The sides of the air shaft were rusty, and it helped my feet get a purchase. It also took the skin off my back.

I held the gun overhead and kept it from banging against the side. Just any noise at all would come out of the funnel above me, amplified like a loud speaker.

I don't know how long it took, because when I came to the bend at the top I got stuck. For a minute I was panicked. Then I wiggled free and my head came even with the funnel mouth. I could see forward the length of the ship.

The *Patty Sue* looked worse than she could have. Her bridge and superstructure were shot to hell, and although the dead men had been heaved overboard there was plenty of blood.

I could see a couple of men on the ragged bridge with rifles trained toward the engine room hatch, and a couple more going in and out of the radio shack. I laughed at that. They'd never get another message going from there.

Just then one of the drunks from last night staggered out of the crew's quarters and stretched. He got one yawn off before the guys on the bridge spotted him and cut loose above his head.

He looked surprised, and it took him whole seconds to catch on that somebody had shot at him; then he dived back inside fast.

I had forgotten about the rummies, and it shook me for a moment. Not that I could do anything for them or they for me. It was just another angle in a hopeless mess.

I waited there watching the bridge, hoping something else would happen to give me a chance to climb out unobserved. In a couple of minutes I got it.

A couple of heads appeared out of the crew's quarters. The first man must have roused the sots, and they were looking to see what was up.

The men on the bridge cut loose with more warning shots, and I pushed against the funnel sides and came out on my face.

I got to my feet and cut to ribbons those guys at the bridge before they even saw me.

I was running for the catwalk before anyone else could get into action and was up there, heading for the ladder to the bridge, before I got an answering shot.

I skidded in against the bulkhead and looked up. A goon was leaning over the bridge, pointing a gun down at my face, but before he could pull the trigger the top of his own head disappeared and he hung limp. I swiveled my head back to the direction the shot had come, and there was Harry MacGill charging out of the engine room. He had Garcia's pistol in one hand, and his own in the other, and both guns were bucking as he fired.

I shouted and charged again for the ladder to the bridge.

The Thompson smoked lead ahead of me, cleaving the way, and I went up in three bounds.

Just as I got to the top my sub-machine gun stopped, I threw it at the first hood who appeared at the wheelhouse door and went in with the knife glinting in my hand.

I stuck him like the pig he was and ripped the knife up his guts as the force of my blow carried us into the wheelhouse.

Captain Croup faded out the other side as we stumbled in, and suddenly I was standing there all alone with a bloody knife in my clenched fist.

It was so quiet I could hear my own breathing. The ship rocked listlessly under her dead weight in a choppy sea. There wasn't a moan or sound of gunfire or even any wind. There was just Croup and me up on that bridge.

That's the way it had to have been all along. Exactly the way I wanted it.

I glanced down at the dead sailor at my feet. No gun!

And did I ever need one. I stepped silently to the door Croup had gone out and I flattened myself there against the wall. I even tried to stop breathing. He couldn't be more than ten feet away. You can't miss at ten feet.

The wheelhouse stood on a bridge that had a railing around all four sides. It was made that way so the captain could stand up there and give orders from any side of the ship.

There were windows all across the front and halfway back on both sides. The only place Croup could be would be right behind me. As bad as I wanted Croup for myself I was wishing Harry would show. Then I saw the gun in the cold early morning light laying on the bridge just outside the door.

I didn't even stop to think.

With a dive I was outside on the deck scooping up the pistol and rolling on my back.

But the gun hand came up to cover nothing but blue sky. Croup wasn't on this side of the bridge.

So we started a deadly, silent game of round and round the mulberry bush.

Croup must be circling to catch me from behind. I got to my hands and knees and crowded aft. When I got to the corner I put my head flat on the deck and peeked around the corner. Empty.

I scooted around just as slugs kicked up steel splinters where I *had* been.

I got to my feet, cocked my wrist around the corner, and fired back.

Now he was forward and I was aft. He would have to be crouched to be under the windows. I ran fast to the other corner, fired a round, and looked. No one. Then I ran back to where I had been and looked. He wasn't coming down this side either.

"Hey, Croup," I called. "How are your knees holding out?"

"I'm okay, boy, how's yourself?"

"Never better. It's going to be a nice day. A perfect day to kill you." He laughed.

"You can't kill what you can't hit," he said.

"Fat boy," I told him, "I couldn't miss you with my eyes closed."

"It won't work, Brody. I'm not going to get sore enough to show myself."

If I could keep him talking I wouldn't have to worry about where he was.

"How's your girl friend?" I asked, and it grated to keep my voice even.

"So you know about Sheba and me? Say Brody, let me tell you about the good time we had in Houston before Ringle showed up."

He was making it work better than I was. It made me crazy mad to think about her.

"Okay, tell me," I choked.

He laughed so hard I though he had gone nuts.

"You really went for her, didn't you, Brody? Don't feel bad. About six hundred other guys have, too."

Suddenly I was noticing something. That something was the great number of holes in the bulkhead that I leaned against. The wall wasn't even heavy enough to stop these slugs. And that was very interesting.

"Hey, lard head," I yelled, "why don't you suggest another partnership? Have you run out of offers?"

He was silent for what seemed like minutes. I was suddenly afraid I had made a fatal mistake and let him sneak up on me.

The sweat broke out on my forehead, and I was trying to look in both directions at once when he spoke.

"No, boy, I have one more to make."

I let the air go out of my aching lungs in a low whistle.

"Okay. Tell it."

"It looks like you win," he said. "I'm all through. Ringle is gone and so are his boys. Let me get away and I'll give up my gun."

"How can you do it?"

"I'll help you navigate a landfall, and before you hit port just give me a boat and I'll disappear."

"We don't need you to make port," I told him. "Why should I do it?"

"Because somebody will get killed if you try and take me. It could be you."

He was right about that.

"Are you on the level?" I asked.

"That I am. It means hanging if I'm turned in. I'd rather go out here than in a dry land prison. I'll tell you, boy, I got a sliver of steel in my hips. I can't walk any more now. It was all I could do to get out of the wheelhouse. Give me a break. Let me fix my hip and get away in a boat."

"Where's Sheba?"

"Well now, that's a sensible question. She's down on the tank deck with one hand on the casing head valve and a match in the other."

My blood went cold.

"… she don't want to die in prison, either," he finished.

I looked down, and sure enough there she was. Croup must have worked this angle out with her after she got loose from Garcia. Only instead of a match she held a lighted blow torch. Would she do it? Was she nuts enough to commit suicide by cremation? There wasn't any question about it; she was.

What could I do, but what I was going to do?

"Okay, Croup, you win. Toss your gun over the side and I'll give you a boat when we sight land."

I looked around the corner and saw the automatic arch up into the air and fall thirty feet down to the ocean.

"I'm clean," said Croup.

I walked around the corner of the bridge, but instead of going all the way forward I stepped into the wheelhouse and sighted the gun down to where he must be on the other side of the steel partition.

I emptied the gun fast, putting the bullets about six inches apart in a row about a foot above the deck. Then I stepped up and looked out the window at him lying there.

My conscience didn't bother me at all, because he was sighting down the barrel of a second gun and there was a very surprised look on his face. He squeezed the trigger in a death spasm and collapsed like so much warm Jello as the gun went off.

"So long, fat man," I whispered.

But I didn't stop to pray. I was outside the wheelhouse and to the railing in two bounds. And I was kicking myself all the way.

Every last slug in my gun had been used to chop Croup, and Sheba was down on the tank deck with a blow torch in her hand and murder on her mind. If that casing head blew ...!

The captain hadn't been lying. There she stood, a demon clothed in beautiful flesh and very little else. The blowtorch was spitting blue flame, as wicked as the blue vapor it was about to ignite. Inches closer and wham, all the carbon tetrachloride foam on the ship wouldn't extinguish the inferno that would burst out of our tanks.

And everything had been for nothing. All the blood and killing and petty scheming had failed. I had won only to lose.

I watched helplessly as Sheba threw back her gorgeous head and laughed. It was a piercing and crazy yell.

I stiffened.

She wasn't laughing at me. Below the bridge a lonely figure staggered toward the girl and her hot glowing torch.

It was the big Panamanian who had hated me so unreasonably. I understood a lot in that fraction of time it took to recognize him. He had hated me because of the girl, a girl he had wanted and never thought he could possess.

Now he knew, as I did, that she was not what we had wanted her to be. And as I watched him struggle painfully toward her out across the tank deck I knew that he was not what I had thought him to be, either. He was a better man than I had given him credit for being.

There was a hole in his back the size of a fist where a forty-five slug had come crashing through his magnificent body.

And Sheba mocked him as he came.

Even with her dying breath she would taunt a man.

Her beauty went sour to my eyes, and I wanted her throat in my hands more than life itself.

But I was rooted to the bridge in fascination as the big man went forward, spilling his blood out, spending his strength. I knew that it wasn't the girl he was after now. It was the blowtorch in her hands that he was going for.

Self-preservation had changed him from a rum-drinking thug to a seaman. This was his big chance to redeem himself as a human being.

And he was doing it for every man still alive, as well as for the ship itself.

He didn't have a chance, but I was pulling for him.

It was Sheba that made the mistake. She couldn't resist a chance to sneer at his puny, futile effort. And she waited too long.

The Panamanian got too close. Suddenly she was trapped without enough time to twirl the valve and apply the flame before he could reach her. She had to retreat.

They started a deadly dance with the girl moving backward, the mestizo slowly advancing. His face was set in grim pain and purpose.

I had to move. If she kept away from him long enough he would fold up from loss of blood and she would be free to get back to the casing head.

I started down the ladder to the tank deck. If he could keep her occupied and if the blowtorch didn't ignite a stray gas fume, maybe I could get there in time to help.

Sheba let herself be worked into a corner at the bow and the Panamanian gathered his last ounce of strength and rushed her. I screamed, and Sheba let her eyes stray for a split second. Then she turned back to him.

She jabbed out with the blowtorch, searing his face, but he was already dead on his feet. He didn't feel it.

His momentum carried them both to the railing where she crashed with the small of her back. Sheba wrapped her arms around the sailor to keep from falling, but the force of the blow was already carrying them over, out into space.

I watched their bodies disappear over the railing, and in a moment came the sound of a gentle splash as they hit the water far below.

I walked slowly forward and looked down. The water was being thrashed to white foam by a school of giant hammerhead sharks.

It was all I could do to turn my back before I got sick.

When I got myself pulled together I went looking for Harry.

I found him sitting up against the bulkhead in the radio shack. The place looked like a slaughter house, but Harry was alive.

"Both legs," he mumbled, and tried to smile. Then he passed out.

We were laying to outside San Juan Bay in the Caribbean waiting for the harbor pilot. Harry was in bed in the captain's cabin, and I was sitting next to him on a wooden chair.

"They're bringing a doc, too," I said.

"You need one yourself," he told me. "Your face is red." Then he gritted his teeth in pain.

It was true. I had a fever and one continuous headache.

We avoided each other's eyes and the question that both of us wanted to bring up.

Finally the pilot's boat arrived, and a couple of medics put Harry on a stretcher after the doc had examined him. I went along in the pilot's boat with Harry to the dock and then in an ambulance to the naval hospital.

They weren't going to put us in the same room, but I went along to see that he was comfortable.

Just before I had to leave the room he motioned with his head and I put an ear down close.

"I gotta know, Brody, what are you going to tell them?"

"Nothing," I said.

He had saved my life and paid plenty for having been one of Croup's men once. It wasn't up to me to know what his record had been. Let the Feds nose it out if they could. There was going to be such a stink raised about this caper back in Washington that they never would be able to sort out all the different bad smells.

"Thanks, Brody," Harry said and went to sleep.

They put me in a room and took away my clothes and I got into the hospital bed.

San Juan wasn't a bad place. I had been on a few shore leaves there. They had plenty for sailors to drink and other things he could do. There was voodoo, and dancing mombas to the bongo drums.

It was the last sound I ever wanted to hear. All I wanted was to save up enough dough to buy a chicken farm in some place like Kansas. I had heard it was pretty dry in Kansas. All I wanted to do was forget Garcia and quit hating Croup. Just plain forget.

And Harry had said "Thanks." Thanks for what? They were going to take off both his legs.

Then the door opened, and a nurse came in.

She looked fresh and healthy in a white starched uniform that couldn't begin to hide the curves.

"I'll have to give you a sponge bath," she said in an efficient yet warm voice. "Take off that nightshirt."

I looked at her big brown eyes and soft black hair. She was a knockout.

"*All* the way off?" I asked.

"You sailors are all alike," she smiled.

As she sponged me clean I watched the supple play of her body, and I wondered if there was anybody in port I knew who could lend me a few bucks … or if she had a place of her own.

THE END

A TRIO OF LIONS

From the early 1950s—the golden age of the paperback!
Three noir crime novels in each volume!

Lion Books began in 1949 as Red Circle Books, part of the Martin Goodman publishing empire that also included such magazines as *For Men Only, Stag* and *Movie World*, as well as various pulps and the early version of Marvel Comics. Lion Books only lasted for nine years, but during that time at least a third of their books were noir reprints and originals, and featured authors like Jim Thompson, David Goodis, Robert Bloch, Richard Matheson and Day Keene.

Kermit Jaediker: Hero's Lust
Shel Walker: The Man I Killed
Clayre & Michel Lipman: House of Evil
978-1-944520-02-1 $19.95
"A real ten-knuckle page-turner."—Kristofer Upjohn, *Noir Journal*.
"Reading these books are like watching late night film noir on late night TV with the lights out."—Rick Ollerman.
Introductions by Gary Lovisi and Dan Roberts.

Kermit Jaedeker: Tall, Dark & Dead
Frederick Lorenz: The Savage Chase
D. L. Champion: Run the Wild River
978-1-944520-75-5 $19.95
"As hard-boiled as they come."—Paul Burke, *NB*.
"…really races along."—James Reasoner.
"…unequivocally recommended."—*Paperback Parade*.
Includes an interview with editor Arnold Hano.

"Lots of tough-guy, wisecracking fun… reads like a 65-70 minute RKO private-eye movie."—*GoodReads*

Stark House Press
1315 H Street, Eureka, CA 95501, 707-498-3135, www.StarkHousePress.com
Retail customers: freight-free, payment accepted by check or paypal via website.
Wholesale: 40%, freight-free on 10 mixed copies or more, returns accepted.
All books available direct from Publisher, Ingram or Baker & Taylor Books.